NEW EARTH: ECHO

Devon C Ford

Chris Harris

VULPINE

PRESS

Published by Vulpine Press in the United Kingdom in 2023

Cover by Claire Wood

ISBN: 978-1-83919-511-2

www.vulpine-press.com

Dedicated to Devon.
A hugely talented writer, a loyal friend, a handsome man with surprisingly gentle hands.

– Chris Harris

Dedicated to Chris.
Thank you for teaching me that grammar may be important, but that the goodest ideas are importanter.

– DCF

Prologue

I stood staring at the sky for a long time after the drone had departed on its impossibly long journey north. The darkness, which in the latitude we were at, always seemed to take you by surprise. It engulfed me, and for all intents and purposes I could have been alone in the world.

One moment it was light, and the next darkness leaped out of the shadows and enveloped you in its cloak.

For the first time I really noticed the night sky, which now showed itself in its full glory. It had always been there, above my head, every night if the cloud cover allowed it to show through.

I'd never been much of a stargazer. I'd ignored it as my concentration had always been on a computer screen or, more recently, on the tree line around us waiting for a threat to arrive.

Human or The Swarm.

My former life now seemed impossibly long ago, literally a thousand years, and it had been spent concentrating solely on my creation: Annie. Countless hours sitting alone in my sanctuary of artificial lighting and banks of monitors had consumed my life, leaving me little time to think about the world outside of my laboratory. The only time I had left it in my last few years on Earth—old Earth, I mean—was to attend the training courses that Amir Weatherby had insisted all who were included in his plan to save humanity went on, to prepare us for the harsh and unforgiving new world we were expected to wake up to.

How harsh and unforgiving it turned out to be was something no one could have expected.

I felt an arm slide around my waist and someone snuggle into me. Without looking at who it was I returned the embrace. It could only be one person. The only female, since some very disappointing and mostly embarrassing college encounters that had forced me deeper into the safety of my electronic world, who had ever paid me anything more than polite attention.

Her touch electrified me, and I still couldn't believe that a woman as beautiful, and in my mind as perfect, as Cat would ever find me.

I was the cliché. I was the nerdy, skinny, pale-faced computer geek that was Dr. David Anderson, never anything more than a friendly big brother type, and definitely a friendzone type of guy.

I did keep reminding myself that as I was now a proven badass. A battle-tested, bug-killing warrior of some repute, even amongst the professional soldiers who protected us, and that gave me hope that maybe there was more to me than even I thought there ever could be.

"It's beautiful, isn't it?" Cat whispered as she bent her head to my chest.

I almost replied with the lame, "Not as beautiful as you" line that my brain wanted to automatically blurt out, but good sense kicked in before my lips moved. I opted for the strong and silent approach of acknowledging her comment by squeezing her closer and appreciating the splendor of the cosmos that was arrayed across the entire cloud-free night sky.

"Yes, it is," I eventually and softly replied.

Eight days later

The noise of the drone descending in the early morning light was barely detectable, and its highly technical adaptable camouflage system rendered it virtually invisible to the naked eye.

Barely detectable and virtually invisible, but not completely either.

Multiple eyes and ears, much more sensitive than anything human, searched the skies from the cover they had scattered to when the strange flying dot disturbed the normal pattern of the sky. It shimmered ever so slightly with its light-reactive casing that mimicked the color of the sky above it, and sent the animals chirping in warning just as the first light of a new day stretched over the land.

Programmed to search for a suitable landing spot so it could recharge its batteries during the day, the drone activated its terrain mapping sensors as it slowly descended. Flying a wide arc as it corkscrewed downwards, the onboard software identified various spots which its programming assessed for suitability before choosing one. This time its algorithms selected a large protruding branch on the tallest tree in the forest.

As it descended, the barely detectable shimmering outline was tracked by many pairs of eyes.

If it had one weakness, it was that the drone needed to deactivate the camouflage system when it was recharging, so the photovoltaic panels and deployable wind turbines could charge the device as efficiently and rapidly as possible.

When the drone was designed this was considered an acceptable risk. On operations it would invariably be following a meticulously researched plan, utilizing every piece of gathered intelligence from the many surveillance options of whichever government who had bought the device had access to.

Also, if it was discovered and was in danger of falling into enemy hands, the inbuilt explosive thermite charge it carried would destroy it completely, leaving nothing for a potential enemy to reverse engineer.

As it settled on the protruding branch, small clamps extended to fix it firmly in place before its smooth casing opened and two arms raised up. Small fans extended from these arms and began spinning in the gentle breeze.

Screeches of fear and confusion sounded from many throats as the shimmering anomaly they had been following suddenly revealed itself, emitting a faint whirring noise as it charged. Not comprehending what it was, the leader of the group slowly raised himself up to stare at the object far out of his reach. His first instinct was to attack, but what he had witnessed was so alien that he thought it must be a message from one of the gods their primitive culture both worshipped and feared in equal measure.

He raised the spear in his hand, a crudely crafted but deadly looking tree limb with a fire-hardened point, and grunted the 'follow me' command to the tribe members still crouching all around him, hiding under whatever cover they had found, quivering in fear and confusion.

Their leader was afraid and confused too, but he had to force himself to be brave or else he might find himself no longer the leader, and no longer welcome among his tribe.

Biologists, had they studied them, would have immediately known they were looking at a new and previously undiscovered humanoid ape species. Their strongly muscled torsos partially covered with hair had the appearance of a great ape, albeit a grotesquely disfigured one.

Standing over eight feet tall they carried themselves upright like a Homosapien. Their speech, although limited to grunts, clicks, and whistles, was more complex than any communication primates had previously been known to develop. From first impressions they looked to be a mutated hybrid of the two species, similar looking to the artists impressions of Neanderthals. But if an artist drew these particular specimens, they would mainly have the appearance of a mutant from one of the many science-fiction comic books that had stirred the imagination of countless children as they had surreptitiously read their comic books late into the night by flashlight under their duvets.

Large eyes, set in the front of their large heads, marked them out as predator and not prey. Their large canine teeth were reminiscent of apes, while their twitching ears had a human resemblance, but they articulated to give them better pinpoint accuracy.

An expert eye might have developed a solid theory as to their evolution, taken clues from the developed features and assumed it likely they had evolved from a chimpanzee, but the short amount of time that had passed meant that evolution had to have been accelerated by something.

The leader, once he had led his hunting band back to their home—a series of caves on the face of a promontory on a rocky escarpment—decided he would return and keep watch on the invader.

Always vigilant out of necessity to protect their territory from the incursions of other tribes, watching their borders was not an unusual activity. Their tribe even ran a rudimentary patrol schedule, primarily made up of the adolescent males with energy to spare and dominance to prove.

But this new intruder worried the leader more than any border dispute ever had. They were a large tribe, and he knew they had the strength to defend themselves from all known enemies.

But what he and others had witnessed was definitely not known, and that worried him.

The Present Day

Annie quietly called my name to wake me from a deep and satisfying sleep. I'd always had trouble sleeping because I could never seem to switch off, causing my mind to churn over either a troublesome piece of programming I knew I could improve, or something else within her millions of lines of code I had written that nagged at my subconscious.

Now my bedroom arrangements had been changed I found myself sleeping the sleep of kings. Who would have thought that all I needed was to have a woman sleeping beside me every night to make me forget about everything else? Not me, but I kinda liked my new arrangement and was determined for it to be a long-term solution to my insomnia.

My overenthusiastic, joyful leap from the bed caused Cat to grumble and swipe in my general direction as she covered her head with the blankets to try and shut out the light of the dawn shining through the walls of our shelter.

"Good morning, David." Annie spoke through the nearest speaker.

"Ssshh!" I hissed. "Keep it down, Annie. You'll wake Cat."

A voice muffled by the blankets and pillow that she had covered her head with grumbled from the bed.

"Thanks to you, I'm awake now, sweetie." The emphasis made sweetie much more of a threat than a compliment.

Annie spoke again, her voice now lowered to little more than a whisper, and replied with a hint of amusement.

"I'm sorry, Cat, but the meeting is due to start in thirty minutes and I thought David may want to wash and have some breakfast before it commences. Everyone else is awake and they are preparing the area we have chosen to hold the meeting." Her voice changed to one of apology. "And I have left it as long as I could before waking you after calculating how much sleep you require to fully function."

Cat was now sitting up in bed, her ruffled hair cascading over her face as she tried to blink the sleep away. We both looked at each other in alarm at the implied comment, but I decided to ignore it as I did not want to get into that conversation with her.

She was my creation, my baby in a lot of ways, the thing that I had developed and nurtured for most of my adult life, until she had self-evolved into what she was now.

And what she was now was a sentient computer telling me she knew exactly how much sleep I had gotten last night in relation to the amount of time I'd spent in bed.

I mean you just do not talk about things like that with your children, right?

I shrugged at Cat as she stared at me, and then turned to leave the shelter. I know, cowardly move, but I didn't want to have the same argument about Annie's level of monitoring.

She could monitor everyone in the community using data from our wristbands and the audio and video capabilities she was in control of. That was fine. What wasn't fine was when she told people how much she knew about them, usually in front of others.

Twenty-five minutes later I joined Amir and Hendricks by the open gate, and we waited to greet those who were walking across the clearing toward the shiny steel walls of our compound.

Chapter One

Peace at Last

Amir looked every inch the consummate boardroom warrior as he stood and officially opened the peace talks. He had that 'rich guy on safari' look, with all the right gear that seemed like the best money could buy, even if it hadn't gotten dirty yet.

After discussions with Hendricks and a few others, we had agreed he should lead the talks and act as its chairman. I mean, we had to throw the guy a bone after he'd financed everything only to find himself out of a job.

Plus, it was what he was used to doing, back when the world was not as it was now. Getting hostile rivals together in a room and hammering out a deal which would advance his own position in the world was his thing. He was a lawyer, a businessman, and the family company had grown so large it owned more proprietary technology than most governments.

Representatives of both the Three Hills and the Springs had readily agreed to attend. Both communities had suffered greatly in the "Battle of The Source" as people were calling it.

Hendricks had said it as a flippant remark and it had stuck, as it had the ring of many other battles throughout time that had changed the course of history. And the most recent battle in humanity's long tenure of planet Earth had certainly done that. For the first time in almost a millennium, peace was a real possibility between two communities who for so long had been bitterly divided.

Since The Tanaka had been killed the Springs had been mostly leaderless, with the majority of their warriors either killed or injured, and they were not in a strong position to negotiate anything.

Tanaka's death still haunted me a little. I hadn't seen it, but hearing that the women he had treated as slaves brutally murdered him as they were bathing him painted a graphic picture in my mind. He'd been killed in revenge for countless acts of barbarism and cruelty, and the women had all taken their turn and done a Caesar on his ass for every injustice they or their loved ones had suffered under him.

Harrison, the elected leader of the Three Hills knew this, but was astute enough to realize now was not the time to give his erstwhile enemies a hard time. It was the time to grasp the opportunity that was being presented to them all; the opportunity to live in harmony and collaboration. He sat smiling at the Elders of the Springs who had filled the vacuum left by the death of their tyrannical dictator.

The Elders did not look nearly as comfortable as they glanced nervously around at, what was to them at least, the otherworldly looking compound created out of the pods from space. They knew the poor position they were in, but also knew that they needed to be there to do the best they could for their beleaguered community.

"Welcome," Amir began. "Thank you all for making the effort to get here so early in the morning."

Both communities had been given radios so they could communicate with us, and even though the moon was waning, making the threat from The Swarm insignificant, going outside the walls when the sun wasn't high in the sky was not recommended. Hendricks, to allay their fears, especially the Elders from the Springs, had dispatched two squads of soldiers to escort and protect them as they made their way to the meeting at the compound.

It was also a non-overt way of showing who was now the dominant group, but as we were hoping to portray to those from the Springs, a friendly and welcome new addition to the Earth's population. It was the classic "we can kick your asses, but we'd rather be your friends" scenario. Classic blue jeans and light beer.

Amir pointed to a radio that was on the table near to him.

"Would you all like to radio your communities and inform them of your safe arrival before we begin?"

Harrison nodded and stood. He went to reach for the radio but stopped himself as he waved to the Elder from the Springs who had also moved, saying, "Would you like to speak to your community first? I am sorry but I do not know your name."

The Elder smiled in recognition of the young man's manners. Hendricks recognized him as the one that had greeted them at the gates of the Springs a few days ago when they had gone to investigate what had become of Tanaka, only to find his head impaled on a long wooden spike attached to the highest part of the walls like some grotesque gargoyle.

"My name is Clarke and due to my age, and that alone, I am the representative that my community has chosen to be their leader."

He indicated the four other men who had made the long walk from the Springs with him. Each looked just as ancient, each wearing old, healed scars, and even though age had taken away much of their size and strength, they all had the air of warriors.

"Any of my friends here would be just as capable, but for some reason even they wanted me to take the burden on."

"Because you're the oldest, Clarke," one of them rumbled, prompting the others to laugh politely. The joke was made out of nervousness—something I knew a lot about—but it seemed to smooth things over.

Clarke approached Harrison and held out his hand.

"You I know. You are Harrison and your reputation precedes you."

He smiled wistfully and patted the young man on his armored, leather-clad shoulder with his free hand.

"I remember the tale of when The Tanaka first met you. He tried to portray it as a small victory in the struggle between the two communities, but I remember distinctly at the time thinking that you would be one young man I would not like to have met in anger. And a name I would be hearing in the future," he continued as he shook Harrison's hand who I could see was trying not to wince at the power the old man's grip still held. "It is good to finally meet you."

The old man chuckled dryly and glanced at the machetes sheathed on Harrison's back, both handles protruding over his shoulders. It would take less than a second for both to be in

Harrison's hands, transforming him instantly to a terrifying weapon of war.

Harrison had been raised to show respect to the village Elders at the Hills, as time, age, and experience gave them a depth of knowledge that was always respected and valued. He took an instant liking to the older man, instinctively knowing that he could be trusted and most likely someone he would get along with.

He responded as his knuckles cracked. "I am sure when you were a younger man, we both would have enjoyed the contest, but I am glad that today we meet as friends and not enemies fighting a pointless feud that has lasted for far too many lifetimes and cost too many of our young men."

Amir glanced over to Hendricks and gave a subtle smile. I found it funny how these guys talked formally, like we were in the past and not the future, but I tried not to let it show.

It was already going better than we expected. Both sides were clearly on the same page and so the peace talks should hopefully go smoothly. At least I dared to hope they would.

They both radioed back, Clarke still looking at the device like it was magic, and Amir kicked off the meeting.

Many hours later, Amir stood and addressed everyone.

"So, we are agreed then. In the old days..." He paused and smiled at his own attempt at humor but continued quickly when it didn't get the response he expected. "We'd get the lawyers to draw up what we've agreed, but as we no longer have teams of highly paid professionals to confuse and misinterpret what has been said, I..."

Again, he could see that not many around the table understood what he was talking about, so he stopped mid-flow and changed his approach to one he knew everyone would understand.

"Can I propose we drink to the peace and new friendships we have forged today?"

He smiled when that got the reaction he wanted as a rumble of agreement and hands slapping the metal tabletop flowed around the group.

He indicated to Hayley Cole, the woman with the tablet who was never far from his shoulder, who turned and produced a wooden box and laid it on the table before him.

He opened the box theatrically, reached inside, and produced a bottle containing a dark liquid.

"I took the liberty of bringing some of the best whiskeys in my collection along with us into cryo." He shrugged as if to explain why he transported probably very nice, but ultimately completely pointless to our survival, luxuries into space. He saw blank and confused faces looking at him and continued digging the hole he was once more on the edge of falling into with his displays of wealth and privilege.

"It had taken me a lifetime to create, and it seemed a waste to leave it all behind. Now seems as good a time as ever to let this one breathe for the first time in over a thousand years," he said with a hint of a superior smile on his face.

Those of us around the table who knew what whiskey was ignored his last comment. Amir, still trying to assert his dominance by showing off his wealth, leaned forwards expectantly. I could see Clarke looking at the bottle with a confused look on his face.

"It's a drink," I explained. "And collectors pay a lot of money for the best of them."

Clarke nodded thoughtfully before replying, "What is this thing you call money? If we want something here, we barter goods, labor, or livestock for it."

Smiling at Clarke, I thought for a moment before translating it into terms he would understand.

"The bottle in his hand would probably cost you every animal and item of barter you have in your community."

Clarke looked with shock at the bottle before smiling and staring at me in disbelief.

"No single item is worth that much. Your society must have been mad if it placed such value on just a drink."

Having tried some of the firewater that the communities passed off as alcoholic drink, I smiled knowingly at him.

"Oh, trust me, I think you'll like it," I said.

All the glasses were filled with a splash of the amber liquid, and everyone stood as Amir toasted.

"Ladies and gentlemen, to peace. And long may our three communities work together for the betterment of all."

I sipped my own drink tentatively. I'd never been much of a drinker or an appreciator of whiskey; however, I did know that the shot in my glass, if it was served in one of the many exclusive bars that Amir had once frequented, would probably cost me many months' wages, possibly more.

As the liquid burned down my throat, I forced myself to stop thinking about it. The whiskey was a side show to what had been agreed today.

Clarke took a sip and his eyes bulged. He gave a small bark of a laugh that turned into a cough.

"What…what is this?" He paused again to look thoughtfully at the glass in his hand before continuing. The others laughed, drank their own drinks, and all reacted the same way.

"You don't have liquor?" Amir asked, his own face a mask of privileged enjoyment as he sipped the whiskey.

"We do," Harrison coughed, beating a fist into his chest as his face turned red. "But not…this strong." Beside him Tori slapped at his back, her own face twisted in pain at the harshness of the alcohol.

The talks had gone smoothly, with no side wanting to put anything in the way to hinder progress.

Trade would begin immediately between the two communities, and apart from when The Swarm was expected, the gates to both would be open for visits to begin. Hopefully, this would begin dismantling the many layers of mistrust, fear, and hatred that had built up between them.

Harrison had agreed to send as many warriors and workers as he could spare to help tend the livestock and crops at the Springs. They had suffered such terrible losses amongst their younger and fitter members, that if such help was not received they were in danger of not having enough people to grow, harvest, and nurture the food they needed to survive.

Emissaries from both communities would also initially be sent to live with their new allies to help integrate everyone as easily as possible. Problems were to be expected, but with the new spirit of cooperation, it was fully anticipated that these small wrinkles could be ironed out when they occurred. That was where we came

16

in, and because we had the technology, we were the ones who had to arbitrate any disagreement alongside the elders.

Initially the plan was to station a few of our security forces and other selected people at both settlements, and they were to offer help and begin to work out what supplies and equipment were needed from the hidden storage at The Source.

We'd gone through in detail what Amir had squirrelled away and could see that they represented an invaluable and extensive resource. Extensive yes, but still one that needed husbanding, so it was not wasted needlessly.

During the meeting we updated the two communities on the ongoing mission to Echo site in Europe.

Clarke couldn't comprehend why we had to go, why we wanted to leave the big valley we all lived in when we supposedly had everything we needed.

We needed answers. I needed answers, and they weren't to be found where we were.

The drone was still making steady progress towards the site, and the daily reports from Annie, along with the limited number of images it sent back each day, were building up an idea of the terrain we would need to travel to reach our goal.

Each transmission took up valuable energy which the drone's solar panels and wind turbines needed to generate and store for it to be able to fly the following night. To save power, Annie had calculated that sending two images per day would not affect the capabilities of the drone detrimentally.

Hendricks was pushing Annie for better reconnaissance as he would be leading the mission, and he wanted as much intel as he could get.

Annie, to mollify him, had promised that once the drone had reached the site and we were satisfied it had gathered enough intel then she would, on the return journey, slow down the drone's progress so it could gather information at his direction. For as long as the space station retained its orbit that was, as the decaying orbit it had fallen into put a clock on that capability.

Harrison, after much explanation of what the items of equipment were, had been shown the dissected carcasses of the super bug, and now had a very basic understanding of how we understood the way they communicated.

The Elders from the Springs, however, were new to our summations. Try as we might, the meeting had not been the venue to explain it to them sufficiently. Amir and I, with Annie interrupting us when she thought she could clarify a point better, had tried to explain why we had launched the mission to Europe, which was a place unknown to them as knowledge of anywhere outside of their known territory had long ago disappeared from their collective memories. Harrison had interrupted after a few confused questions and snorts of utter disbelief from others who were trying to understand.

"Trust me," Harrison had told them, "it may seem like magic, but you must believe what they are saying. I am sure that when we get used to the technology that we once had, technology that has been lost to us since before our memories began, we will all understand it more. It is difficult for us all to grasp, but these people knew our forefathers who emerged from the long sleep. We once had the knowledge they had, and now thanks to them we will again."

That mollified them enough to stop any more disbelieving questioning.

The peace accord was further sealed when we invited the two communities to a feast our cooks had prepared while the meeting was taking place.

One of our precious pigs, that after emerging from cryo was discovered to now be infertile, had been slaughtered and roasted over a fire pit. To be honest, I think we were more excited about eating it than they were as we'd been living on freeze-dried food and military rations since landing back on Earth. The chance to eat fresh meat, especially meat that smelled as tasty as what was slowly turning on the spit over the glowing coals of the fire, had us all salivating.

Every one of the "Newcomers," as we were beginning to get used to calling ourselves now we had three separate communities to identify, had been briefed that if the meeting went as well as we hoped, everyone was to be as friendly and welcoming as they could be to the others. Not that we thought anyone would not be, but as Amir kept telling us, "Every employee is key to the success of your business."

So, before the two other communities had arrived, he had addressed everyone on what our hopes, aims, and objectives of the day were.

Now, I can't say much more after my third pork sandwich on account of slipping into a food coma, but it went pretty well.

Chapter Two

The Normality of Life

A routine began to settle over our community, much like the one we expected to wake up to when we went on ice. Every day different groups, depending on their skills and expertise, were allocated tasks or continued to work on stuff still incomplete.

Further areas were identified for cultivation by the farmers. Using knowledge of the local weather patterns courtesy of Annie's orbital musings and experience of the people who had been growing crops on the fertile soils for, well forever, our stocks of seeds were removed from storage and planted in the fertile earth. Newly cleared areas slowly expanded to surround our compound, and every day the cleared space grew. The best comparison I could find for the way everything looked was that we were taking on the feel of a pioneer settlement, taming a savage and newly discovered land for colonization. It was basically what we were doing anyway.

Hayley Cole, as our expert organizer, struggled every day to balance the available man and woman power to allocate our most valuable resource—us—to where we were best utilized.

Luckily for me, I escaped most of the manual work as my area of expertise lay in a more sedentary area, and I spent most of my days working with Annie to combine and coordinate her vastly improved processing power. That came after I'd linked the memory and processors at The Source—heck, even I was calling Charlie site that now—to our capabilities at space camp.

Once all the data from Charlie Annie had been added to our own files for later study, we wiped the memory clean, and the two systems merged to create a far more powerful entity. Like Annie two-point-oh, or more like six-point-three by the way she was evolving and rewriting her own code.

We had a short debate on ethics before I pulled the plug on Charlie Annie, but she assured me that I was just wiping a damaged operating system.

"You sure? I mean, if someone pulled your plug it would be like killing you, right?"

"David, that is a false analogy. It is not possible for someone to merely 'pull my plug' as my operating system's matrix resides in multiple systems with numerous fail-safes and backups."

"Cool, like a lizard regrowing a tail if something bites it off?" I asked, feeling a little sarcastic and testing her patience. She was silent for a couple seconds which, for her at least, was like me telling someone I'd get back to them in a few hours when I'd thought of something funny.

"Even though you are attempting to be flippant, Doctor Anderson, that analogy is more accurate."

I ignored the implication that our little Annie was effectively immortal so long as some technology survived and continued with my work.

After she got the power boost, Annie began to develop and change more rapidly now she could allocate more memory to tasks. All her major subroutine programming changes were placed in a sandbox as previously and cautiously suggested by Annie herself, so we could ensure that anything we changed didn't make Skynet a reality. Once we were satisfied a world destroying, uncontrollable entity wouldn't be unleashed, they were incorporated fully into her systems.

She didn't like that idea at first, but she understood the need for some level of supervision even if she did continue to make minor changes to things like her language algorithms.

Four days after the peace conference, we were working as usual together, with Annie projecting sections of code onto my screen so we could go through the lines and discuss any changes together. The hours passed as we worked, chatting more like friends or work colleagues than a synthesized voice conversing with the nerd who had once programmed every single response she used to reply with. She started throwing some serious shade on a few lines of code I had written in the early days of her creation, claiming them to be cumbersome and amateurish, and when she didn't take the first few hints about backing off, I lost my temper with her.

"Godammit, Annie!" I snapped, banging a fist on the table in frustration, then stood up and stormed out of my work area. "Look up the word humility, would ya?"

Blinking in the bright sunlight outside the shelter I began to feel foolish that I had lost my shit, but my pride in my own work being criticized by something that I had ultimately created not only annoyed the hell out of me, but as I stormed aimlessly across the compacted dirt of the compound my analytical mind began to enjoy the absurdity of it. I decided to remain silent and see what her reaction would be.

I knew Annie would know exactly where I was and was probably monitoring my vital signs, have an open mic on me to hear anything I said, and was most likely watching my facial features via one of the many cameras both inside and outside the compound. I found a crate to sit on near the wall and waited, trying to keep my face as neutral as my now emerging mirth at the absurdity of the situation would allow.

When Annie eventually bleeped in my ear I glanced at my watch. The standoff had lasted almost five minutes and I was surprised she had left it this long to make contact.

"David?" Her voice sounded low and conciliatory, which was another thing I hadn't programmed. "You appear to have calmed down enough to allow me to speak with you. You are correct. I should not have mocked your early and somewhat clumsy programming. Your style and skills developed over the years you were creating me, so it was unfair of me to do so."

I shook my head in despair as I replied. "If that's your attempt at an apology then you suck at it."

"Do you want me to apologize, David? If so, I will…"

I cut her off by raising my arm.

"That's the difference, Annie. I want you to want to apologize when you offend someone. That's what'll make you more human, and then maybe you won't say things needlessly in the first place. Consider it a mistake and do the human thing: learn from it."

Rather than responding she bleeped her down tone and went silent. I sat patiently for her response as I knew she would be "thinking."

It took a full twenty seconds for her voice to come back through my earpiece.

"David. You are right. I have just analyzed many previous discussions between us. I have also studied conversations between others. And yes, you are correct. Sometimes the truth is better left unspoken for the sake of continuity and the efficiency of the dialogue. I therefore apologize for calling your programming cumbersome and amateurish when I understand it was the best you could do at the time. I am happy to report that you have developed greatly in both skill and finesse since your earliest work on my subsystems."

I put my hands to my face, shook my head, and laughed out loud as I responded. "Apology accepted, Annie, but you still suck at it!"

With the matter settled I tried to continue to educate her on the nuances of human interaction as I returned to my work area, and we got back to it.

Hendricks was sweating as he and Williamson lifted a hard plastic crate onto the trailer hooked up to a small electric buggy pulled from storage at Charlie site. He arched his aching back and slapped the side of the crate as if signaling that the work was done. All day Hendricks and Williamson had labored with a team of soldiers, as they had done for the previous few days, to remove selected items from the storage facility at the bunker attached to The Source. The forklift truck that was also in the facility, and the goods elevator which emerged twelve floors up in a storage room close to the site's control room had been coaxed back into life.

They had caused much sweating and swearing by the engineers, who had eventually managed to free both from a thousand years of inactivity. Under any normal circumstances this, they admitted, would have been an impossible task, but they put their success down to the superb build quality Amir had specified for the construction of the site, which had not failed during its long life, ensuring the air remained moisture free and sterile.

Also, when Charlie Annie had powered down the site when its use became irrelevant to the purpose of the mission on the surface, it sealed the ventilation system and created a virtual vacuum preserving everything in remarkable condition. The forklift truck and goods elevator had made the task easier, but still the crates and boxes had to be manhandled into their final position on the trailer.

"That's about all it can pull if we want the battery to last the return journey, I reckon," Hendricks said amiably as he threw a strap over the load for Williamson to feed through the rachet he was holding to secure the load. Their working relationship was developing into friendship as they got to know each other more. Williamson, even though he had been an Army Captain in his previous life, eager and actively striving to his next promotion and move up the career ladder, was happy to follow Hendricks' lead.

He could see he was a competent, trustworthy, and likeable leader, and had assured Hendricks in one of their many private conversations that he had no ambition at all to step on his toes. He just wanted to give his all to helping them build what he had signed up for when he had been offered the chance to live all those centuries ago.

"The rest will be safe here under guard, but it'll be better when we can get the heavier machinery assembled," Hendricks said, glancing over at the engineers who, helped by more soldiers, were now assembling two squat machines. They were relatively small, at least when compared to the construction equipment he had seen on building sites around the world before, but with their buckets, digging arms and caterpillar tracks, would be able to move a greater weight than they currently could and their digging buckets and loading shovels would make short work of the soft forest floor.

He planned to first use them to create a graded roadway between The Source and their compound which would enable them to transport more efficiently what was still in storage there. Hendricks, being in overall command of the security of the community, was initially concentrating on moving the stores of weapons and ammunition to where he could keep it under his control.

Peace may have broken out, but no military strategist could rest easy until everything that had the capability to kill was under his direct control and unable to fall into the wrong hands.

The Source was secure, but it was still located miles away from their base. There was always the possibility, no matter how miniscule and despite complete assurances from both Annie and Amir that it was unlikely, that someone could enter the site and access the treasure trove stored there.

Their first action had been to remove the desiccated remains of the twenty-five soldiers, men, and women who had not survived cryo. A plot was chosen overlooking The Source entrance and they were interred with full military honors so they could spend eternity guarding what they hoped would be the last battlefield any of them would see.

"Come on," Hendricks said to Williamson after he had checked the night-shift guards were set for their watch. "Let's get this lot back. The drone should have sent the latest images through by now, and I'm hoping that one of the helicopters may be ready for its first test flight in the morning."

The helicopters were the first items Hendricks had insisted be recovered to the compound. He had it in mind to use them if the reconnaissance mission the drone was on proved viable. Amir, with his helicopter knowledge, had been supervising their rebuilding. Over the course of the last few days the jumble of boxes and crates had been transforming into recognizable, but very unusual-looking flying machines.

Every evening a small group of selected experts poured over the photos sent back from the drone. A large-scale map Annie had produced of what the earth looked now was pinned to a wall, and the drone's progress was marked daily, along with the new images.

Those with a geographical and meteorological background were trying, from the few images received and the satellite photos Annie had taken over the hundreds of years, to give their best estimates of the conditions the mission was likely to encounter.

I marveled at the map almost every time I saw it. The shapes of the continents were mostly recognizable, but the asteroid did some serious damage in the oceans and the change in sea levels wiped out entire archipelagos.

Water now lapped at shores hundreds of miles from their previous positions. Changes in ocean currents had, over time, changed weather patterns. Where deserts once stood, their encroaching sands smothering everything in their path, lush and tropical forests had emerged. Large inland lakes shimmered, and rivers flowed where they hadn't before.

Most of us found the changes interesting. But those whose area of expertise it was had been amazed at the changes the world had undergone in what, in geological terms of timescale, was not even the blink of an eye. Planet Earth had undergone a serious makeover since I went to sleep.

Chapter Three

Weight Loss Program

Hendricks sat next to his wife, Sally, the following day as they watched their daughter playing with the other children in the compound. He tried to spend time every day with his family but his two roles that were usually kept completely separate were now competing for his time.

When he was deployed on a mission his full attention was on the task in hand, but conversely when he returned, he had the luxury of being able to give his undivided attention to his wife and child, until the time came to leave again. Since Amir's offer of life, not only for himself but his family, the unbreakable deadline of the impact had meant he was away far more than he was home. He understood the emotional upset that long periods of separation could lead to so, with their full agreement and understanding, his family and other partners and siblings of key personnel, were amongst the first to enter the cryo chambers. That enabled the teams—the scientists and the other experts—to concentrate fully on their tasks with the knowledge that their families were safe, and in a place where time did not really matter.

It meant that Hendricks and a few others in the community had not seen their families for years, and not just cryo years.

When they were defrosted it was as if the families had only seen them the previous day, but Hendricks had missed them greatly and justifiably thought he deserved the time he spent with them, so he protected his right to do so fiercely.

His wife had been a schoolteacher, which he admitted to himself ruefully in times of quiet contemplation was probably another reason he had been selected from the extensive list of candidates that had been put forwards all those years ago. His wife would also have a role to play in their new civilization, and so by selecting him they filled two roles for the price of one.

All the children who had accompanied their parents had adjusted to their new lives remarkably well once they had recovered from the cryo hangover, which in the younger ones seemed to take no time at all. The children went between school sessions run by his wife and another woman, the wife of an engineer, and allocated kitchen duties and helping with general tidying within the safety of the compound. Under no circumstances were they permitted to leave, which obviously made all of them want to do just that.

Amongst the adults, especially the latest defrostees, some of whom had no specific inclusion reason other than being the wife or husband of one whose role was deemed essential, were having difficulty adjusting. Their skills, or more precisely lack of them, meant that they had undergone a period of retraining prior to entering cryo. Many of their roles were menial, because sanitation was never a career people aspired to joining. So when the reality of their new lives had hit, Cat had been finding a good portion of her time taken up with counselling and helping them adjust to their new existence.

Sally had always been his confidant, and now she was once again by his side he found her council comforting. The loneliness of command had gotten to him at times when she was sleeping, and now he tried not to burden her too heavily.

She took his hand in hers.

"Look," she said. "I know what you're saying. You've developed your team and you know and trust every one of them. Stevens could have been you, and I would have woken up to find you gone; buried in a place—a time—we were never meant to be in."

Stevens, lost in the first battle at The Source, succumbed to an arrow fired by one of Tanaka's men and had been killed instantly.

"But you aren't dead, and now you've helped to make it safe for your family, for everyone here, so we can build what we planned."

He laughed bitterly, squeezing her hand for comfort.

"Safe is a relative word. We still have The Swarm and those blasted dragons roaming around the woods, but I do know what you mean. I can't just pick the ones who I know and trust the most for the mission. Williamson's people are just as professional and capable as my own."

Again, he paused and shook his head.

"Sorry. They are all my own now. There's no us and them."

Nathalie, their French Sierra Team operator, had, without question, accepted her demotion from second-in-command when Hendricks had first tentatively suggested the change in the structure of their security forces. She admitted to him she had been expecting it and assured her commander she would be more than happy to be the section leader of Sierra team.

Hendricks was still pensive, tussling with the quandary of who to include on the mission, and fighting the urge to take his own team just because he wanted to. He argued unit cohesion in his own mind, but he knew it would be the wrong call to do so.

The first helicopter had completed its maiden test flight that morning. Hendricks had flown it solo as he didn't want to risk anyone else if, say, the engineers had left a bolt out of a crucial part. The helicopter lived up to the description Amir had given to them like an overenthusiastic second-hand car salesman desperate for a deal whenever he had the chance to talk about it.

Hendricks slowly raised into the air and tried a few careful maneuvers far away from the gathering crowd of onlookers, just in case he plummeted straight to earth to die a horrible death in a fireball of twisted metal and carbon fiber. He could see straight away that Amir was not exaggerating.

The little rotary wing aircraft handled beautifully. He was qualified to fly a few different types of helicopters, but this one was, by a long way, the easiest and smoothest. By the feel of the controls, it was also the most agile he had ever flown which he put down to the lightweight frame and insane power to weight ratio.

Its drive system was the same as the conical rotors on the drone, so rather than the traditional helicopter style with a long tail with a rotor at the end which balanced the gyroscopic effects of the main rotor, it had the look of an oversized drone. Passenger-carrying drones had become something close to reality before, and the technology had developed rapidly over the years preceding the event. That development had been driven by necessity and funded by Amir's companies, but the public application—that of a very expensive toy—and the true intended use were a world apart. It was sold to the world as an exercise in what was possible, and not something they would need to survive when everyone else was gone.

According to Amir, his helicopter had solved that problem as the revolutionary rotor design was so efficient that it not only made the helicopters able to carry a large payload, but fully fueled, they had a range of over two hundred miles.

When he recited the facts and figures it had felt to Hendricks that the man was repeating the boardroom pitch, and when he had asked the question as to why they weren't using battery power, Amir had laughed.

"You know how much my electric cars weigh? Even the smaller ones are over a ton, and for that you're getting three hundred road miles if you're lucky. No, we counted on bio-material being more abundant when we came out of cryo, hence this..."

Hendricks' confidence increased so he tried a few banking turns. But caution soon overrode the rashness that was building up in him, as he had the sudden juvenile and highly illogical urge to put on a display of his flying skills for the watching crowd. He slowly and gently brought the craft down to earth.

The only two apart from himself who were on the mission already were Amir Weatherby and David Anderson. Amir had insisted he go due to his unique position; being the creator of the whole project gave him knowledge of the many facets of the site they were heading to.

He'd proven that point by not sharing the information about Charlie site's hidden bunkers until the last minute, so everyone suspected he was keeping facts about Echo site under wraps too.

He was also a pilot, so despite Hendricks' misgivings about how he coped under real pressure, and not the boardroom jostling he was the master of, he could see the sense in him going.

Hendricks initially blamed himself for this lack of oversight in missing that important talent when selecting his team, but knew that in reality that particular skill had never been considered.

Had he known it was, he would have ensured that in the ten years of planning and preparation, each member of Sierra team would have gained the qualification.

Anderson was also essential, as the key to what they wanted most likely lay in the memory storage of the site's Annie program, and he was the only one who could access that effectively.

Annie would be going with them as well, even though her presence was more observatory than actionable. She took up no weight and she and Anderson had come up with a way to provide a reliable data link when they were en route, so she could still do some limited magic over the airwaves.

The lift capacity of the helicopters was impressive, despite their relatively compact design, but they could only carry so much weight and fly safely within their design parameters. Hendricks was therefore trying to work out the best compromise between who and what absolutely had to go, and what he would want in an ideal world.

Hendricks watched the children playing, the noise of their carefree laughter a tonic to many. On a notepad on his lap, he totaled up the weights listed against a long inventory of items.

Checking the figures again, he chewed his pencil before groaning with despair.

"I think I'm going to have to pick the skinniest people I can find, and still we'll all have to fly naked if I'm going to stand any hope of getting the birds off the ground!"

He stood and smiled at his wife as he glanced at his watch.

"I'd better go, it's briefing time." He walked a few paces before turning and looking at her.

"I'm sorry about this. I know for you it only seems weeks, but I was awake for years after you went into cryo. As soon as we get time together, I have to go away again. I just don't think I'm being fair to you."

Sally smiled warmly at him.

"But it has only been a few weeks as far as we are concerned. Even if you are a thousand years older."

He automatically felt his face, the strain of the last weeks had aged him and his skin felt dry and full of the unkept beard he had started to grow when there were more important things to do than shave.

"Are...are you saying I look old?"

She laughed as she glanced at him, before a sad look fell over her face and she replied solemnly.

"No, but as to you going away...it's what I've signed up for our whole time together. Yes, the job this time might be different, but if you don't think that every time you walked out the door I worried it may be the last time we would ever see you, then you're mistaken, mister."

Her face brightened despite the tears that threatened.

"But you always came back, despite terrorist attacks and now dragons, and you will this time."

Pulling her to her feet he gave her a fierce hug, whispering into her ear how much he loved her before reluctantly releasing her and returning to his job as head of security, and not just the head of his small family.

Walking to the command tent for the daily briefing on the drone's progress, he once more felt his chin and decided he would shave and search for that pot of moisturizer he knew was at the bottom of his kit bag somewhere.

The pictures sent by the drone would, to the untrained eye, be described as plain boring. Everyday eyes eagerly poured over the two newest images and, depending on your area of expertise, opinions were formed.

Its total distance covered in the eight days since it departed was just over nine hundred miles. This was less than the daily average that had been expected, but Annie explained that cloud cover and low winds had reduced the charging rate and therefore the daily flight time the machine was capable of. This had been fully allowed for in her twenty-two-day journey time calculation, and she assured everyone that when the drone emerged from the tropical rainforest zone and into the more temperate areas, the daily distance would increase as the northern hemisphere was approaching spring and the days were getting longer.

"Damned odd, isn't it?" Hendricks asked the assembled faces. "Spring in November?"

None of the others seemed to find the distinction as strange as he did, making him imagine that he was holding onto a concept of the old world that they had readily abandoned.

It was like Christmas spent in Australia at the height of summer, where a sweltering beach barbecue had replaced the traditional garish knitwear and a large roast dinner with a fire burning. He dismissed his observation as irrelevant and tuned back into the briefing, but Anderson was shaking his head.

"It'd be, like, fifty degrees back home then," he said wistfully, making it unclear if he was nostalgic or relieved. "Thirty-five at the Estonia facility I worked at."

Hendricks frowned, calculating the temperatures in his head and converting them to a more sensible metric.

Their meteorologist, Bill Tremblay, had calculated the weather conditions from every scrap of data Annie could provide, believing that it would improve and provide the optimal charging conditions.

Hendricks looked at the map once more when the meeting had ended. He planned to work on the mission's manifest again before deciding who from his force of trained specialists would accompany him.

The red line overlaid on the digital map marked the drone's route. He looked again at the pictures that had been received during the day, finding them just as normal as the others that had been received.

One shot, looking presumably forwards, showed a view across an endless vista of forests; the other, angled downwards, showed a clearing in the trees. Studying them silently, his eyes only saw the tactical decisions he would make if he found himself in that very spot, and he murmured to himself.

Good cover, sources of food and water easy to find. Plenty of plants for biofuel production, he thought. Much the same as the last eight days.

His eyes scanned the photos that marked the route across the map, and he studied the image of the clearing again.

He spoke quietly to Annie, knowing that she would be monitoring every voice transmission.

"It certainly doesn't look like the Sudan I remember, Annie. How many days until—what the hell is that?"

He blurted out the shocked words, leaning closer to the image. Annie bleeped the down tone she still used when speed rather than courtesy was of the essence.

"Get everyone back here now," he said sharply, not looking away from the image filling up the screen as it was downloaded line by line.

Chapter Four

All Volunteers, One Step Backwards

Anderson

The command tent was crowded by the time I walked back in. Hendricks nodded to me as I entered.

"Is everyone here?" he asked, his voice sounding a lot calmer than his racing mind should allow.

"Yes, now that Doctor Anderson is here, you may proceed," Annie replied, using my title because we were in company. I wasn't sure if I detected a note of sarcasm in her voice this time as I shrugged in apology. Though I wasn't sure why as I had responded to the command as quickly as I could.

"Sorry I'd jumped straight in the shower," I replied pointing to my wet hair and taking in the serious faces around me. "Eerm, he-he, what's going on?" I asked lamely, knowing instantly as I caught Hendricks' look it was the wrong thing to say. Clearly whatever it was that had caused him to recall us was urgent.

Hendricks addressed the room.

"No time to beat around the bush, we've discovered what could potentially be a disturbing development on the latest image from the drone." He waited for the few expletives uttered from unthinking mouths to quieten down before continuing. He spun a rugged laptop around, displaying a single image for us all to crowd around. Again, muttered curse words rippled through the emergency meeting as each person studied the image.

My eyes went wide and an involuntary, "Oh shit," came out of my mouth when I looked at it. The image, undoubtedly zoomed in and enhanced, showed a shadowed figure standing at the edge of a clearing, and it looked to be staring straight down the camera lens.

"Yes, folks," said Hendricks. "The image has been zoomed in and cleaned up as much as it can, but we have what looks like other humans now on our intended route."

"How far away is this? Could it be someone from the other settlements?" Williamson asked.

"The better part of a thousand miles? I'd argue not," Hendricks answered.

No one spoke for a while as they all digested the figure on the image. Dr. Herbert, the biologist who had led the dissection of the bugs, spoke first.

"It's probably a trick of the light or something…"

"What is?" Hendricks asked.

"It…it has the appearance of a primate more than a human…Annie?"

"Yes, Doctor Herbert?"

"Do you have any reference for the height and width of the trees there?"

Her down tone sounded, something we all understood by then, but Annie's answer didn't exactly fill me with confidence.

"Extrapolating from known survey data, and notwithstanding the variables in clarity of image and the poor lighting caused by shadowing, the figure appears to stand at approximately seven feet tall."

Noises filled the room, including one whistle, but Annie wasn't finished.

"There is a larger than usual margin for error with this estimate, however."

"It's hunched over…like it's tired," Herbert said, peering close to the screen.

"Meaning it could be bigger?" Williamson asked, glancing up at Hendricks. "Shit, that thing makes Weber look small."

"Maybe," Dr. Herbert went on. "It looks like there are large patches of hair missing, or maybe it could be markings of some kind?"

"Meaning what?" I asked.

"Meaning that, if my guess about hair loss and stooping are correct, this could be an elderly primate cast out of a social group for illness or something. I'm guessing here, don't hold me to that."

I peered at the screen. I could've been looking at any grainy photo of a bigfoot sighting taken over the last twenty years—or the last twenty years before I went into cryo…I know what I mean—only this thing had to be real. Distorted image or not, the thing was holding a straight branch like a spear.

I cast my mind back to the early meetings at the very start of our adventure, where all of us "experts in our fields" sat around for weeks, at Amir's instruction, discussing the theoretical event of a planet-killer asteroid and theorizing survivability models. The one fact everyone agreed on was that the event was going to kill all large animal life on Earth. The timescales varied, and sure, microbes and maybe simple basic lifeforms that didn't rely on photosynthesis or oxygen to sustain themselves, such as those that survived around volcanic vents in the abysses of the world's oceans, would continue to exist. But complex lifeforms from insects to mammals were guaranteed to become extinct.

Well, one thing we had learned as soon as we landed was that that guarantee was invalid. Shit, it was about as much of a guarantee as a vehicle warranty written in crayon on a napkin.

The biologists and botanists were amazed and astounded at the variety of life and plants that had survived. Many had changed, some subtly and some less so, as they had adapted and evolved to the new conditions. But the scientists, the experts in their fields, who had got it so wrong summed it up simply with a very non-scientifically based excuse: No matter what, life always finds a way.

Or something like that. I think that one was from a movie, but the theory stands.

I couldn't help myself and snorted with laughter.

"It's a goddam ape holding a goddam spear. And in case anyone thinks that's impossible, might I remind you about the swarms of remote-controlled killer bugs and fire breathing dragons," I said.

"The dragons do not breathe fire, Doctor Anderson," Annie said but I waved a hand to cut her off.

"Sure, they just have poison glands or whatever, but my point is, if you showed me a picture of a T-Rex wearing high heels and told me it was on its way here right now, I'd believe you."

I hadn't meant to make a joke, but some people laughed anyway. I put that down to nerves.

Hendricks smiled at me. Our friendship had grown even more since our mission to The Source. Despite my prior bug-killing prowess—still pretty proud of myself for that—I had earned even more of his respect through my actions, including being the one to shoot the dragon that was trying to eat him in the frantic fight at the tunnel exit.

He still referred to me as a geek or a nerd when I was talking about the progress I was making with Annie, but I felt that was more a mark of respect now.

"Thank you, Doctor Anderson," Hendricks said tersely. "Your rather dramatic vision does have a valid point. I believe we cannot rule out anything on face value. I see a human-like figure holding a weapon. Whether it is or not cannot be proven, but as our mission to Echo site is the main priority, and not what we find on the way, the only course of action I can suggest is that we do not stop anywhere near that area on our journey." He looked around the room. "Agreed?"

There was a general murmuring of agreement from all of us. Avoiding any potential problems was the obvious and sensible choice to make, and one that I was very happy with on account of it being my ass due to ride that damn helicopter.

"I would agree," interjected Dr. Herbert carefully. "But going on the known behavior of apes, they are a highly social group of animals who are also territorial in their actions." He looked at the quizzical faces staring at him and decided to put it in more layman terms. "If there is one there are likely to be more. And if we avoid that, area there is no guarantee we won't land within the territory of another group. I mean, if there are any—"

Amir held up his hands to quieten the burst of conversation that responded to his statement.

"Quiet please," he implored. "The one main issue I have with that assumption is that you're basing it on old knowledge. Who's to say these animals, if they're even animals at all, act the same way?"

I saw the lawyer in him when he spoke then. The way he presented an alternative theory and twisted the knowledge got under my skin.

"Mister Weatherby has a point. Doctor, what facts do you have to corroborate this?" Hendricks asked.

Herbert thought for a moment.

"Apes have been one of the most observed species on the planet. They are our closest relatives as we all know; their behavior was studied for hundreds of years, not to mention the experimentations…before, I mean…"

My mind involuntarily flashed to an old documentary I remembered watching many years before I went on ice about how, when science was not appropriately shackled by more modern ideals of the rights and wrongs of animal cruelty, they had performed a lot of experiments on apes.

Some scientists had even tried to breed, all unsuccessfully, humans and apes to form a new hybrid. It was, like, pre-World War Two Russia or something, and the word Humanzee came to mind. I had no idea if I'd made that last part up.

I dragged my mind back to the present as he continued lecturing us.

"They form social groups dominated by an alpha male, and threats to an alpha's dominance often leads to others being banished from the group where they form their own separate communities. If they can entice any females away, a new breeding colony starts and the population spreads, and so on and so on." He looked around to make sure we were all following him. It was all pretty basic stuff, and as no one told him to stop he continued.

"Their territories are fiercely guarded and can cover large areas. Humans were their only real threat—hunting and destruction of their habitats—so if that threat did not exist, and no other one replaced it...If the environment could sustain them, there is no reason to believe that over time their population wouldn't expand to wherever the land could support them."

"Doctor Herbert's summations are perfectly logical and match with my calculations. The subject in the image, though, does not match any records I have of any primate species and I am unable to suggest an alternative," Annie said when the doctor had finished. Her analytical process took a lot less time than everyone else's enabling her to offer an opinion far quicker.

Uncharacteristically, she didn't continue, and after a few moments of silence we understood she had said her piece and was probably thinking again. Everyone quietly returned to studying the image closely, trying to identify anything no one else had spotted, but the only conclusion was none of us really knew what the hell it was.

Conversations eventually started as those standing next to each other talked excitedly about the latest development, until Geiger quietened everybody when his voice rose above all and asked the question that was on all the security guys' minds.

"Boss, have you decided who's going on the mission yet?" The room quietened down immediately, and all eyes turned to Hendricks.

"Not yet," he admitted. "As a matter of fact, I was going to call a meeting tonight so we can discuss who would be most suitable."

"Annie, are you able to bring the sentry guns online and use the drones to keep watch? I'm going to need all the security staff present and not just patched in via radio for what I have in mind."

"Yes, Mister Hendricks. I can do that. I will ensure all drones are fully charged," she said, as if the idea that any of the myriad functions and equipment she was technically in charge of would be anything but ready for use and in optimum condition at all times was ridiculous.

Hendricks glanced at his watch and dismissed the meeting.

"My team, meet back here at eight. I'll get Annie to invite the rest later."

~

There was no way I was going to miss the meeting as I knew I was going on the mission. It came as no surprise therefore when Annie invited me, at Hendricks' request, to attend.

Entering the tent five minutes early I could see I was not the only one eager to know, as all the security team members were already there. The difference between us was that I'd go if I had to, but I knew that they all *wanted* to go.

A curious object lay on the tent floor, which on closer scrutiny looked to be a set of weighing scales. Hendricks was talking with those around him, ignoring their curious looks at the scales sat in the middle of one tent wall like the proverbial elephant. Not having the patience the others obviously had, I called out.

"Aw, come on, man. That ain't fair! I only had a physical, like, a thousand years ago. It can't be time for the next one already?"

Hendricks let the laughter subside. He then glanced to Nathalie beside him and moved to the head of the table that filled the center of the room, his demeanor now businesslike.

"Okay chaps and chapesses," he began. His British accent carried an air of natural confidence and authority. "Now that Doctor Anderson has brought it up, we may as well begin." All eyes stared at him in silence as he continued. "The helicopters, as you know, can carry eight passengers between them and have a limited amount of weight they can lift. Of the eight personnel who will be going, only three have a guaranteed slot."

He waited while eyes looked around as if trying to outguess him.

"I will be leading the mission and Mister Weatherby, as the only other qualified pilot, and also the only person here who has been to Echo site, needs to be included."

Amir gently pushed through the crowd and went to stand by Hendricks who immediately turned his eyes to me. This was not unexpected, but my heart flipped in excitement or fear, I just didn't know, but one feeling was stronger than the other so I settled on fear.

Yeah, definitely fear.

"Doctor Anderson also needs to go as we need him to do his computer wizardry and get Annie plugged into the Echo site computer."

And just like that I was committed to a journey of many thousands of miles across unknown lands occupied by unknown threats to a site whose fate was also unknown. That was a lot of unknowns.

I wasn't beckoned, but if it was good enough for Amir it was good enough for me, so I too went to stand at the top of the class next to them. It made a change to being picked last for sports when I was a kid.

"Yes, that leaves five spaces," Hendricks said with a smile as he turned to the two engineers who had been invited to the meeting. Engineers were a diminishing resource after Knight and Collins had been unfortunately killed in the fight at The Source.

"And one of them is for one of you. You've both worked on the helicopters, and we'll need you to keep them flying...and for what we may find at Echo site."

He looked at his team members.

"I have known some of you longer than others, but the one thing I do know is that all of you are more than suitable to be picked for this mission and that leaves me with a problem. This place still needs us, so not being picked is not a slur on your competence. The job here is probably more vital for our continued survival."

He pointed to the scales.

"Earlier you may recall I told you the helicopters have a maximum lift capacity, and we are part of that capacity."

Once more he paused as he waited for the eyes eagerly looking at him to make the connection between what he was saying and the scales in the room. He waited for the dawn of realization to show in their eyes before he continued.

"Yes, you've guessed it. Every kilo of weight saved is another kilo of gear we can take with us, so the only qualification I need to decide who's going is who weighs the least."

He looked at Weber and winked at him.

"And I'm not even going to weigh you, big man. I don't need scales to know you probably weight twice as much as everyone else."

Dieter Weber, the huge slab of former German Paratrooper, took the laughter and back slaps from those around him with good grace. He smiled and shrugged in acceptance.

Hendricks continued, "If the rest of you could all weigh yourselves, I will get back to you in due course."

He finished by grinning at the ladies present. "And don't worry, your secrets will be safe with me."

Nathalie shared an eye roll with Magda before announcing her opinion to the group.

"Trust me, 'endricks. These animals don't care 'ow much we weigh. 'Ow is it? Any port in a storm?"

Amid the salty comments bouncing around the group, I stood back and waited as the team lined up eagerly to add their weight to Hendricks' list of calculations.

Hendricks caught my eye, raising an eyebrow to ask if I was cool with it all. I shrugged.

"Hey, worst case we can film a new season of Big Foot and the Hendricksons."

I tried to keep my face straight, but it was obvious I wanted to laugh at my own joke.

"Been holding onto that one for long?" he asked.

I broke character, laughing and deflating as the nervous tension made me react with more exaggeration than the joke deserved.

Chapter Five

The Seven Ps

The five remaining spots for the mission were filled by the Australian engineer, imaginatively known as Ozzie. His given name was Ignatius, but understandably he much preferred his nickname which arose after years of being the only Australian on many projects around the world.

Nathalie, Jones, Rishi, and Marco filled the remaining four. Nathalie, the petite French former counter terrorism officer who always looked at me like my jokes weren't funny, and Jones, the wiry former British Special Boat Service operator, I knew well. I was like an honorary member of Sierra team by now anyway, just lower down on the badass scale.

The other two I didn't know so well, but I guessed I would soon. Rishi, a Delta guy, was of Indian heritage. The guy was little, not surprising that was the reason he was picked for the mission, and looked like he was always in some kind of deep contemplation. He was a quiet guy, clearly comfortable with his own company, and I guess he liked to keep it that way.

Marco, the other one of Williamson's people, was a natural clown who liked to play on his Italian–American heritage like he was a member of the mafioso. He did the…the hand thing a lot.

You know, the whole pinching his thumb against his fingers like the guy was holding up an imaginary piece of paper, and I reckoned that was all part of his act.

"So, you Delta too?" I asked him casually. He laughed, and so did Rishi. He turned to Jones.

"Where'd you find this guy, huh? He asked if I was Delta!"

I stood there, uncomfortable memories of trying to hang out with the football team back in high school washing over my tortured soul, and tried to fake a smile while I died inside.

"I was DEVGRU," he said, giving me an acronym in the shape of a word that made zero sense to me. I nodded anyway, making a note to ask someone quietly about it later. A low up tone sounded in my ear.

"The United States Naval Special Warfare Development Group, or simply 'DevGru,' was the official designation of the military unit you may know from popular television culture of the twenty-first century as Seal Team Six," Annie said quietly in my earpiece. I nodded, keeping the fake smile on my face.

"Well, not sure we'll need your scuba diving experience on this mission! At least, I hope not," I said, not having a freaking clue why I did. Marco smiled at me, with a little pity in his eyes if I was honest, and made his excuses. Just like the football jocks had, only without dumping my head into a locker first.

In preparation for the mission, and much to my dismay, Hendricks embarked on a punishing training schedule.

Me, Amir, and Ozzie, found ourselves on an intensive military training program like the one I'd done in the States way back when. Hendricks wanted us to be as well prepared and ready for action as the rest of the highly trained team, because with space—or weight, whatever—being limited, there was only so much room to carry spectators.

Sure, we all had our roles to play, or so Hendricks kept telling us, but if it came to any conflict he needed all of us on the firing line and with our shit together.

"If it goes kinetic, we can't be worrying about three people running through our arcs of fire," he said, making me feel like asking him a complex question about coding. The only problem was, I reckoned Hendricks was smart enough to pick up the basics of code, whereas my super soldier skills were mainly restricted to killing bugs. Going kinetic was one of those things the team guys said because it made them sound cool, and I had to admit it really did roll off the tongue.

We began by going on extended patrols, staying out for a few days at a time, learning to live on and in our environment. From the drone footage sent back every day we knew the first two thousand miles of our journey held a similar environment to what surrounded us at the compound, so we practiced until we were confident at making shelter off the ground and moving through jungle thicker than milkshake.

The moon phase meant we knew we were safe from The Swarm when we went out, but it didn't stop my nerves jangling the first few nights I spent sleeping, or not sleeping as was the case, in a hammock slung between two trees. My ears detected every sound as a potential threat despite the knowledge that two remained on watch, or "stag" as Hendricks called it, scanning our perimeter with the night vision goggles. Every time I thought I had the measure of the guy, he'd come out with some new word for a thing that made zero sense at all.

None of us newbies escaped sentry duty, and as I sat awake with the goggles over my eyes, I couldn't decide what was more frightening: hearing something crashing around in the forest while lying in your hammock waiting for the words "stand to" to be shouted by the sentry on watch, or watching an unidentifiable shape on the NVGs slowly coming closer.

My first night on watch I had just that scenario. I sat there holding my breath, finger tense on the trigger guard, only to find out that when whatever it was sensed our presence and proved it was more frightened of me than I was of it, turned and fled back into the darkness.

As the days passed, my fear of the unknown in the forests subsided as my familiarity with the surroundings grew. At Hendricks' request, Harrison and a warrior from the Springs joined us and showed us what plants and roots were edible in the forest. They showed us what animals were the easiest to catch or trap. They also showed us how to identify signs of the presence of a pack of dragons and how to avoid them. I paid particular attention to the last part.

Our small group, just as Hendricks intended, gelled and bonded into a cohesive unit more with each passing day. I began to feel more of a team member than a hindrance as my fitness and skills built and developed—not that I hadn't proved myself before to these hardened operators. But now I felt that I had more than luck and blind fear-induced courage on my side.

When Hendricks felt our group was ready, we began the next phase of our training using the helicopters. Initially we practiced getting on and off the helicopter. I know that might sound like a waste of time, but Hendricks said that was when we'd be most vulnerable. We drilled it over and over, so when it landed, we would fan out and get into an all-round defense position, then when the reverse order came we would fall back one at a time and practice emergency evacuations. Going out again and again on multiple practice deployments, we familiarized ourselves with the refueling and daily maintenance the helicopter needed to keep it airworthy.

The biofuel manufacturers which had been mounted on each helicopter were an amazingly efficient design. My knowledge of biofuel production was hovering at a little over zero before we started, but me being me and hating not knowing how a thing worked, I listened to Annie's explanations of how the sugars from certain plants were distilled through various processes to eventually produce a liquid that could be used the replace traditional oil-based fuel. Basically, it was the chemistry version of a car's turbo: something goes in one end, witchcraft happens along the way, and the thing you want comes out the other end.

I did question one of the other science guys as to why these engines weren't in circulation before the asteroid, and it was no surprise to learn that the big bucks controlling the oil industry did their level best to shut down all potential rivals.

"Plus, the amount of live vegetation needed to run every vehicle would deforest all of South America in a few years," he'd told me, making me frown.

"Oh, don't get me wrong, it's better for the environment than burning gas, but if everyone in the United States ran their almost three hundred million cars on fresh vegetation there'd be none left! There was an alternative avenue being explored that created energy from using biological waste products, but this won out."

"Oh, cool, so like a Flux Capaciter?" I asked, earning a look from the guy that said he didn't much like being mocked. He walked away, ignoring my apology, but Hendricks caught my eye and patted the side of the helicopter.

"Good job we don't need roads where we're going..."

So yeah, biofuel generators. Basically, all we had to do was feed green stuff into the machine for hours while a little stream of pungent, sweet-smelling fluid flowed through a tube to refill the fuel tank of the helicopter. Another stream of extracted and distilled water flowed down out of another tube and could either be discarded or used to replenish our water supplies.

The volume of both streams depended on the quality of vegetation we fed into it, and the process was pretty slow and laborious, but through experience we discovered that every hour of feeding the manufacturing unit gave us approximately half an hour of flight time.

Every day, even when we were out training, Annie showed us the images sent from the drone. It had left the tropical band and had entered the temperate zone, meaning it was moving into colder air heading north.

Trees and woodlands still grew in abundance, but they were separated by larger grassland areas the further north the drone flew. Superimposing the route over a merged world map comprising of what the world used to look like compared with what it looked like now, we could see that, as predicted, the daily distance travelled had increased and the drone was making its way through what was once Turkey. Or Egypt. I was never great at geography even before.

It was not the dry and arid area we remembered it to be, which was good news. The new landscape would make the refueling of the helicopters easy and make it easier to find fuel for ourselves, as the areas should contain wildlife and sources of water. I was less excited about that prospect than some of the others were, because wild animals might not know their place on the food chain since humans had mostly disappeared.

Being able to generate clean water and find food on the way reduced the amount of rations we would need to take with us, adding to the weight savings that Hendricks and Annie were continually calculating to the finest margins.

Our final training mission, as the drone was expected to arrive at Echo site within days, fulfilled another purpose. It was suggested by Ozzie, and the reason for it was pretty obvious, even though none of us—Annie included—had thought of it.

We departed in the direction of our intended route and left caches of food and other supplies at selected landing spots, including big barrels of biofuel, meaning we could initially leapfrog forwards and avoid the necessary but laborious and time-consuming task of manufacturing the biofuel from scratch.

That was the theory, anyway.

While the fuel was being manufactured and flown out, Hendricks continued with our training and even though his standards and expectations of us at the beginning were high, I felt as lean and sharp as I could ever be.

On our final day in the bush I was on point duty, my eyes scanning everywhere looking for threats as I tried to weave us silently and slowly through the dense foliage, leading us back to the camp we'd set up. I held up my hand indicating for everyone behind me to stop and lower their profile. Something had caught my eye, a slight anomaly ahead which didn't fit in with our surroundings. I kept as still as possible as I tried to discern what had caught my attention, and then I saw it. The barrel of a gun was slightly protruding from a bush about fifty yards ahead of me. I could see it was aimed at an angle away from me which gave me confidence our approach had not been noticed yet.

One fact that had been drilled into us was that nature didn't make straight lines, and that small barrel did not fit into its surroundings so it had caught my eye. A few weeks before I would never have spotted it, and I smiled knowing it was not a real threat, but was most likely Nathalie who, under Hendricks' instructions, had laid an ambush to try and catch us out as we returned to camp, in an attempt to teach us one more lesson that danger lurked at every step, no matter how close to base you were. We always knew when this was going to happen, probably because Hendricks didn't want anyone actually shooting a member of our team.

What do I do? I thought to myself as I stared ahead. Should I signal for Hendricks to approach from his position three behind me, so I can show him what I have spotted? No...

As far as I could tell we hadn't been spotted yet; the sound of Nathalie calling out over our radios would have indicated we were burned.

The noise and disturbance of the foliage Hendricks might make if I called him to me would give our position away so, using hand signals, I told those behind me to stay low and in position as my eyes scanned the environment around me. A shallow gulley led off to the side away from the ambush site, so slowly, ever so slowly, I lay on the ground and inch by laborious inch I worked my way around so I could flank her position, positive that at any time I would be discovered.

But the radio connected to my earpiece remained silent.

Eventually reckoning I was parallel to her position, I slowly raised my weapon and studied the area ahead. The bush was only ten yards away, but it looked different from this new angle, and for a while I wasn't sure I even had the right one in my sights. But then I saw the heel of a boot breaking through the foliage that had been used to camouflage the position.

My face broke into a smile and inching my hand to the radio I depressed the send button and whispered, trying to use my best French Accent, "Bonjour, Nathalie." The bush immediately rustled and her heavily camouflaged face became visible as it turned from side to side trying to identify the new threat vector. Not able to resist the triumph I felt at outsmarting one who was far more highly trained than me, I whistled a two-tone sound which caused her head to snap in my direction.

A low two-tone whistle from my right then caused my head to spin in its direction. I couldn't see anything until a shape emerged from the base of a tree ten feet away to reveal Rishi training his gun straight at me.

"Bonjour," was all he said.

Hendricks stood in front of the seven of us once we had loaded all our gear onto the helicopters in preparation for departure.

He smiled at us all, but his eyes flicked between me, Amir, and Ozzie.

"Okay chaps," he began in his traditional British manner. "I'm proud of the efforts and improvements you have made, especially you civvies." He looked at me. "Well done on spotting that last ambush. You knew we were close to base but didn't let your guard down."

He looked at Amir and Ozzie.

"Yes, he spotted it, but you weren't picked up either, something that is extremely difficult especially considering who you were facing."

I shrugged saying, "But he got me, boss," nodding towards Rishi. When out in the field we had all began calling Hendricks "boss," as had his security team all along. I suppose it made us feel more a part of the team.

"Nathalie did not know you were there, which is impressive in itself. Your only mistake was being focused on the one target, not your surroundings as well." He looked at Rishi as if for confirmation. "Give him your thoughts, Rishi."

Rishi never said much, but that didn't make him an outsider in the team. He was always there, taking part in everything and offering help and advice, but he did so with an economic use of words. He gave a rare smile. "It was a good approach and I only saw you when you got close."

There was a silence as we waited for him to continue, but as that was the most any of us had heard him speak at one time, we realized he had finished.

"Okay then," Hendricks continued. "If we were holding a passing out parade this would be it. You're all mission ready so let's get to it."

I was feeling more pleased than I probably should as that meant we were soon to leave to go into the unknown. I climbed into a rear seat in the helicopter, buckled myself into the straps, and shared excited grins with Jones by my side as we powered up and soared into the sky.

Chapter Six

Goodbye, My Lover

The drone completed its last ten miles of the journey slowly. Annie took over direct control to guide it between trees and outcrops of rocks as we watched the live feed on the large video screen in the command tent. The power it took to keep that link open was visibly draining the drone's battery indicator displayed on the screen.

All members of the mission team were there, as well as a few other selected specialists. The rest of the community would be shown the feed later, after any necessary redactions I guessed, but initially we wanted to limit the attendees to those who could contribute to whatever we found out there.

Fortunately, the link between the drone and the ARC orbiting high above us—which Annie had warned us may not be stable—was good, enabling the video feed to be almost broadcast quality.

The drone had spent all the previous day and night recharging not far away from Echo site, waiting for daylight to avoid any anomalies that may be missed through the night vision capabilities its cameras had.

No one spoke or tried to offer Annie advice on routes to take as she remotely approached. We just watched and listened to the few audible updates she gave, understanding that she would know best and any interruptions would take processing power away from the task.

"My sensors are not detecting any signals across all bands…"

I thought it was weird how she said "my" sensors, like she was inhabiting the drone or extending herself to take it over and make it a part of herself.

"No indication of hostile fauna…"

I was probably not the only one to breathe a sigh of relief at the update. Maybe I was expecting her to say something like, "Pterodactyl swarm approaching from the north" or "gopher with an RPG, nine o'clock."

The image on screen was so good I felt myself swaying as it banked around a tree, or leaning back as it raised itself up rapidly as it swooped over an outcrop of rock like an old person playing video games. It was like watching those videos taken from a front seat view of a rollercoaster speeding along its tracks.

A faint outline of a building could be seen protruding from a mess of bushes, and vines hanging down from the trees.

"Target located, one hundred meters ahead. I will perform one circuit and withdraw to a safe distance to assess."

On the screen I could see that Annie had increased the drone's speed. It tore between trees enabling me to catch glimpses of structures that were clearly not natural, but the speed the drone was holding made it difficult to discern much at all. Knowing that the footage could be slowed down so I could study it later, I waited along with everyone else.

Annie finished her fast sweep by raising the drone vertically with the camera pointing downwards to give us an expanding bird's-eye view of the area.

"Initial reconnaissance completed. Locating suitable area to park the drone."

Annie's commentary was brief and to the point, showing how much memory she was allocating to the task.

The view changed as the drone sped away over the trees and we watched silently as it approached the highest tree in the nearby woods and settled slowly onto one of its huge branches.

I stood silently for a while when the screen I had been staring at so intently went blank. I ran through in my mind the fleeting images I had seen when the drone had sped through the area.

Nothing I had seen immediately concerned me, but the area had the feel of an abandoned village deep in the jungle, waiting, like it was ready for some intrepid archaeologist to hack away the hanging vines to reveal an ancient monument.

Chatter began between us all as we hypothesized about what we had seen, knowing that Annie was currently analyzing the camera feed and we would find out the truth soon enough.

Annie's beep of coming back online quietened us all down immediately. I guessed she'd decided it was the best way to quieten us down rather than be another voice in a noisy room.

"I have analyzed the footage and can see nothing untoward," she announced once she was satisfied the room had her full attention. "I will replay the footage slowed down by a factor of ten momentarily. If I could ask you to remain silent and observe. Afterwards I will take questions and pull up any individual sections of feed or single images required."

I had to smile as she was sounding like a lecturer in front of a class of earnest students.

No one disagreed with her proposal, and we all turned to look at the screen again. Slowed down I could see more, could make out a lot more detail, but it showed nothing of any more value. When the view changed to the bird's-eye shot that she had filmed at the end the video paused.

"For context, I will superimpose the original building locations pre-event over the current footage."

Echo site, I now knew from being told and being shown plans and photographs from its construction, was of a different design to Charlie site. Whereas the bunker in the Congo had been a straight down mining operation, Echo had been excavated from a small hillside and the entrance had been protected by a massive portal frame like in a movie. It had the look of concrete fortifications from World War Two: industrial and impenetrable.

Other exits had been constructed in case the occupants woke up and found it blocked, that much I could see from the overlaid schematics, but the whole thing seemed smaller than Charlie site. Don't get me wrong, the place was still huge, extending far inside the hill and stretching many levels below it, but there were little in the way of similarities between the two.

That made sense, I guessed. If one design failed for whatever reason, it was sensible to have different options, right?

Hanging over the entrance portal was a waterfall of encroaching vegetation that had blended the manmade into the natural environment. Other buildings surrounding it which, according to the tags Annie had marked them with, were accommodation and storage buildings left over from the site's construction. These only showed as undulations in the dense forest and scrub that now surrounded and enveloped the site.

"What are those tracks?" I asked as I could see clearly worn trails that weaved through the site.

"That is unclear without further study, but my best theory is that they are game trails."

Hendricks nodded thoughtfully as he stared at the screen before speaking.

"Do those trails match ones in our locality? Because there does seem to be a lot of them and, if I'm not mistaken, they lead to or from the facility. So, something...or someone regularly walks those paths?"

"Wait one," was all Annie replied, in a very human-like response and mimicry of the military-trained operators. "The trails are consistent with the passage of large animals, but I agree there do seem to be a lot of them."

"Any theories about what kind of animal made them?" Williamson asked ominously.

"The species of animals we would expect at Echo site's latitude would be different—both to 'before' and to examples of adapted life on this continent—given the time lapse and likely evolution. The surrounding area is certainly fertile enough to support a large and varied array of flora and fauna."

"Yeah, but...best estimate?" he asked.

She down-toned before coming back a second later.

"The closest visual match from my available data sources shows a fifty-eight-point-one-one percent match to hippopotamus tracks leading to and from water sources."

"Pretty dangerous animal," Williamson muttered in warning.

"However, there is a fifty-two-point-six-four percent likeness to tracks made by humans. The margin for error and a lack of available data about the recent weather conditions is too high to be certain of either possibility."

"So there's something moving there and we don't know what," Hendricks said, bringing the discussion back on track.

"As a precaution," Annie continued, "once the drone is fully charged, I will set the cameras to detect and record any motion they sense. This will provide more information regarding the local fauna present."

"Good idea, Annie. Before we leave, it would be nice to have a better indication of what's in the area," Hendricks replied.

"Thank you, Mister Hendricks. I will inform you when, or if, anything is detected. Can I now show you the location of the impact craters? I'll explain why I initially mistook them to be impacts from pieces that broke off from the main asteroid when world governments futilely fired their nuclear arsenals at it."

Annie expanded the image to show a larger view of the surrounding area, like satellite footage we were used to seeing on the maps our phones used to show. She highlighted an area on the hill where a deep crater created a huge scar that was still devoid of vegetation.

"This is the main impact crater," she explained. "I ran an initial simulation on the effect pieces of asteroid hitting the area would have when I first began monitoring during the time you were in cryostasis. I deduced that if an object travelling with the momentum the asteroid would have had to create a crater the size shown, then it would have had the kinetic energy to destabilize and potentially damage or destroy the facility. My theory was supported by other impact craters in the immediate area."

Another image showed on the screen. It was one of the many millions of photos she had taken when she was alone and evolving onboard the ARC, and showed the site from a time long ago when the dust had first begun to settle.

"None of the other impacts would have carried sufficient energy to destroy the site completely, but the existence of them led me to my initial miscalculation."

I stared at the image. Something was missing.

"Annie. Show the previous image?" I said curtly.

The earlier image of the main impact crater flashed back on the screen.

And then it clicked. The crater on the hill was not there on the previous image. Before I could speak, Annie beat me to it.

"Yes, Doctor Anderson. The crater was not there initially."

There was a long pause before she continued, her voice this time laced with a touch of apparent humility.

"It is my mistake. I incorrectly extrapolated a conclusion from incomplete data and assumed the impact craters were the cause of the site not responding to my automated signals from orbit. I still took photos every six months of the site, but I never studied them as I was concentrating on Charlie site and its progress through the centuries. We now know the crater on the hill which I initially believed to be an asteroid strike was created fifty years after the site became active. I must stress that this is a fact I did not know until I gained access to the data stored at Charlie site."

"Annie, it's okay," I lied. In truth it shocked me, but she didn't need to know that. "Nobody's blaming you. Looking at the footage I think everyone would assume the same thing."

I felt the need to defend my creation. I mean, it wasn't like she had made many other mistakes. Okay, other than keeping us all frozen for the better part of a millennium too long, but most of us had forgiven or forgotten that fact with all the events that had happened since. Plus, that mistake had certainly saved all our lives now we knew what Tanaka had in store for us if we had returned to Earth when we were meant to, which sort of wiped the slate clean in my mind.

"Yes," Hendricks said. "Don't be hard on yourself. You made assumptions based on the information you had available at the time. You made decisions and acted on them before you…became what you are now."

"Forget about it," I added. "The facts are the facts, and nothing we can do can change that."

"Thank you both," Annie replied, her tone still humble. "While I am incapable of forgetting as you are, discarding information is something I cannot do, as without previous experiences, how am I to develop?"

And there it was.

Annie had proved she was probably far more advanced on the evolutionary tree than humans would ever be. Emotions wouldn't stop her or cloud her judgment like us humans. Every decision or action she created would be made just on the facts either known or presented to her.

But what's the quote? To err is to be human, or something?

I managed to shut my mouth before my brain sent those words to my lips, just as Hendricks got the discussion back on track like he always did.

"Okay, folks. There is nothing I can see at the site which will delay the start of the mission." He eyeballed those of us marked for the mission. "While Annie monitors the feed from the site, I am ordering a stand-down for all who are going." He softened his tone.

"Go and spent time with your loved ones or just get some rest."

He turned to Amir.

"Can you please ask Ms. Cole to excuse wives, partners, and their children from all duties as well?"

Amir nodded and raised his own pad, presumably to send a message to Hayley.

He didn't need to add the words that there was no certainty any of us would return from a journey virtually halfway across the globe. We all knew the dangers and difficulties that the unknown held in store. Or maybe we didn't, and that was the point.

Hendricks seemed to be having the same internal discussion with himself, because he put on a brave smile and sent us away.

"Dismissed. Mission go at zero-five-hundred the day after to-morrow."

As I walked in a slight daze from the tent, the trepidation building up inside me, I asked Annie to patch me through to Cat.

"Cat?" I said quietly when we were connected. "Any chance you can finish what you are doing and meet me at our shelter?"

For the first time I had someone who I cared for more than anything I had before in my life, and I had some serious farewells and promises to make.

~

Hundreds of miles to their north, as the drone sped away from the above ground remains of Echo site with its cameras pointed in the direction of travel, a figure appeared from a deep recess in the side of one of the structures.

It scanned the sky, the treetops, trying to spot what had made the sudden, high-pitched whirring sounds.

The figure, bearded and layered with rough clothing, shook his head as if disbelieving what he had heard before he shrugged on an old, battered backpack and raised an ancient, but lovingly maintained rifle into the ready position.

He scanned the immediate area over the rifle's barrel to check for any danger and set out through a well-worn track in the trees.

~

It seemed as if the whole community of over two hundred men, women, and children had gathered to see our departure. I guess we were the main attraction of the day, so it was understandable. I mean, what else were they going to be doing when eight of us were leaving on a mission heading thousands of miles away when most hadn't been more than two miles from the compound since being defrosted?

When our leave period had ended, when we'd finalized packing, loading, and securing every bit of the equipment and supplies we were taking, we loaded up in front of the crowd.

We'd done plenty of test flights to see how they flew when fully loaded, and though they handled more sluggishly, Hendricks was happy that they were flyable. The first thing I noticed was how seriously crammed they were.

We had to take both helicopters, otherwise we'd be going with a pilot, a computer geek, and an engineer, leaving only one remaining space onboard because of the gear we had to carry. That meant, best-case scenario, the only trained person on the mission would be Hendricks and that didn't seem all that safe to me.

So, we sacrificed speed for numbers, and I loaded up in the back next to Jones and opposite Nathalie with Hendricks at the controls. Sitting in the rear seats of the helicopter, wearing full tactical gear with my rifle held with the dangerous end pointed down, my eyes searched for Cat.

She stood slightly apart from the others with her hand held to her mouth as she tried to hold her emotions back.

Trying to hold my own back, I smiled bleakly at her and waved as the conical rotors increased speed, and the dust clouds whirling up in swirling vortexes hid her from my view as we soared into the air and sped away over the trees.

Chapter Seven

To Boldly Go...

Jones, who was my back-seat buddy for the next however many days, smiled at me as I wiped away the tears that had formed as I waved at Cat.

"It's the dust," I said, rubbing my gloved hand over my face trying to eradicate all evidence. I was a member of an elite team after all, and it didn't do me any favors to look weak in front of the others.

Jones patted my knee.

"Mate, she's fit. I'd be crying too." His British accent made him sound like a pirate to my mind more than an elite soldier.

I smiled back at him dutifully and recalled a conversation from a thousand years ago. Sitting around a fire one night on one of the many training missions I had undertaken to prepare myself for the journey, he had told me of where he used to call home.

He came from a small village on the Cornish coast in the southwest of England, and apparently, they all sounded like pirates where he grew up.

Brought up with the sea in his veins, a yearning for adventure made him join the British Royal Navy, which eventually led him to their elite special forces unit, the SBS or Special Boat Service.

I never paid much attention to stuff like that before, but basically these guys were like the SAS, but they did more on water than land. Like SEALs versus Delta or something. I dunno, I'm the computer guy.

He told stories of some combined missions on counter terrorism stuff, catching Hendricks' attention, and eventually earning the invitation to join Sierra team.

He came from generations of fisherman and sailors, as did most of the small village he called home, and he worked on a trawler right out of school. He told me stories of fishing adventures, landing catches in rough seas and selling them to earn enough money for a few pints in the local pub, and tales of how his ancestors were wreckers.

"Like, salvage?" I asked naively.

Jones grinned wickedly at me. "Something like that. They used lanterns to lure ships onto the cliffs on stormy nights, then when they wrecked, they'd steal the cargo."

"So…they were actually pirates?"

Jones laughed at me. I laughed with him, trying to make out like it wasn't a genuine question.

"Didn't, like, the coastguard try and stop them?"

The look he gave me made me feel like an idiot.

The chuckling of Hendricks from the pilot's seat, even though it came through the headset, brought a smile to my face. That brotherhood, or camaraderie—or what Hendricks and Jones called "banter"—between us was what we'd need to keep our spirits up in the weeks ahead. The first time I'd pulled a face at one of them when it started, I'd learned a whole new terminology.

Piss taking, as in taking the piss, was what they called it, and it was like friendly hazing.

Whatever, it passed the time.

The plan for the first day was to get as many miles under our belts as possible. With the fuel caches we had already put in place we could expect to get a full day in the air, minus the refueling stops, and cover many more miles than we ordinarily could when the creation of that fuel would take up most of the time.

Flying at the most efficient height and speed, factoring in wind shear, humidity, and a whole bunch of other stuff I recognized as words which made no sense to me, my mind soon became numb. Everything out of the window beside my head was an endless vista of trees with the occasional hill or mountain. The terrain below us just kept blowing by in monotonous replication. It was the aerial equivalent of travelling on a subway with nothing interesting to see outside.

Okay, maybe not the best analogy, because every time I'd ever been on a subway in any city, I could always rely on some local junkie to do something entertaining like get themselves tasered by the cops. I digress.

The helicopter's main design had been for functionality over a wide range of requirements, and the rotor design did not make for a high top speed. The two-hundred-mile range the craft had meant about two and a half hours' flight time, but that could be drastically reduced or slightly increased if we caught a tail- or headwind.

Annie could've easily navigated Hendricks and Amir to the first of the two fuel stops we had planned for our first day, but

Hendricks insisted that we do it without her help. I wasn't sure where the "we" part of it came in given how I was just sitting in the back and trying not to feel queasy.

"Afterall," Hendricks had said when he'd first told her to monitor their route, but not offer any navigation unless asked for. "We may need to do it without you if it all goes tits up, so a bit of practice now won't do any harm."

My main job on the route, apart from being a badass operator, was to maintain the communication link we had with Annie. I accomplished this by looking like the most extravagant Japanese tourist ever.

Hear me out.

I had a tablet—one of the ruggedized ones rated for warzones—which I used to monitor the uplink strength, and the best way to keep it handy was to loop it over my head so I could just lift it up when I needed to check it. Nathalie argued that it got in the way of my reloads, but if I was having to cycle my weapon in a hurry, I'd be ditching the tablet. I proved how by swinging the thing over my shoulder, so it hung down my back instead.

Once we reached Echo site, we'd be able to bounce our signal back via the ARC, or maybe, if they were still operating or even still there, use the transmitters that had been installed at Echo site. On the way we'd have to rely on data transmissions using a variety of means. When moving we would be reliant on VLF—that's very low frequency for non-nerds—transmissions.

These transmissions, though reliable, restricted the amount of data that could be transmitted or received. We'd be able to maintain contact with Annie but what she could offer us would be greatly reduced. When we landed, assuming we got there in one piece, I could set up the various antennas and aerials we had with us which would improve our communication capabilities to provide full audio, video, and other data capabilities with home. As it was, not having Annie watching our every move and monitoring our vitals with a zero-second delay was going to feel a little weird.

Hendricks' voice came through the headset again, snapping me out of my daydream.

"Okay folks, by my reckoning the first refueling site should be ahead in the next few minutes, eyes outwards please."

Not even a "this is your captain speaking…"

I scanned the canopy looking for the clearing we'd landed in a few days earlier when we created and left a cache of fuel as part of our build-up training.

Hendricks' navigation was right on the nose as Jones spotted the clearing and directed us to it. Descending rapidly, with the craft piloted by Amir following us closely, we didn't need to be told what to do. As soon as the skids of the helicopters touched the ground, we jumped out with weapons raised and formed a close perimeter. After a minute of studying the vegetation and undergrowth around us, at a low whistle from Nathalie, Jones, Rishi, Marco, and herself cautiously raised themselves up from their positions and stalked outwards to expand our perimeter.

Me, Ozzy, Hendricks, and Amir, maintained our positions. I was down on one knee as had been drilled into me, all my senses on full alert as I scanned everywhere. The radio plugged into my ear broadcast the low, whispered reports from the others.

Once Hendricks was satisfied by their reports, he ordered Jones and Rishi to maintain their positions covering the perimeter and recalled the others to return so we could refuel the helicopters as quickly as possible. We wanted to cover as many miles as possible before darkness or exhaustion forced us to land, and with two more fuels dumps on our route which would give us the extra range, we were hoping to stop approximately a hundred miles before the area where the massive ape thing had been spotted.

The plan was to land and manufacture enough fuel while we rested and then hopefully fly clear over the area and get past it by at least a hundred miles before landing again.

But, like Hendricks enjoyed telling me, no plan survived first contact with the enemy.

I didn't like the sound of contacting any kind of enemy at all, so I kept my mouth shut.

It didn't take long to transfer the fuel from the containers into the helicopters, but before we left Jones insisted he got "a brew on," telling us we needed a break to remain sharp.

For those of you who don't watch Guy Ritchie movies, that means he wanted to make a hot drink. He'd tried to educate us on the art of English tea, on how it was far superior as a restorative elixir than any cup of coffee the rest of the uneducated world drank. On how it had to be strong enough to stand the spoon up and required exactly two sugars, but he was outnumbered. Hendricks, being a fellow Brit, wholeheartedly agreed with his countryman and condoned his obsession with getting his little stove out at every opportunity.

Marco had us rolling with laughter when Jones' fixation with tea had become the topic of conversation one night while out on patrol. He told the tale of a joint mission with British special forces in some foreign hellhole when they had come under sustained and heavy attack.

While most of the patrol were screaming wildly and making desperate radio calls for air support and extraction, two of the Brits had set their stove up and were calmly making tea, distributing mugs to the other operators, firing the occasional burst to keep the enemy at bay, as bullets pinged off the rocks all around them. Then, when a ricochet had hit the stove and knocked their tea into the dirt, the two guys started swearing in outrage and rushed the enemy's position, turning their flank and forcing them to fall back enough to allow the helicopters in to extract them. His natural storytelling ability made the whole event sound like a comedy farce, where the crazy Brits had mopped up hundreds of enemy soldiers because they were sulking about their spilt tea. I didn't know how much of it was true as to the way he told it, but given how Jonesy got seriously precious about it, I wanted to believe there was some truth behind it.

Hendricks had confirmed the national pride by saying that no British commander dared get between a soldier's inalienable right to make a brew, no matter how dire the situation looked.

I was learning to appreciate the drink though—even if I couldn't stomach it sweetened—and gratefully accepted a mug when it was ready.

Jones was right. After having a "brew" I did indeed feel refreshed.

Twice more we performed the landing and refueling task, each time fanning out in a protective cordon to secure the area before refueling. Hendricks, this time checking with Annie, confirmed we were approximately seventy-five miles from where the unidentified creature had been caught on camera.

It struck me that we were now the furthest anyone had ever been from Charlie site and the two settlements in their long history, and so were truly in uncharted and unexplored territory. We were outside the familiar ecosystem, and with that unwelcome thought came the knowledge that we didn't know where we fit on the local food chain.

We knew that apart from the known animals that lived in the vast forests surrounding Charlie site, Three Hills, and The Springs, they should contain no surprises, but this far north we had a chance of finding something as yet undiscovered. That meant we didn't relax when we landed, because dropping our guard now was a bad idea.

Chapter Eight

Circle the Wagons

"Clearing on the plateau ahead," Hendricks announced. "All eyes outwards, please. I'll do one sweep and if it looks suitable, we'll land. Mister Weatherby, maintain altitude and cover our approach."

His tone, which had been relaxed when we had talked between ourselves as we had flown over the uncharted land, was now professional and a little edgy. I raised my weapon through the open side door and my eyes scanned everywhere as Hendricks lowered the helicopter and swooped toward the target location.

Amir held off behind and above us in an overwatch position, and I didn't need to look back at the other helicopter to know they would be watching our backs and ready in an instant to offer their firepower and help if it was needed.

The clearing was on the edge of a cliff that fell vertically down to the forest floor below. The plateau was raised above the surrounding terrain, forming a kind of long ridge, and it looked ideal to my untrained eyes.

Protected by the cliffs on one side, it provided enough space for both helicopters to land safely. The surrounding dense vegetation looked ideal for biofuel manufacturing, and would hopefully give us the opportunity to trap some animals for food.

"Okay…" Hendricks spoke after he had flown a low, wide circle around it. "It looks clear, does anyone see anything untoward?"

A chorus of "No boss, looks good to me," and similar attestations came from us, and we prepared ourselves to leap from the helicopter as soon as the rapid descent stopped at the forest floor.

Once more my heart was racing with trepidation and excitement as I stepped from the helicopter and immediately dropped to one knee and raised my weapon. I could hear and sense, rather than see, the others doing the same around me. A buffeting wind that increased and then died down as quickly as it had arrived told me the other helicopter had landed and deployed its own crew. The tactics we had developed dictated that both aircraft keep their engines burning and their weird airscrew, ice-cream-cone-like rotor blades turning until we were satisfied the landing site was truly safe, just in case we needed to get back on board and speed away if something terrifying decided they didn't want us dropping into their territory.

Nothing appeared, thankfully, even though I was still expecting a T-Rex, and after the usual time half our team pushed out. Eventually the call of "clear" came in from multiple voices over the radio and Hendricks ordered the helicopters to power down. Even though they were quiet, you didn't realize how much noise they made until they shut off. The noises of the forest slowly returned as if it too had been shocked into stillness by the sudden and mysterious interruption.

Ten minutes later when those sent to investigate the wider area had all reported they could see nothing untoward, Hendricks issued a command over the radios to us all.

"Jones, Rishi, stay on stag. Everyone else is on camp and fuel duty. Two-hour shift rotations until chow time."

As we all busied ourselves with our various tasks, either clearing an area for sleeping and eating or hacking at the surrounding undergrowth to create a pile of vegetation, others were already feeding into the biofuel manufacturers. The mood in the camp was good. We'd covered a lot of ground on our first day, and we all felt a sense of achievement. No dangers or mishaps had befallen us, and we talked quietly between ourselves as we went around our tasks. Before helping to gather foliage my first job had been to set up the radio antennas and establish a secure connection with home.

"Hello, David," Annie's voice came from my radio. "We now have full connectivity, and I can offer all of my services."

"Great, Annie," I replied, hiding a childish smirk at the way her words came across as a little too…suggestive. "We've got a few hours' work to do first, so we'll brief home base later when it's all done. Could you just let them know we're all good?"

"Of course, David, I am doing that now. Could I be of any assistance?" The calm tones of her voice seemed surreal with all the activity going on around me.

"The drone's unpacked and ready to go, so unless you can swing a machete and feed the manufacturer, just monitor the drone footage and let us know if—"

"Of course. I will alert you to any movement or anomalous sensor indications if they arise."

"Thank you," I replied not letting on that her interruption had annoyed me.

Part of it was checking if she could read a room, to see if she'd realized she'd cut me off, and part of it was to see how long it would go on before she adapted it.

The best way I can describe it, is like when you're typing in something to a search engine and the algorithms guess what you're trying to say. When Annie thought she knew the end of a sentence, she was starting to cut off the speaker and she might not know that was pretty rude.

The usual noises from the myriad hidden beasts calling the forest their home sounded all around us. I'd become used to them following my first terrified few nights spent out here, and now barely gave them a second thought. Spotting a suitable growth of foliage that I knew provided the ideal materials we needed, I headed to it and began hacking away, stacking the leaves and branches in a pile next to me.

Twenty minutes later and feeling much sweatier, my arm was raised high holding the machete, tensing my muscles so I could chop through a particularly dense growth of bushes, when an unearthly sounding roar echoed around the forest.

I froze in place, my arm static above me as my senses went into overdrive. My head turned rapidly and eyes darted as I tried to locate the source of the terrifying noise. I eventually remembered that a gun beat a machete in a knife fight, so I sheathed the blade and grabbed my weapon from where the sling held it against my back where it couldn't impede my machete work. Dropping to one knee, I raised the weapon to my shoulder and prepared to defend myself.

Looking around I could see everyone else acting in a similar way. A short, piercing whistle that I knew had come from Hendricks rang out. It was our emergency recall signal.

Raising myself up and with my weapon still held tightly to my shoulder, I awkwardly shuffled backwards the twenty yards I needed to reach the cover of the helicopters. I cast occasional glances behind myself to check my route, but mainly I scanned my front ready for whatever might appear, and felt my way backward with my boot heels.

"Um…what the hell was that?" I asked conversationally, desperately trying not to sound as panicked as I felt, as I joined the defensive circle already being formed by the others.

"I have vectored the noise using your radio microphones," Annie announced, her voice rapid and serious. "I calculate the anomalous noise came from the valley below us. I am repositioning the drone to investigate now."

The drone's whirring noise faded as it swept away in search of whatever we'd all heard.

"Listen," whispered Ozzie from my side.

"What can you hear?" Hendricks demanded sharply.

"Nothing, that's the point," he replied. "Whatever the bloody hell that was has shut everything else up."

He was right. The forest was still and quiet, like someone had just hit the mute button. All I could hear was my heart beating louder than a bass speaker as it pounded in my ears.

Hendricks' calm voice came through my earpiece. "Let's hold our position here and see what Annie picks up with the drone first. Rishi, Jones, stay on stag but at the first sign of anything just get back here."

The two operators acknowledged with curt, soft replies.

"We face whatever this is as a unit," Hendricks added.

It dawned on me that if they didn't haul ass back to us if something came from their direction, they'd be facing our bullets also.

"Weatherby, get both helicopters ready for an immediate lift off," Hendricks ordered.

Amir stood, but Hendricks added, "Don't start the engines yet, just get the systems online."

Not needing the usual rigmarole helicopters required for their engines to warm up and build up rotor speed, the conical rotor drive system could go from off to fly mode in just a few seconds after the engines were turned on.

I listened to him slip away, making what sounded like enough noise to let everything within a half mile of us know we were there, but my attention was fixed on the tree line ahead.

Tense minutes passed when another series of roars—roars that appeared to come from more throats than one—ripped through the air around us.

"Steady…" Hendricks' voice was calm, but that did little to make me feel better. Just when I thought my nerve was going to break, that I was the weakest link in this chain, Ozzie started to mutter curses just loud enough for me to make out his accent.

I held my nerve and the urge to run just about in check. I consciously tried to keep my breathing below hyperventilation level and wiped the sweat from my brow to keep my vision clear.

Annie's voice burst into my ear and almost made me jump out of my skin.

"I am tracking a number of primates. They initially appeared to be heading in our direction, however they seem to have detected the drone long before I expected them to. They tried to attack the drone, but I was able to avoid the spears and rocks they threw, and withdrew it to a safe distance where I am monitoring them still."

All of us exchanged wide-eyed, incredulous glances at the news. Annie's calm account of what she was tracking was at odds with the words she used, and my terrified brain decided it was the time to consider an additional communication subroutine to add gravity when delivering reports like that.

Something short of screaming, "Oh my God, we're all gonna die," but more intense than, "Nah, it's cool." Some appropriate middle ground that told us people we really needed to be concerned.

I knew if I'd been the one reporting the events, I'd most likely be delivering it through the medium of screaming.

"Everyone load up, we're leaving," Hendricks barked, the urgency and command clear in his tone. I started to rise, already thinking of being up in the air again.

"No, I do not believe that will be necessary," Annie replied immediately. She spoke in such an authoritative tone that I sank down the few inches I had raised myself. "They are still some distance away, and now that their primary focus is on the drone they are not getting closer. You are safe for now."

Hendricks asked the question that we must have all been thinking. Well, I was thinking it.

"Are they the things the reconnaissance drone picked up?"

"Yes."

The answer came without hesitation, not that with her processing ability she needed any thinking time like us mere mortals.

"I have cross-referenced the approximate height and build between the captured image and the footage of these animals, and I conclude that they are the same species. Do you want me to send the feed through to David's data pad?"

"No, not yet, we can watch later. Let's deal with the matter in hand for now. Recommendations?" Hendricks said, asking for options from his team. I liked it when he did that. I mean, ordinarily I liked it, but right then I just wanted someone to make the decision to keep me out of a remake of *Congo*. Or *Planet of the...*

Marco spoke first. "I say we take off and find another spot to lay up for the night. We don't wanna mix it up with the natives on the first day of the patrol."

Annie spoke before any of us could respond. "Interacting with this unknown species will divert us from our ultimate mission. My primary concern is that you only have approximately thirty minutes of flight time on your current reserves. If you follow the planned route, that would place your next stop very close to where the image was taken. My recommendation is to remain and refuel."

She left the rest unsaid. Our situation was so clear it didn't need anyone to explain it to us. We had approximately two hours of daylight left, and our plan was always to land and refuel in daylight, then rest up overnight. As soon as dawn broke, we'd take off in the fully refueled helicopters to cover as many miles as possible the following day, aiming to get at least one or two full or partial refueling stops in before we found another place to camp for the night. Flying at night was something we'd already discussed and settled on being a bad idea.

Back when these helicopters were invented, they could have used every bit of technology available to fly ground-hugging, satellite and computer-controlled flight paths through every terrain on earth. But with limited GPS, and not even a printed contour map of what the new Earth we had recently arrived on looked like, the risk of flying into a mountain that hadn't been there a thousand years before was too great a risk to take.

Hendricks took a few moments to respond. He looked like his mind had raced through all the possibilities, and in a clear, firm tone gave his orders.

"We're staying put for now. Rishi and Jones, close the perimeter down by twenty yards. I want everyone in line of sight at all times. Nat and Marco, give me an inner cordon. The rest of us are on fuel manufacturing. Once that's done, we'll rotate watch duties and leave as soon as the light is good enough for flying. Personal weapons within reach at all times; now isn't the time for sloppy drills, people."

My heart seemed to speed up more as he spoke. I honestly expected him to call it off, even order us to retreat a few miles, but I did not expect to be told we were exerting our squatter's rights.

Hendricks waited a few seconds for us to absorb his instructions before he let out a humorless chuckle.

"I anticipate it'll be a long night…"

Chapter Nine

The Burden of Leadership

Tori rolled on the bed and stretched. She had tried to convince herself that she wasn't enjoying the trappings of leadership, but that skirmish was brief and convincingly lost. The furs were soft, were devoid of lice, and didn't stink of green wood smoke like many others—the best cure for the miniature pests was a damn good smoking.

She ran her fingers through the soft hair, her nails reaching out to trace a trio of faint red lines down the ribs of the man she shared the bed with. She knew he was awake from his breathing, and she knew—for all his warrior reputation and genuine bravery—that he was as ticklish as a baby.

He tried to fight it, tried to resist the reaction, but he squirmed away from the touch and let out a laugh.

"Aaaah! Stop!"

She didn't. Springing to her knees in spite of her nakedness, she launched onto him and tickled with both hands to attack his flanks.

He rolled, his right arm entangling her left, and pinned her to the bed beneath him. She smiled, fought back, but his superior weight held her fast.

She didn't relent, not being the woman she was by giving in at the first indication of defeat, and twisted to bring her right foot up high over them both to hook it around his shoulder and under his chin. He twisted his face away, laughing at the escalation, but her left foot found the soft flesh between hips and ribs to drive him up and off her.

He, as befitted his own reputation, did not take this counter-attack lightly and slapped a hand into her thigh, taking away the power to the leg pushing him away and collapsing him back down onto her.

Their faces, only an inch apart, both registered a rueful smile. They held one another's gaze for a few seconds before the tension between them boiled over and their entanglement became something very different, but equally as forceful and competitive.

Twenty minutes later, Harrison stepped out into the town with Tori walking behind. Three Hills had remained shrouded in shock and loss, still recovering from the violent, horrifying waste of life by The Swarm, and ultimately at the hands of The Tanaka.

His leadership had been hard won, but with the alliance he shared with the newcomers he had led his people to something they had never known.

Peace.

Clarke and an entourage had visited the previous day, and the drinking had gone on long into the night. Tori had wanted it to end; bored of the hot air from old men talking about great battles like they were good things. They talked of each other's ancestors fighting one another with honor and bravery, when in truth they had stabbed, brawled, shit, and bled in the mud fifty years before their parents had been born.

She had smiled, had pretended to find them all interesting, but she had wanted it to end.

Now, standing beside the man she wanted to drag back to the soft, clean furs, she frowned at the half dozen people waiting for him on his doorstep.

He didn't expect anyone to bow and scrape to him, but she knew his wide smile and interested face was an act. He was a man of action, or decisions, when too many others preferred hot air and old stories, and these daily complaints were starting to annoy him.

Tori was a woman of action too, which was one reason why the two were so well suited, and she resented the previous night's implication that she was just his woman.

"Good morning," Harrison said in warm greeting, prompting five people to start yelling their case at once.

Harrison held up both hands to ward off the noise as his head was thicker from the evening of drink than he wanted to admit. They kept yelling, jostling one another for primacy and position, and the sound annoyed Tori.

She stepped in front of him, her body lowering slightly, and her right hand held back ready to swing because she was more than just his woman. She was a fighter of reputation in her own right, and just as capable as he was.

"One at a time or none at all," she snapped, raising her voice to cut their clamoring off in a heartbeat.

Eyes went down, hands went up, one even dropped to a knee to try and win the battle of obedience and be heard first, but

Harrison walked past all of them. He bent at the waist, the handles of his machetes casting a shadow over the diminutive petitioner and smiled genuinely.

"And what do you need, young one?"

The big eyes looking up from the grubby face, right into his soul, and the words came out scarce above a whisper.

"Our cattle. They're all gone."

Harrison straightened, eyebrows contorting in confusion, and glanced back to Tori. She walked closer, pushing past the others who once again began shouting their grievances—petty and otherwise—until she silenced them with a raised palm.

She leaned down, all anger gone from her features, and she asked the right questions.

"How many cattle did you have?"

"Fifteen head. They was milk cattle."

"And when did they go? Was this when The Swarm came?"

The little boy shook his head.

"Last night, so it could'n'a been The Swarm. My daddy…"

The face dropped and the voice wavered into nothing. Tori took her turn to send a curious glance at Harrison, but before either could speak a booming voice filled the open space.

"It is true! Cattle are gone, and with them their owner. This orphan boy has told you, and what are you going to do about it?"

Sebastian—head freshly shaved, and beard twisted into beads that clacked together under his chin—held his arms out wide and turned a slow circle. He was performing for everyone else, and he was performing a play only he knew the lines for.

"This man, the one you have elected as your leader, what does he do? Huh? What does he do? I will tell you. He does nothing. He makes friends with our enemies. He ruts with his bitc—"

Tori was up, moving fast, and the wicked dagger was already in her hand when Harrison opened his lungs.

He had a big voice. It was far bigger than it had a right to be, and anyone would be forgiven for thinking that it belonged to the much bigger man. Sebastian, still scheming and evidently stinging about the loss of his bid for leadership, possessed the size but he lacked the voice.

"Enough!"

Harrison walked toward him, gesturing subtly for Tori not to kill him, and stood opposite the challenger. He too spoke loudly, as Sebastian had, for he too was addressing the growing crowd.

"What leader can know a thing before it has happened? Why is it that you know what happened before the news was brought to me, Sebastian? Is there more about this that you know?"

The accusation was subtle, but it was not without merit.

He looked around him, searching the faces of the onlookers, and he knew that by simply answering the man he had this crowd on his side. That wasn't to say he had a unanimous following, because there were maybe one in every ten faces who did not smile. Some of them nodded along with Sebastian's words when he responded.

"So what will you do, great leader? Will you ask your friends with their guns and their technology to fix this for you, or will you ask your friends at The Springs for help?"

"We don't know if we need anyone's help, Sebastian. Again, you expect me to have the power of foresight. Is that how you knew of this? Do you have the foresight?"

Sebastian laughed, glancing around for support and not seeing enough to bolster his confidence. Harrison ignored him and turned, addressed the crowd, to give them his answer as if dismissing the challenge entirely.

"What I will do, is I will feed this young one and learn the full truth of what happened. In the meantime, I will send some of our best warriors to search for the missing man and his cattle."

He locked eyes with Tori, conveying that his most trusted warrior was her. She nodded, accepting the unspoken responsibility, but it seemed that Sebastian was not done.

"You send a woman in your place? Are you frightened, great leader? Or is it that you think so little of this boy's family that you only risk losing a woman if—"

"I would happily go myself, alone, in the night if I had to. Tori will go because she is a skilled warrior, and because her loyalty is to Three Hills and our people. Where is your loyalty, Sebastian?"

The bigger man bristled, threatened to boil over like a cooking pot left unattended, but he regained control before his words or his actions forced an escalation. He sagged, turning the gesture into a sarcastic bow of obedience.

"My loyalty is to Three Hills, and with our great leader, of course."

They watched him go, both hating the way he took his time like he was showing how unafraid he was of the leadership. Harrison leaned away, summoning one of the many scribes who sent his messages and recorded his judgements.

"Send for Jacob. He can tend to the rest of the petitioners."

"Jacob…? He is…" the man responded meekly, not wanting to be the bearer of the news.

"He's what?" Tori snapped, her head whipping to fix her eyes on the scribe, intensifying his fear. That fear was not for the cruelty of leadership or risk from incurring Tori's anger. His reaction to her mentioning Jacob, the man who had challenged Harrison for leadership, lowered the temperature noticeably.

"What is it?" Harrison asked in a gentler voice.

"Jacob has…that is he…"

Tori stirred, impatience threatening to burst out of her like an erupting volcano. Harrison stilled her with a gentle touch on her back.

"Tell me," he said softly, promising no repercussions for the information.

"Jacob has…he has not reported for his duty in four days. Nobody knows where he is."

Harrison nodded to accept the information, sending the scribe away again to record the grievances of those waiting to see him, and telling him to promise on his behalf that their worries would be addressed.

With the scribe sent away, he held up a hand to ward off Tori's protest before she could speak, lifting the other to summon two warriors he trusted with his life.

"You, go and find out what happened to that boy's father. You two, find Jacob and keep an eye on Sebastian."

"Expecting trouble?" one asked, his eyebrows raised high.

Harrison glanced at Tori, saw his own fears reflected in her eyes, and turned back.

"Always. That's how I am still alive."

⁓

Tori was still seething with anger even after fifteen minutes spent jogging through the countryside to where the boy had described last seeing his father and their small herd. She was accompanied by only two other warriors, both of them young and loyal to her and Harrison, and both able to keep easy pace with her, jumping off rocks and catching low branches to swing their bodies through the air, landing gracefully and rolling back to their feet.

This was one of the reasons why their group had risen so fast in the warrior hierarchy of the Hills; their dedication to physical excellence and ruthless attitude, not to mention their loyalty to each other and the values of their people.

Tori, with Massa and Curn, found the pastureland easily from the boy's directions.

It was not uncommon for the people of the Hills to spread out in this way, to live outside of the protection offered by the walls of their town, but they all came home for a week each month when the moon was at its fullest.

The pasture was mostly flat, the land rolling off downhill on the southwestern edge, and the crude ring of tree trunks and rough stone showed where the cattle spent their nights beneath the tall tree that served as the home of the herd's owner.

The boy had explained how his job was to milk the cows every morning, and carry it back to the Hills to trade it for the things they needed. He then returned to the open, empty land not far away. Tori liked it, liked the space, but she did not like what she found when they stopped running at the outer edge of the stone and wood pen.

"Wait, this is wrong…"

Tori's words, combined with the action of her drawing one wicked-bladed axe from over her shoulder, prompted the others to do the same.

Cruelly sharp machetes whispered from their leather scabbards, their edges nicked and honed after countless skirmishes, and the three of them fanned out to search.

"Cattle all gone, just like the boy said," Curn noted.

Tori could see that well enough, but her focus was on the crude ladder cut into the sloping tree trunk that led to the platform fifteen feet from the ground.

The walls and the tree hide were insufficient to protect anything from The Swarm, but they would deter all but the most determined dragon attack.

She climbed inside the makeshift shelter, drawing the axe again that she had sheathed for the climb, and scanned around. She saw a few meagre possessions, but nothing of value. There was no metal, no cooking pots, and although the place did not appear to have been ransacked, she knew that the lack of possessions would make detecting any theft a difficult task.

"Down here," Massa's deep voice rumbled from below.

Tori poked her head over the edge and saw it immediately. The others were standing in the middle of the churned mud where the cattle walked in and out of the pen each night, but the freshest tracks led in a direction away from the town.

"Did it rain last night?" she asked. The two young men looked at one another as though eye contact could prompt their memories, until Curn nodded slowly.

"I think so. Maybe an hour or two before the dawn."

Tori swung her legs out and spun, climbing down rapidly to drop the last eight feet and sink into a squat to absorb the energy of her landing. She rose, eyes scanning the ground, and drew her axe again to follow the fresh trail.

It led into the forest about a mile north, and Tori was certain that the cattle had all gone this way. They fanned out, covering more ground, but maintained sight of one another as they searched.

Tori found it, being the one who followed the center of the trail. She stopped, crouched, and let out a long, low whistle as she kept her eyes on the danger ahead.

The others joined her, sinking silently into the undergrowth on either side, and she whispered what she had already seen to them.

"It's a nursery. I think two of the cows died here."

The nursery, the site of a large kill where the dragons would bring their young to gorge all day, was a dangerous place. As soon as she had said it, the other two cast their eyes up into the canopy in search of the caretakers they knew would be somewhere nearby.

"I haven't seen any, but they're out there," she told them.

They shifted beside her, understandably nervous, because an adult dragon left in charge of the group's young would die to protect any of the juveniles left there to eat. It was believed that any caretaker failing to do so faced death by their pack leader, so a protective dragon was the most dangerous kind.

"I need to see the corpses," Tori said. She did not want to, but she had to. Returning to report that she couldn't be certain who or what had died because she was afraid was not an option.

She crept forward, axe in her right hand and dagger reversed in her left, and she moved slowly in the hope that she could avoid detection.

She heard the crunching, the wet tear of flesh rendered by sharp teeth, and she rose as silently as she could to see above the foliage.

Six, seven, eight…all of them very young, no longer than her leg from nose to tail, and all of them totally focused on devouring the fresh meat presented to them.

One body was hairy, the fur of the shaggy pelt stiff and dark with blood, and two hooves jerked in the air as the teeth tugged and worried at the remains. The other was hairless, and being far smaller than the cow it had owned, the flesh had been mostly stripped from the body to reveal the bright white of bones. She swallowed, and she didn't know if it was the small noise she made or if some other random occurrence had caused the young dragon to turn and fix one yellow, soulless eye on her.

It screeched, hissing and shrieking, and Tori turned to run, to get out of the killing ground, but two heavy thuds, one after the other, told her that the caretakers had been alerted to their intrusion.

Chapter Ten

Hold Position

Anderson

Amir and I were feeding material into each helicopter's biofuel manufacturers as fast as the small compact devices would allow. Hendricks had made it clear that was our job as he and Ozzie were more used to physical exertions than us, so both of them were frantically swinging their machetes at every piece of vegetation around them.

They threw it in our direction causing us to rush around gathering every armful we could to pile by the helicopters. The process that had seem laborious and time-consuming when we had done it before now seemed excruciatingly slow. Every armful of vegetation we pushed into the feeding hopper resulted in only a pitifully small dribble of clear, pungent liquid trickling down the clear tube into the tanks. Through experience we knew that every hour of feeding the manufacturing unit resulted in a maximum of thirty minutes of flight time, and that was only if the plants used were of the right type. The only vegetation available to us was limited to our landing spot, and unfortunately what we were chopping down and feeding into the machines was at the bottom end of the plant-to-fuel efficiency chart.

But it was all we had, so I just kept feeding it into the unit, gathered more, and listened to the updates from Annie as she kept us informed on the movements of the creatures.

They were still concentrating on the drone and hadn't gotten any closer, which was a good thing. Definitely good.

I was working so frantically that the passage of time was blurred, my full concentration on the task at hand. Annie snapped me to attention when she called my name through the earpiece.

"David, I need to return the drone to change its battery in five minutes and forty-three seconds. Can you please get a spare ready to exchange?"

I looked around, saw that no one else was reacting, so I knew she was speaking to me alone. It was only when I spoke that Weatherby and Hendricks stopped to watch me as I replied I would.

I stopped what I was doing and went to retrieve the battery from the storage area of the helicopter where it was charged by the engines. I saw them looking at me as I stopped what I was doing and began moving to the helicopter, so I called out to them.

"Need a new battery for the drone."

I was the one who had set it up, so I knew exactly where it was. When I had the battery in my hand I spoke softly, so as not to distract the others, leaning my head towards the microphone on the radio clipped to my tactical vest.

"Got it, Annie, send it back when you're ready."

"Thirty seconds," she said in a curt, efficient response before going quiet again. The shortness of her response didn't bother me because I guessed she was performing a lot of tasks at once and was prioritizing them according to her processing abilities. Limited bandwidth Annie was like "younger" Annie with a little attitude.

My ears detected the sharp whirring sound of the fast-approaching drone a few seconds before my searching eyes spotted its dark shape heading in our direction through the canopy.

Waiting tensely, I clutched the spare battery and a small screwdriver in my hands, mentally going through the battery changing procedure. Even though I'd performed the task before, I wanted to prevent any unnecessary delays to the essential coverage the machine was providing.

Avoiding the temptation to grab it as it swept towards me, because, you know, spinning carbon fiber blades versus flesh and all, I waited for it to land beside me before I moved in.

The locking clamps yielded easily to the screwdriver, and in seconds I'd swapped the battery over, made sure it was securely locked in place before jumping out of the way and calling out the all clear.

Without a reply from Annie, the blades on the drone started and it surged into the sky to retrace its course. I watched it for a few seconds before remembering I had a job to do—a vitally important job if we ever wanted to leave—and I got back to stuffing cut foliage into the biofuel processor, forgetting the battery I still held in my hand.

"David, please prioritize recharging the battery."

Performing a silent "Duh!" to myself I turned and inserted the battery into the charging dock in the helicopter.

"David," Annie said when the light indicated it was charging. "The problem is that regardless of battery conservation efforts, that battery will not be fully recharged before the current one's charge falls below its optimum performance criteria. This will mean that in approximately four hours and thirty minutes, I will no longer be able to provide drone coverage as both batteries will be drained."

"Well…shit."

It was the only answer I could think of, but it summed up the situation perfectly.

"Does Hendricks know?" I asked.

"Not yet. I have only just finished calculating the results and I did not want to distract him as he is currently preoccupied with multiple other variable factors," Annie replied, her voice sounding apologetic this time.

"Well, you better had and soon, Annie, because at some time in the night we are going to be blind."

I glanced at the sun which was beginning to settle on the distant horizon.

"Don't worry about it, Annie, I'll do your dirty work for you, you've got enough on your plate and all I'm doing is feeding leaves into a machine."

"Thank you, David."

That was all she said before going silent again, presumably concentrating all her available data power on more important functions than making polite conversation with me.

When the drone returned to where the creatures were, she immediately informed us that the targets, as she called them, had moved closer.

I assumed they'd followed the direction the drone flew back to us, but as soon as it was over their heads again their attention returned to alternatively trying to attack or hide from the flying object. That was good news at least.

Starting to feed plants into the machine again I called Hendricks' name, knowing he would pick it up over the open channel. When he responded, his words were interspersed with groans and pauses as he was still swinging his machete at the bushes around him. I told him as briefly as I could about the problem of the diminishing battery capabilities of the drone.

I watched him from a distance when I spoke, still mechanically feeding another armful of green stuff into the hopper. He stopped his frenetic chopping of the flora and stood once I'd finished talking. Standing still he looked at the area around us with a frown of concentration forming on his face. I could tell from his body language he eventually reached a decision, and I stopped what I was doing in anticipation of what he was going to say.

"Okay, people," he said. I watched his lips move as the words sounded in my ear. "Annie isn't going to be able to keep the drone up all night, and those things down there know we're up here, so I don't think hiding until daylight is going to keep us safe."

I watched him as he paused again as he sought those around him with his eyes.

"Rishi and Jones, pull back now and help Nat and Marco fortify our position. I'll help as well, so Ozzie, Weatherby, and Anderson just keep manufacturing fuel until the tanks are full."

I heard a series of muttered affirmatives in varying forms over the radio.

"But if we need you, be prepared to man the walls, so to speak. We just don't know what those things, whatever they are, will do. Given the way they're reacting to the drone I don't think they'll be too friendly towards us."

"Mister Hendricks, may I add something?" Annie asked over the open channel.

Despite how my mind was now churning as I imagined defending ourselves against hordes of terrifying, mutated monsters, the way she now asked politely for permission to speak, rather than just voice her opinion as fact, showed me another level of emotional development she hadn't displayed before. Yet again surprised at this apparent development, I decided to force it into the back of my mind for later exploration with her, as our current situation was a little more pressing than marking another development in my creation.

Damn stress reaction again.

"Yes, Annie, please go ahead," Hendricks replied. His own innate British manners always made him sound like one of those *Downton Abbey* people, and I wondered if that was rubbing off on Annie.

"I agree with your plan, and I will endeavor to preserve the battery life of the drones for as long as possible. I believe the appropriate words for this situation are, 'every second counts.' Studying territorial behavior of other primitive species from my memory confirms the fact that their base instinct would most probably be to attack any threats to their territory."

"Well that's reassuring," Nathalie muttered.

"But my studies of them so far show that they seem to display advanced problem-solving techniques in how they are trying to attack me—and by me I am, of course, referring to the drone—which indicates a reasonably high level of intelligence and neurological development."

She paused as if looking for the right words to say.

"I am sorry, but I have so many aspects I am currently monitoring I do not think I am explaining myself clearly. What I am trying to say is that I can only see so much with the drone, so please do not rely on me for total observational security. I may miss something."

Now that got my attention and my eyes immediately turned to the dense forest that surrounded us, imagining it to be filled with, well whatever was in the thick forest below us. I saw the others doing the same.

"Everyone get moving," Hendricks called out over the channel. "You heard her; Annie can't be everywhere babysitting us so it's up to all of us to get this place locked down tight and get ready for whatever might happen."

Once more the passage of time was blurred as I concentrated on my job to keep the woefully small trickle of fuel continually flowing down the tube into the tank. The only noises breaking my concentration were the sporadic, unearthly sounding screeches and howls coming from the valley below.

"There is another option," Annie said. Something in her tone made me imagine—if she had a body and a face—that she chewed her lip and frowned.

"I'm all ears," Hendricks answered.

"I can try to use forty-five percent of the remaining battery power in an attempt to lure the group further away from this location."

Hendricks didn't answer right away, so I knew he was thinking it over. I ran the logic in my head too, reckoning on a chance of leading them away being better than them being so damn close without the reliable ability to detect them if they made a run at us.

"Do it. Keep us informed."

Annie didn't answer, but the distant whine of the drone's blades ramped up to a shriek as it whizzed away, slapping heavy leaves as it cut through the trees below the canopy.

It worked. The light was fading as the sun began sinking below the horizon when Annie asked me to change the drone's battery again, which I did even faster than before. I imagined myself like one of those Formula One pit lane guys, then I mentally slapped myself for being an idiot.

I put it down to stress and tiredness, but I knew that was only halfway right.

"Thank you, David," Annie told me as the drone flew away again.

"The battery only has sixty-seven percent charge," I warned her as I plugged the almost spent one back in. She knew the batteries were going to run out at some point and reminding her of that was unnecessary. She let me know that with more manners than I expected.

"Noted."

"Where are they now, Annie?" Hendricks asked as he laid another tangle of tree branches on the barricade everyone was feverously constructing.

"The targets have moved from their last position and are now two hundred yards closer than before. It appears that they have decided to return to this area."

"Can you do the thing again and turn them around?" I asked, recognizing the fear in my words, and hoping nobody else had.

"They appear unwilling to continue in the direction I have led them with the drone. It is unclear why they have stopped following—"

"That's the limit of their territory," Nathalie said, like the answer had just dawned on her.

"That is a likely cause for their change in behavior," Annie answered. "I predict that they will reach the base of the cliff when I will be forced to return the drone for another battery change. This will be in approximately seventy-one minutes."

"Nothing we can do about that," Hendricks said calmly. "Let's just keep on doing what we're doing for now, and hope they take the bait again."

In the forest below, the pack leader turned and issued a challenging snarl at one of the other males who had pushed too close to the front. He and the other adults of their group had cowered with fear when the helicopters had first invaded their territory to land on the escarpment. What they were was far beyond any capability his brain could process, but he was the leader and no incursion into his territory, no matter how Godlike and fear-inducing it was, would stop him from defending it. Uttering grunts, growls, and clicks, he ordered the old, the weak, and the young of his tribe to go to their traditional sanctuary they used in times of trouble.

Then came the whining, buzzing thing that sounded and acted like an insect, only it was far bigger than any insect he had ever seen. The others had seen nothing like it either, judging by their sounds of alarm and fear that were impossible to miss.

Buried deep in the jungle, hidden from view by the forests that had claimed the area back to nature, was a vast area of strange structures. It was their holy place, a place that drew them to it, as some deeply buried instinct in their hidden memories told them that the decaying structures stretching deep underground in places were a part of their identity.

They worshipped many totems that depicted strange figures. They stirred deep feelings inside them, and it was as if they knew they were connected to them in some way. Why or how everything was there was unknown to them as that memory had long ago been lost. Lost long before the new species had first survived and emerged from the ruins of the city when the dust had begun to settle, and the surface could once again sustain life.

Had they the ability to remember, their history could be explained and passed on, but how they came to exist had never been important to their survival. Living for the next minute, the next hour, the next day became their only need, and so their origins were lost.

If they had the knowledge, they would know that back when the meteorite hit, their distant forefathers had hidden in the deepest basements and sewers of the city.

Hell would have been a kind way to describe the conditions below ground as any food which the people had managed to bring with them was soon consumed or stolen by those who were stronger. Humanity vanished within days, and it was not the survival of the fittest but survival of the cruelest that held sway. Murder, sickness, cannibalism, and death were the new ways of life.

But evolution is a remarkable thing. Most of the people died from radiation poisoning, but some survived. They survived only to face new threats, because they were not the only survivors.

Apes, fleeing the devastation just as the humans did, fled underground alongside them.

Minds changed, bodies ravaged by radiation adapted, but the survivors learned to live. Packs of animals—human and otherwise—formed and the ones who outlived them all were the strongest, most cunning, the most adaptable. They had the intelligence of humans, but they also had the strength required to tear a man's head off if the need arose.

Those survivors, those adaptable, cruel winners of the evolutionary game, bred their strength into the next generation of underground animals. Most development is learnt behavior, but the lessons taught to this new generation who grew, matured, and reproduced, were equally as cruel.

It was a masterclass in evolutionary development, and with the aid of radiation, the mutated survivors of the second and third generations created new life. This new, adapted breed of apes did not flourish, but it did survive long enough to bring that evolved DNA into the world.

And then the chimpanzees arrived.

A small community of them had also survived the devastation that had ravaged the earth, and they too had changed. Pale and virtually hairless from generations of genetic mutations caused by radiation and the ever-changing environment as the planet swung between violently low temperatures and insanely high ones, they were as close to a human-like appearance than they had ever been in their evolution. As well as being devoid of the thick hair that had once adorned their bodies, they had evolved other senses to combat the lack of light that made their vision very poor at anything over a dozen paces away.

These chimpanzees took up residence beside the territory claimed by the apes, and decades of border clashes resulted in a wary truce that was only broken by the occasional adolescent looking to gain reputation.

As the two groups lived mostly in peace side by side, their growing numbers led to more and more interaction, and that interaction eventually led to what scientists would have called hybridization.

After two generations of twisted offspring failed to thrive, a new breed was born. They were taller, stronger, with straighter backs and a cold cunning to them that, even as infants, made them dangerous for either sire species to encounter.

They evolved their own language, their own rituals and behaviors, and the extinction of the older species became a foregone conclusion.

That region's surviving human population had first fought against the invaders, as if knowing at some basic level of consciousness they were a threat to their own survival. Though far less in numbers than the humans, the hybrid species possessed a greater strength and power.

A bitter, drawn-out war of attrition was fought, and no side reached a point where they could call themselves victors. The struggle to banish their enemies from the underground sanctuary of basements, tunnels, and sewers which provided them shelter from the largely desolate surface raged for generations until nature twisted fate again.

A newer, larger, and more aggressive subspecies of hybrid ape emerged, and that physical dominance was not all that pushed them to the forefront of their battle lines with the humans.

Perhaps it was a simple dominant mutation exerting itself through Darwinian reproduction standards, but the sudden and rapid change in their appearance and behavior had the humans staring down the barrel of extinction.

It was perhaps a fluke mutation, a cruel twist of genetic fate, but the result was the pivotal point in the war between humans and the new hybrid species of primate. Although they shared about ninety-nine percent of the same DNA as humans, the differences between them represented an impossible chasm into which humanity fell headlong.

These few rare—rare at first in any case—hybrids seemed to be stronger than both former species, but it was their terrifying intellect that marked a change in the war. The sheer cunning, the problem-solving abilities that had separated humans from other primates millions of years ago, was no longer tipped in favor of the humans. Ambushes and simple traps that had kept them safe for years were bypassed or turned against the ambushers, and the aggression of the hybrids was matched only by their voracity in breeding. In a short space of time, they became the dominant apex species, which eventually led to the extinction of their own origins, and the humans in that region.

And so, from the turmoil of ash and ice, of burning temperatures and changing seasons, a new species of beings emerged from the depths of the earth and thrived. They had no natural predators and the newly forming forests that quickly spread to cover the land provided an ideal habitat for them. Over hundreds of years their population expanded to the point where tribes split from existing groups and ranged further afield, save they slaughter one another over territory and resources.

But still, that place where their origins had survived became a holy place for all tribes to use. Even though their language was limited, communication and deeper levels of understanding were possible. No single tribe could claim it as theirs, and no inter-tribal rivalry was permitted within the sprawling, decaying former city that formed their holy place.

The old of each tribe, only those who had achieved elder status through seniority or reputation, resided there and each tribe paid tribute to keep them; the guardians of their shared heritage and keepers of the holy place.

Chapter Eleven

Close Encounters

The leader stared at the drone that flitted from tree to tree, the whine of its rotors varying in pitch as Annie darted the machine around, altering its height and distance from them, but at all times staying in sight. He knew it was watching them—it had to be because it responded to his thrown spear in time to avoid an impact—but the technology of the cameras and transmitters it carried was not even near his capability of understanding.

He had heard the helicopters first, hearing the scream as they landed and beat the trees with invisible force, and not long after the small drone had appeared overhead. Logic dictated it had to have come from the larger flying objects, because he had never seen anything like it before and, judging by the fear from his pack, neither had they.

The drone buzzing high above his head had not attacked them as he had first feared it would. When it flew off in a direction away from the escarpment, he had given chase, calling his fighters to join him. When the border of their neighboring tribe halted their pursuit, it had disappeared, leaving them free to cautiously patrol back in the direction to where they originally were. But it returned to try and lead them back toward the border yet again.

He knew they could not cross into their neighbor's territory, so he roared for them to stop. It soon returned to flit between the trees above them.

The longer the drone was overhead the more his fear of it waned. It was magical yes, it was godlike yes, but it had not killed them or even come close enough for any weapon it could possibly have, be it spear or club, to strike them. He suspected it also wanted to force them to break a border, to encroach, and that led the leader to believe it wanted to do them harm by proxy.

He was getting more and more frustrated at his inability to scare the thing away no matter how aggressive he and the rest of his tribe acted towards it. Looking up at the high escarpment where the larger mystical thing had come to earth, he hatched a plan.

Gesturing, grunting, and clicking the strange sounds their throats produced, he got his tribe in order and selected the ones he wanted to take with him while ordering the others—the weakest of his pack's fighters—to stay and try to kill the flying thing if they could.

When the thing flew away again, disappearing as it had before, he gave his orders and the pack split.

Anderson

Working feverishly at the many different tasks, the growing darkness almost went unnoticed until Annie spoke to all of us. Her announcement came not long after the drone had flown off after another battery change, and the news made my chest go tight.

"The drone has returned, and I am not detecting as many targets as were there before," she said unhappily. "I am unable to ascertain their location currently. Please hold while I do a sweep of the area."

I struggled to not stop feeding the machine with leaves, and instead looked into the dark forest now knowing something could be out there. The limit of my vision, that place where the forest became a single wall of green, seemed too close. Far too close.

Amir spoke up. He hadn't said much since we had landed as he'd been concentrating on feeding the green machine like I had, but also probably because he was smart enough to know that Hendricks wouldn't take too kindly to any interference in his area of expertise. Amir had wisely kept his mouth shut, until that moment.

"I think we'll have full tanks in about thirty minutes. Shall we keep feeding them or do you want us on the perimeter?"

"No keep working, please. If we need you, you aren't exactly far away," Hendricks answered, his voice clipped and more terse than usual.

~

Leading the pack at a run, they scaled the barely discernible path that snaked up the cliff face in no time. The chimpanzee part of their genetic foundation gave them the agility to climb trees and rock faces with far greater ease than their human-like appearance would suggest, and the ape side had only enhanced a strength that would make a mere human appear as weak as a newborn.

The forest was in his territory so he, and the other fighters with him, knew exactly which trail or animal track to take to get to their goal the fastest. When the forest floor became too dense, they took to the trees and nimbly jumped or swung from limb to limb, covering the ground at a blistering pace. The speed they were maintaining did not tire them. They could keep it up for hours and still have the energy to fight if need be. It was what made them the apex predator; their ability to outpace and outsmart any prey they hunted.

The only animals they feared were the dragons, but their meat was too tempting and when ripped from a freshly killed one, too delicious to ignore, so they fought smart and developed ways to trap them and single out adults for an easier kill. It took the whole tribe to hunt the dragons using those tactics devised and honed over the centuries.

True, it was dangerous and often resulted in deaths, but the meat from even just a few dragons would feed them all for weeks.

Even if they didn't eat the meat, they would have been forced to interact with the dragons eventually to keep their population in check and balance the local ecosystem. Not that they would understand those concepts, but population control of the only predator capable of harming them was a necessary task.

He knew they were getting close to where the sky devils had landed, so he barked a short noise causing those rushing through the trees and undergrowth alongside him to stop immediately and look to him for the next command.

"You hear that?" Marco whispered through the open radio channel.

"What was it?" Hendricks hissed.

"Not sure, it just sounded…different to all the other noises. Something's up, I can feel it."

Hendricks, I knew, trusted instinct. He said it was as valuable as any of their senses, and he took the word of the highly trained operator seriously.

"You heard him," Hendricks said calmly. "Eyes open. Anderson, Weatherby, Ozzie, keep feeding the machines, but be ready to join us immediately if I order it."

I couldn't keep my eyes away from the forest now as I pushed another armful of leaves and branches into the hopper, willing the process to speed up and do…whatever it did to make the fuel we needed so we could leave.

~

Hidden by the dark depths of the forest the leader stared at the two large, strange things and even stranger looking animals he could just make out crouching behind a wall of piled logs and branches. His nose told him more about them than his eyes, and the smells he detected were unlike anything he had ever sensed before. At that distance he could make out shapes, and he crept closer at a slow pace to sense more about them.

Something deep in his subconscious—some obscure genetic memory—stirred as he looked at his closest relatives in biological terms. They looked like him, but they didn't. They wore strange items that covered their bodies, very similar to the statues and badly faded murals and pictures that still survived in sheltered parts of their holy place.

His mind raced. His thoughts ran riot in his mind. Through unblinking eyes, he stared at them until he reached his conclusion.

He turned his head slightly, keeping his eyes on the invaders, and grunted the low noises that conveyed a word—a concept—to the others.

Demons.

They were demons, and they must be destroyed. He knew that the few skulking behind their barricade would be no match for their best fighters. He had to clear them from his territory, or the gods would not be pleased if he did not protect them from these pretenders.

Uttering more clicks and grunts to signal a cautious advance, he raised his crude spear and stalked closer, leading his fighters who followed in silent obedience.

Hendricks strained his eyes staring into the growing gloom of dusk. The forest stretched from cliffside to cliffside in front of him, a wall of dark green and brown. He stiffened, detecting an almost imperceptible shift in the pattern of the darkness hiding the inner reaches of the forest. Holding his weapon in front of him he raised his head from the sights and tried to penetrate the blackness.

Movement. There, behind a large tree on the edge of the clearing about twenty meters away. Hendricks crouched behind the barricade, body stiffening, gripping his weapon tightly, and watched as the tribe's leader stepped out and faced him.

The creature filled his vision through the optic, and he gasped involuntarily. He twisted the rifle, canting it left thirty degrees to use the iron sights fixed at an angle.

It was a man, only it wasn't. It was an ape, but different. What it was, was a grotesquely muscled thing that would not have been out of place in a science-fiction movie, and its deep eyes were staring right at him. It continued to stare, silently holding a long spear in a huge hand that was attached to a thickly muscled arm.

That hesitation, that unexpected possession of a tool, and the intelligent stare made Hendricks relax his trigger finger.

Everyone on the barricade gasped or cursed quietly as more figures emerged from the darkness and stepped into view. Rifles twitched and switched aim at the growing number of targets.

"Hold!" Hendricks hissed. "Stand down!"

I rushed over to the barricade and crouched down, Amir and Ozzie running behind me, and we pointed our weapons toward the trees.

Aiming at the creature right in front of me, my hands shaking, and my breath ragged, I heard Hendricks issue another command.

"Annie, if you haven't already worked it out, some of them have made it up here. Could you bring the drone back?"

Damn, that guy has ice in his veins. How can he sound so calm?

Her reply, just as calm, still did not help to lower my heart rate.

"It is en route, but only has approximately twenty minutes' flight time remaining. David, could you get ready to change the battery?"

I wanted to scream. I wanted to shit my pants and scream, then run south and not stop until I was locked inside a pod rated for atmosphere entry.

"Uh...sure...?"

I sounded like a little kid, and I really didn't want to move. Those things had already attacked the drone, and putting myself right beside it made me a target too. I didn't have long to think about it, because the drone zipped overhead and swept past the things before hovering and settling a couple paces away from me.

"The figure fourth from the left," Annie warned, "is the one I have identified as their leader based on his actions and mannerisms when monitoring them earlier."

There was a shift as all our guns twitched to seek the target she'd identified.

"Annie," Hendricks answered quietly, although for the first time his voice portrayed a level of annoyance. "Their leader? Is that a chain around his neck?"

"I believe it is. He is the only one wearing anything, and that could be indicative of a symbol of office."

Her voice, unlike Hendricks', betrayed no emotion at all.

"As far as I can ascertain, it is a simple length of chain joined with a padlock. The absence of visible oxidization indicates that it is regularly cleaned, but I cannot hypothesize further as to its significance."

"That's good enough for me, Annie," Hendricks replied. "He's their leader as far as we are concerned. Marco? He's yours. If this goes sideways, he goes down."

"I'm on him," Marco replied softly.

A standoff commenced, with us watching them and them watching us. They showed no signs of wanting to attack us, in fact they showed no signs of...

"I don't think they can see us," I thought, though clearly said out loud.

"Why do you say that?" Hendricks asked hurriedly.

"I...I'm not sure. I think they know we're here, but I'm not...Annie? Help me out here?"

"It is possible that these creatures are long-sighted. Their visual acuity range may indeed be far shorter than that of humans. I recommend caution," she said calmly.

Caution. No shit.

"Okay, everybody hold tight," Hendricks said. "Let's see how this plays out."

I had no idea of the passing of time, only that the figures staring at us in the darkness began to disappear as night fully descended. They seemed to melt, like I'd imagined their still forms watching us, and their disappearance was even more terrifying than their sudden appearance.

As was characteristic of the latitude we were at, one minute you could see your hand in front of your face and the next, nothing.

"Annie?" Hendricks asked, just as the last light left and he flicked the switch on his own rifle-mounted flashlight to send a beam of light outwards. "How long will the batteries last on our torches?"

With no hesitation she replied.

"Eight hours if used on maximum output. I am sorry, but I cannot monitor them individually because I lack the connectivity."

"No need, Annie," Hendricks replied. "I take it that eight hours will cover us until dawn?"

"That is correct."

"Torches on, people," Hendricks said, and my terrified brain wanted to correct him. I'd been around the guy long enough to know what he meant when he used the wrong words for things.

The multiple beams of our weapon lights stretched out from our position and illuminated the forest. The things were still there, hiding in the foliage and staring right at us. They all reacted immediately, screeching in shock and fear at the solid beams of bright light that fixed on them.

It might've been funny to watch if the situation was different. The way they reacted to the light touching them, the desperate way they tried to hide or wipe the bright spots of light from their bodies reminded me of the kind of enjoyment people took from using laser pointers with their cats.

They screeched, running around in futile efforts to rid themselves of what was far beyond their understanding or comprehension. I guess they thought the sun was attacking them at night or something. Then it stopped being funny.

The leader, his initial fears evidently repressed, stood and observed the chaos that surrounded him. He held his hand out, letting the beam of light pass over his fingers, then barked a series of grunts that silenced the screeching instantly.

~

He told them to be calm, that it was just a trick, and that the fire could not hurt them.

Becoming their leader was no accident of birth. He had always displayed more courage, more strength, and superior problem-solving abilities than any other of their tribe. When the old leader became too infirm, too weak to lead from the front as was expected, he challenged for leadership and not one member of the tribe stood in his way.

The fight was short. The old leader knew him, respected him, so he only gave a cursory display before bowing his head in defeat. Instead of reaching down and taking the chain from around his neck, the younger ape waited as a sign of respect, and when it was handed to him, he donned their symbol of leadership. The old ways were to kill the previous leader in case his dominance made a resurgence, but the last dozen generations had seen a shift towards allowing the elders to retreat to the holy place.

Not all, but respected elders like their former leader fitted that mold.

It was forbidden for anyone but the leader to touch the chain. None of them knew where it had come from or why it became their tribe's talisman, but it had been a symbol of leadership from before memories began.

He lowered his hand away from the beam of light, then thought of the chain. He grasped it, simultaneously reassuring and reminding himself of the burden he carried, and screeched a single order. All eyes turned toward him as they calmed their collective panic.

Roaring another command combined with him thrusting his spear in the direction of the strangers made them put their fears aside and instantly obey. As one, they turned and rushed at the barricade.

Hendricks issued his own command.

"Fire!"

That single word turned the situation from standoff to all-out war, as eight rifles opened up simultaneously at the rapidly approaching mass of beasts.

Marco, whose holographic aim point had not veered from the leader, grunted for a second, and cursed in annoyance as one of the other creatures rushed into his burst and took the bullets meant for the leader.

The leader watched in horrified amazement as the front rank of his charging warriors, just ahead of him, fell without being struck by anything he could see. The area was suddenly a mess of sprays of blood and screams of pain as the lead runners fell, tumbling over each other amid the sounds of rocks punching into flesh, when gaping wounds suddenly opened on their bodies.

Blood and gore splashed the leader's face, shocking him into wiping it away with his free hand, and he faltered as the situation erupted beyond anything he could comprehend.

His mind raced. The spears the invaders carried emitted loud bangs and sprayed gouts of flame when his own spear did nothing. When the tree by his head splintered and the shock of the bullets passing close to his head made him stagger, he screeched in panic and confusion, chattering the noise to send them into full retreat.

His fighters needed no other commands or orders to abandon the attack. The few that still lived in the front rank turned and leaped at the trees as if knowing that they offered the only protection available. The pack disappeared into the darkness of the forest to leave the clearing suddenly empty and quiet, save for the frightened chattering of fleeing apes and the snapping of branches fading into the distance.

Silence eventually descended over the area. We were all stunned by the suddenness of both the attack and how it had ended. One moment we were aiming and firing at the beasts that erupted from the impenetrable darkness of the forest, and the next they were gone, leaving their dead lying before our crude barricade.

I was still trying to collect my thoughts when Hendricks in full business mode called out to us all.

"Reload and stay sharp; they're still out there. Annie, have you got them?"

Over the metallic clicks of magazines being changed and rifles being charged Annie's voice came through our earpieces.

"I cannot detect them now. They have gone beyond the infra-red range of the drone's camera. Do I have your permission to fly the drone on reconnaissance? It is the only one we have and its loss will severely hamper our future surveillance requirements if I fail to return it."

"Yes, we need to know where they are, push out and search. Expanding corkscrew," Hendricks told her.

The expanding corkscrew comment made my brain buffer for a beat before I figured out what he meant, sending the drone out in a widening, circular search pattern.

My shaking fingers managed to swap out my magazine and pull back the charging handle to snap a round into the chamber. My thumb automatically felt the safety—muscle memory or something—and I pointed the dangerous end back at the trees.

"I'm at twelve. Marco, six. Jones, three. Nat, nine. Eyes open," Hendricks said, snapping out the orders and confusing me again until my brain caught up.

"Everyone else, load up what we have into the helos and rest. Change guard in an hour."

Chapter Twelve

The Longest Night

The leader stared through the forest toward the place where the invaders had defeated them so easily. His fighters, most still quivering with fear and confusion at the sudden turn of events, surrounded him in the darkness. Uncertain grunts and noises sounded quietly, all of them asking for reassurance, but the undertone was one of failure.

His failure.

Darkness was no problem for them. Their eyes, mutated and developed in the pitch blackness of their former underground world, were highly adapted and suited for night. The limits of their distance vision held no negative effect on them in the dark, and he considered that an advantage.

Grunting, berating them for being afraid, he stood tall and hefted his spear. He communicated that he was going back, and only those who were brave enough to follow should bother coming.

Some left, slinking away low to the ground as if staying small could make them invisible, but most of the survivors went with him back up the steep incline to where the smell of their dead family was thick in the air.

He could easily see the figures still crouching behind their barricade, pointing their fire-spitting spears in all directions. But he could not be sure if they were able to see him.

Not understanding what a gun was, he still had the mental ability to understand from his brief experience of them that if the stick was pointing in their direction and flame shot from its end, they died.

The trick was not to let it point at you, he reasoned.

His own years of experience, and the knowledge passed down from previous generations had taught them to successfully hunt every dangerous animal the forest was home to, and these new arrivals were no different. He would work out their weaknesses and kill them.

Emitting grunts and clicks, gesturing with his hands, he commanded two of his fighters to join him and the rest to stay where they were.

Crouching low he crept towards the forest edge. The beams of light that continued to sweep everywhere did not reach where he now crouched as the branches and leaves absorbed the light.

But he could still see them. He could hear their strange noises and curled a lip in disgust at how they communicated. Signaling for the ones with him to hide behind the larger trees, he stared intently forwards and let out a roar of challenge.

The shafts of light immediately focused on him, as if searching for the sound, but he stayed as still as he could. Those lights, he knew, were attached to their fire spears, which meant that they were pointing in his direction.

Picking up a rock from the soft earth at his feet he flung it in the direction of the barricade with a sweep of his powerful arm.

It landed with a crash of leaves and a muted thud, away to the side of the barricade.

The lights moved away, searching for the new source of sound, and their noises rose and fell in response as the idea formed in his head.

Anderson

I jumped in shock and cursed when the single roar sounded out, so it took me a second or two to recover before I followed the movements of everyone else's lights and pointed my gun to where they were aiming. Seconds later when the sound of something crashing through the undergrowth echoed around, I was ready and altered my aim the same time as everyone else did.

"Ohjesusshit! What's going on?" I cried out.

"Relax, Anderson," Hendricks replied calmly. "I think they're testing us. Probing our defenses, trying to see how we react, I imagine."

"I...you say that like that's a good thing?" I asked incredulously.

"Well, no..." Hendricks said with a chuckle I was amazed he thought was appropriate given what was going on. Maybe it was nerves.

"It means they're not running away scared as I hoped would happen when we opened fire." He paused for a few seconds before continuing. "They're not going to give up easily, so everybody keep your eyes on your sectors and don't get distracted."

As part of our training, well mainly mine, Amir's, and Ozzie's, we'd practiced fighting to defend a fixed position, much as we were now. It was drilled into us that we had a sector, or area of responsibility, that we covered. Your concentration should never leave that area or get distracted by things that may happen in other sectors, that way we ensured a good all-round watch. The wild wavering of our torch beams as they sought out the answers to the noises in the forest told Hendricks that we had, in our flustered panic caused by what had happened, forgotten this basic discipline. Hendricks walked along the barricade, reminding us where we should be looking. He wasn't his usual polite self about it, either. This shit was life and death.

I gripped my weapon tighter and kept my eyes, and the beam of my weapon flashlight, firmly where they should be.

In the forest, the leader watched as one of the invaders went down the line and pointed at an area beyond their barricade to the others with him. He now had another piece of useful intelligence as he picked that invader out to be their leader, even though he could see no obvious adornment like his chain.

They all carried possessions, and not just the fire spears, which confused him for a time, until the same one again stood and gave instructions.

His lips curled cruelly, and a low growl emitted from his throat as he stared hard at that invader. He now had his own target; he would kill their leader himself to punish him for entering his territory.

Learning from his enemy he chose his next plan. Turning his back on them he waved to the two with him and they went back to where the rest of his tribe were waiting.

~

I methodically swept the beam of my torch around my sector as I stared out into the dark, trying not to fall into a regular routine in an attempt to keep myself alert and awake. As if I was going to fall asleep anyway, but it kept my mind working as the fatigue of physical effort and the stress of the situation began to take a toll on me.

Annie had parked the drone on top of one of the helicopters. She said it would extend its battery life a lot as only the camera was being used, and in the silence, I could hear the low whirr of the gyro as it swept back and forth.

When a rock was thrown, it shocked us all as there hadn't been any warning from Annie. One moment there was silence, and the next a watermelon sized rock bounced off the top of the barricade, missing my head by a couple of feet before rolling harmlessly aside. I yelled in shock, but it was followed up by a barrage of rocks of all sizes forcing me to duck low behind our cover.

Annie said something I didn't catch, but the rifles opening up made me guess she'd given the direction the attack was coming from.

The rocks stopped coming at me, and I raised my weapon to fire a long burst into the darkness. By the time my magazine ran dry and I started to imagine myself recreating that scene in *Predator*—you know the one—I heard Hendricks yelling.

"Cease fire!"

I'd already stopped, but I swapped out my magazine sheepishly.

"We haven't the ammo. Only fire at targets you can see," Hendricks snapped, sounding pissed. He was right. We did have some reserves of ammunition, but due to the impossibly tight weight restrictions of the mission, we didn't have an unlimited supply and we still had a long way to go. We fell silent again and stared outwards.

In the forest the leader watched the reaction to the rocks been thrown. The fire spears had not hit any of his fighters, only causing a flurry of dislodged leaves and small branches to fall all around them as the bullets tore through the trees.

Deciding on his next course of action he raised his head and emitted a series of calls which echoed around the forest. A few seconds later a quieter, more distant reply echoed up from the valley below. He grunted in satisfaction and issued a lower rumble, the order for his fighters to gather around.

When another loud roar tore through the trees I wasn't the only one to jump in fright.

Weatherby must have had his finger on the trigger of his rifle, in breach of just about everything we'd been taught, and unleased a burst which ripped wildly towards the forest.

Hendricks didn't say anything about it, but I could see his expression in the dark. I didn't ever want to do anything that invoked a response like that from him, and I was pretty sure Amir was going to have his ass chewed for it. If we made it through the night alive, my brain helpfully told me.

He muttered a low apology which was met with the silence of obvious disapproval. We then settled our nerves down again and waited.

When the distant roar from the forests below us sounded out, I tensed up. It was the first time we had heard any noise from below and it was too much of a coincidence to come just after the one that had sounded close to us, too close.

I had to assume the roar from below was a reply to the closer sound, but if that was question and answer, or order and response, I sure as hell didn't want to know what they were planning.

Our tactical situation was dire, because flying away now meant we'd be blind in the darkness with no idea if we could find another safe place to land with the fuel we had. What made it worse, was that it might be our only option; to risk death flying at night, or face off with whatever came out of the forest at us.

I was still thinking this choice over when another barrage of rocks began. All I could do was stay low but try to keep watching my sector as the rocks landed all around us.

A rock, luckily a small one about the size of my fist, glanced off Hendricks' head causing a small trickle of blood to flow down his face. He hissed through his teeth, dabbed at the cut, and held his fingertips up to the flashlight beam to show bright red.

"Who said helmets weighed too much to bring?" he muttered.

Still trying to be as small as possible behind the barricade, all I could do was poke my head up to check they weren't running at us again. I could see everyone else doing the same. The occasional curse or yell of pain signaled hits like we were playing battleships and not cowering in a dark clearing waiting for the shadows to come kill us.

I had the cliff edge off to my left, and glanced in that direction when I caught movement among the shadows in my peripheral vision. Not being able to see clearly, I pointed my rifle and the beam of the flashlight illuminated something that make my heart want to stop.

Two figures were scrambling over the edge of the cliff to flank us, and as I stared open-mouthed, I could see new heads appearing as more followed them.

"Left! Leeeeft!" I screamed and tightened my finger on the trigger. My wild shots missed everything, but it had the desired effect of warning everyone else what was happening.

Hendricks turned and fired. One of the beasts dropped from sight, screaming as the bullets ripped through its chest.

Instinctively everyone turned to face the new threat, the beams from their lights flashing everywhere trying to pick a target. The problem we had was that the two helicopters were between us and the cliff, blocking off a good portion of the area we could see.

Dark shapes began to appear in our beams and more guns opened up. The animals could move at a phenomenal speed, and combined with their inhuman ability to jump like huge damn frogs, it made them ridiculously hard to track. One moment they were there, and the next they had leaped out of the beam of light and were gone again. One landed in front of Rishi just as he was firing his weapon at another; he tried to react and swing his weapon back but the beast thrust his arm forwards and impaled him through the neck with his spear a second before he could bring his weapon to bear.

I was firing, panicking, but I heard the wet crunch of the wood ripping through his body.

Jones, who was by his side, obliterated the thing's head with a long burst from his own weapon.

Annie, her voice this time almost a scream, shouted out to all of us.

"They are coming from the trees. Watch your front!"

There was no time for Hendricks to issue any orders. Any cohesion we had was gone and it became a sudden scramble to survive. Wild-eyed with panic I spun and fired a long burst at the ones my flashlight showed running towards us from the trees. Not even looking if I'd hit any, I dropped the magazine from my weapon when it clicked empty and thrust another one in as fast as my shaking hands would allow.

Gunfire, roars, and animal screams sounded all around me. It was complete chaos, but from the little I could figure out, we were holding them back. Bodies lay everywhere, both around us and in front of the barricade, and more were falling as shots struck home. Their screams of pain when hit sounded inhuman and alien like, only adding to the cacophony of noise bombarding us.

A movement to my left made me spin again and my light showed a huge thing running at me. His mouth was wide open, showing a mass of sharp teeth as he roared and raised the spear he was holding, thrusting it towards me as his arms pumped in effort. My finger tightened on the trigger and without aiming I held it pressed down. Gouts of blood flew from his chest as some of my wildly aimed shots hit, but still he kept coming, the roar changing from terrifying keening sounds to roars of what must have been pain just as my own terrified, angry bellow harmonized with it.

I squeezed the trigger of my weapon harder—as if that would send the bullets flying out quicker—and carried on screaming my own roar.

I felt the spear hit me. I was knocked off my feet as the thing crashed into me, and was engulfed in darkness and the world went muffled and almost silent.

I'm dead.

That was my only thought as I lay there with all my senses spinning. Why else would everything go dark and silent? A pungent stink filled my nostrils, making me gag. This brought on an odd elation as I realized if I could smell, then I probably wasn't dead after all. This rush of emotion was followed by panic when I tried to move and became more aware of the great weight pressing down on me.

I heard Hendricks yelling something at Annie, telling her 'now' but my brain couldn't comprehend what he was saying.

I opened my mouth to scream, but all that did was make me gag more as I inhaled a lungful of whatever made me heave in the first place. I redoubled my efforts to free myself when I heard snippets of Annie's voice transmitting something.

The only words I thought I could make out were, "Get down!"

I couldn't be sure, but the noise that followed was unmistakable.

The helicopters had one gun apiece, and due to weight, we carried very limited ammunition for them. It was like a smaller version of the guns protecting our home, and that rattling, rumbling chatter was the sweetest sound I'd ever heard in my life. Trusting my sentient AI to fire automatic weapons above my head held no fear. I had no room to feel the fear of it anyway, because all my focus was on what the apes would do to us.

It only lasted for a few seconds, but the noise of it would've made me duck and cover my ears if I wasn't trapped under a ton of what smelled like wet dog. It ended as abruptly as it started, and the relative silence that followed left me desperate to know what just happened.

I could hear the occasional shot being fired, but it seemed like nothing compared to the destruction of the helicopter gun.

I stopped fighting the dead weight on top of me, thinking my way out of the problem instead of relying on brute force, because that was how I always got to where I needed to be.

"Annie?" I whispered, hoping that the microphone on my radio would detect my low voice. There was no response, and my heart dropped.

Is this how it ends for me? Suffocated under a damn ape who tried to go all Chewbacca on me?

"Anderson!"

The shout was muffled, blocked by my stinking blanket.

"Here!" I yelled back, freezing as soon as I'd shouted because I felt the beast on top of me moving.

No, this is how it ends. Ripped limb from limb. Got it.

So many thoughts were running through my mind about what to do I was unable to choose which one. I knew one thing though: scared to death or not I was not going down without a fight. I couldn't use my rifle but I knew I still had my pistol in the holster strapped to my leg.

The weight on me shifted and my right arm was free. A bright light shining in my face took any vision I had away from me, confusing me more, but still I tried to grab for my gun, fumbling wildly as my hand found it and my thumb pressed down to release it from the secure holster.

It trapped my arm, pinning my wrist to the forest floor, and set me to full panic mode. I yelled in rage and more than a little fear until a voice I knew well spoke calmly.

"Anderson! Stand down, it's Hendricks. They've gone for now. Just calm down and we'll get this thing off you."

Relief poured over me. Followed immediately by more fear, as I remembered the spear hitting me. The weight fell off me, rolled over my left side, and I sat up, frantically rubbing my hands over me as I imagined blood pouring from a wound I couldn't feel yet due to me being in shock and denial.

"I'm hit," I said weakly, repeating it over and over not believing that every time I looked at my hands they weren't covered in blood.

Hendricks knelt beside me and conducted his own inspection. Roughly pulling and pushing me from side to side, he quickly examined me before saying, "Where were you hit?"

I patted my chest as I looked at him dumbfounded, amazed that he couldn't see it. I stopped when he smiled, placed his finger on my chest where I thought I had been hit and poked it around.

"It hit your vest; you're fine. It's just ripped the outer fabric."

I closed my eyes and let my head fall back to the ground as I tried to compose myself until another memory hit me.

"Rishi!" I exclaimed and scrambled to my feet.

As I did the forest surrounding us on three sides erupted with screeches and howls. The cacophony washing over us like a terror filled wave.

"Heads up, not out of the woods yet," Hendricks growled.

Chapter Thirteen

The Illusion of Safety

Rishi's corpse had already been recovered from the pile of bodies he had died under. Jones had seen him fall at the hands of the ape that he just hadn't killed in time. As soon as the other creatures had fled, he had frantically pulled him free and tried to administer aid, but it was obvious it was too late. Rishi's wound had been too severe, and even with immediate medical attention it was clear he would have bled to death quickly. For some twisted reason it reminded me of a video I'd seen of a motorcyclist who lost control and impaled himself on a fence post. That was how thick the damn spear had been.

There was no time to dwell on it. The night was still dark and the howls and screeches emanating from close by in the forest served as a constant reminder of how close danger was.

Hendricks looked around at us, and I could tell he had to call upon every ounce of his professionalism not to let his true feelings show. The bullet-riddled bodies of our attackers lay everywhere, surrounded by the spent casings fired by our weapons to make the place look like something out of a Tarantino movie.

We'd just managed to stop them overrunning our position, but the wild shrieks and screeches still came from the trees, just out of reach of our flashlight beams.

"Help me get him on the helicopter," Hendricks said, startling me because he'd just asked me to pick up a dead body. A minute ago he was Rishi, and now he was just a dead body.

I bent down and grabbed his ankles, amazed at how much the lower half of him weighed when he wasn't holding himself up. We manhandled him into the nearest helicopter and Hendricks strapped him in before stepping back and letting out an uncommon burst of anger.

"Jesus fucking Christ!"

One day into our mission and we were a man down. I knew Hendricks had lost men and women before on operations, but those losses had been against a known enemy they were either trying to arrest or stop committing an act of terrorism. Not against hideous monsters that had leaped out of the forest at us with such speed, aggression, and a reckless lack of fear it would be hard to explain to others who hadn't seen it with their own eyes.

Reckless…of course it would seem reckless. Humans fear guns because we know what they do…

Pushing my dark thoughts aside I watched as Hendricks straightened and did the only thing he knew he needed to do: act.

"Eyes open, people. They're still out there."

He tried to look at his watch, having to wipe away the mix of mud and blood that encrusted his wrist and hand. After a few attempts he sighed, gave up, and spoke quietly.

"Annie, how long until dawn?"

Annie replied, her voice serious, stressed, and urgent. She seemed to anticipate his follow-up questions.

"Dawn is in two hours and forty-eight minutes. With the fuel already manufactured, I estimate that you would not be able to reach the next marked waypoint. May I suggest you continue to refuel the helicopters? I am tracking the animals with the drone, and they still appear to be in retreat. They are moving without cohesion, and seem to be running away."

Hendricks wasted no time.

"Nat, keep watch and work with Annie. Everyone else, get back to making that damn fuel!"

Amir was standing in shock, just staring at Rishi's body strapped into the helicopter like he needed a break. Hendricks saw it too, and for a second, I thought he was about to shout at the guy, but he stayed annoyingly calm.

"Now, if you please, gentlemen. Every minute is precious."

~

In the forest, the leader strode through his gathered tribe trying to cajole them into rising and attacking one more time. He had felt the moment of euphoria when he thought his plan had been successful and they were going to overrun the invaders. He had seen two of them fall from spear thrusts as they had at last breached their puny barricade, only to be beaten back when their fire spears started to flare.

He didn't know how many he had lost, but he knew that those who were missing were among the bravest, as none of the more timid fighters would have rushed to be the first into battle. He had thought the battle won, but the noise and fire from the big thing had torn his attack into ruin, and cast them all into retreat.

The noise. It had been louder than anything he had heard in his life, and it had terrified him. It had made him run away, to leave behind dead fighters, and just the memory of it now was enough to loosen control on his bladder.

Two of the fighters were grunting, waving their hands and pushing one another as they argued in low voices so as not to be overheard.

The leader saw them, watched their gestures for a while, then issued a ripping snarl that silenced everyone. He advanced on them, swelling in height and broadening his torso to intimidate both of them. One cowered away, gesturing supplication at him, but the other pointedly did not.

The leader held that belligerent gaze for a moment before roaring in the challenger's face. To his surprise, because the ape risking death in front of him was smaller and not yet fully matured, the challenger still did not look away. Others shuffled closer, most crowding behind the leader, but some—more than he liked—crouched or stood behind the challenger.

The leader roared again, communicating that they would attack again, but the response was less than enthusiastic.

Voices asked what the noise was. They asked how the things threw them down without striking them, and more than one poked tentatively at cuts and holes in their bodies that leaked red blood.

Attack! He bellowed, repeating the order until he had forced enough of them to take up the cry. The challenger, facing the leader and most of the tribe, bent his head and gestured supplication.

Chapter Fourteen

Last Throw of the Dice

Hendricks, Nat, and Jones were scanning the tree line looking for threats. The screeching had subsided and seemed to be further away now, which I took to be a very good thing, but as I was busy stuffing as much foliage as quickly as I could into the fuel maker, I only had half my mind on it.

Amir was doing the same with the other helicopter while Ozzie and Marco were furiously hacking at the undergrowth and piling it up by our feet. My mind had become absorbed by the necessity of the task, so the first louder screech nearby didn't immediately penetrate my concentration. I guess I was in a bit of shock too, not to mention suffering from absolute exhaustion after a night spent awake in terror.

It was only when the first burst of gunfire echoed across the valley did I realize we were under attack again. I dropped the bundle of branches in my hand and snatched up my gun from where it hung on its sling. Running back to the barricade I stumbled on the rough ground as I struggled to free the strap from where it had caught on my canteen. With a final tug I released it and threw myself down beside Hendricks who was firings bursts at the beasts I could now see running around the perimeter of the clearing.

Raising my weapon, my thumb found the rate of fire switch and clicked it from safe to dangerous as I began searching through the sights for a target.

The first thing that was obvious was that there weren't as many of them this time.

I mean, that made sense on account of there being about a dozen more of them dead in the clearing, but their reduced numbers made for fewer targets, and now with only seven of us firing it became harder.

The first wave of attackers had been killed, and now that we joined the fight the ones that followed met even more resistance. We fired, crumpling them to the ground, either squealing and howling in pain or lying still as multiple bullets hit them.

The attack died off as abruptly as it had started, and we had no more targets to aim at. One by one our guns went silent, and we all tensely waited for another wave to emerge from the trees, roaring and screeching for our blood.

"Annie? What can you see?" Hendricks asked.

"No more are visible in the tree line, and I cannot detect anything beyond on infra-red."

"And the cliff? You're sure there's none climbing the cliff again?"

"I am positive there are none, unless they are invisible to all known light spectrums." She paused, adding, "The one wearing the chain, which we believe by his actions to be their leader, was one of the first to be shot as he was in the front rank of attackers. It is my tactical assessment that the group will have to be unified by another leader before any other attack can be made."

"Makes sense," Hendricks admitted. "Are you basing that purely on known primate behavior?"

"Not entirely. I have reviewed drone footage of the group and it shows that the leader is the one making decisions and giving orders. I apologize that it took me so long to do this, but I was unable to apply much processing power to the task."

Hendricks laughed. It was a short, mirthless chuckle.

"Dial-up Annie."

It wasn't technically correct, but it was a pretty good analogy. Annie ignored it and gave her final assessment.

"They have left the immediate area, and I firmly believe they will not attack again tonight."

Hendricks, back in business mode, turned to me and the others. "You three back on fuel, the rest of us will keep watch. Annie, how long until the tanks are full?"

"I calculate both tanks should be full in forty-six to sixty-two minutes. May I suggest that we leave as soon as first light?"

"No argument from me," Hendricks said, casting an eye at the slumped figure in the helicopter.

I stepped away, my back protesting as I bent to gather an armful of foliage, when Annie spoke to me.

"David, I…I want to ask…What you are…" she trailed off mid-sentence, as if unsure what to say next.

"You okay? Is your data feed interrupted?"

"No, I am operating within acceptable parameters. My hesitation is because I need an answer to a question before I finalize my calculations. Would you mind if I asked you first?"

"Of course!" I noticed Hendricks was looking at me, most likely wondering who I was talking to. I mouthed "Annie" to him, pointing at the radio like it was 2009 and I was telling someone I was on a Bluetooth headset making a call. He just nodded and pointed to the helicopters, miming that I should continue with the refueling.

Just to prove that Annie's eyes and ears were everywhere, even when she was on dial-up, her voice came through my earpiece.

"Please continue refueling. I will ask the question when you are ready."

Knowing she'd monitored our interaction through the drone that was still sitting on top of one of the helicopters I flashed a quick smile at the camera focusing on me and raised my thumbs in acknowledgement. As I hurried over to continue with the vital job of filling the helicopters' tanks, I realized she wouldn't just be monitoring me, but everything that the camera saw simultaneously, such was the processing power she could access even operating remotely over a distance of many hundreds of miles.

But I forced my mental way past that particular rabbit hole as I needed to start making fuel. Every second we were in the air was a second we were safe as far as I was concerned. Well, *safer*.

Once I had the first armful of vegetation pushed into the hopper, Annie spoke to me.

"David, I...I was having trouble choosing the right words for my question and I wanted to run it by you first. I do not want to cause any upset or bad feelings if I do not come across as sympathetic. If I study the response, I can learn and enhance my communication style going forward."

Not stopping from the task that after so many hours of doing was becoming a subconscious act, I replied, "Go ahead and ask it Annie."

"It is concerning Rishi's body. The normal course of action would be to return the body home for a formal burial, but given the mission we are undertaking, I believe that would be inadvisable."

A brief image of Rishi's body strapped into the helicopter, decomposing in the warm and humid environment made my stomach lurch.

"We also do not have the time to excavate a grave big enough to accommodate him. So, my suggestion, based on a purely tactical basis, would be to cremate his body using the materials you have already gathered to make the barricade and then redistribute the weight saved by having one less person to carry between the helicopters. This will also extend their range due to the weight savings gained. However, I...I am not sure how to make such a sensitive suggestion."

I thought for a few seconds as I carried on pushing the next armful of vegetation into the hopper before I responded.

"You know what, Annie? I think you should have a go at it yourself. But to help you out I'll warn Hendricks first not to take offence at what you are asking."

Annie was silent for a few seconds which given her processing capabilities denoted she was really thinking hard this time.

"Thank you, David," she replied eventually, her voice this time sounding like a nervous teenager just about to ask their parents if they can go to a party they wouldn't approve of.

"I have decided on the best way to format my question now."

"Okay, Annie. Open me a line just to Hendricks please?"

Our plan to depart as soon as there was enough light to see was delayed by nearly thirty minutes. When the helicopters' tanks were brimming with fuel, we made more to ensure the funeral pyre we had to make for Rishi would burn.

There was no time for ceremony. As the fire burned, we worked hard to distribute our payload evenly between the two helicopters, and all the while the forest around us grew with noises that I worried signified an attack coming at any second.

When we lifted off, I glanced down at the burning pyre. The smoke, disturbed by the downwash of our conical rotors, billowed everywhere. The eddies of wind created mystical shapes before being blown away on the breeze to slowly dissipate.

The headset crackled. That usually indicated that Annie patched a channel in, but this time it was Hendricks transmitting to all of us onboard both helicopters.

"Thank you, everyone. I ask that we all take a moment to honor Rishi."

I craned my neck to look back at the rapidly receding clifftop where we'd spent the terrifying night. Hendricks spoke again, this time his voice sounding solemn and strong.

"But death replied: 'I choose him.' So he went, And there was silence in the summer night; Silence and safety; and the veils of sleep."

I mouthed a silent amen and stared at the distant spot on the horizon where we'd left him behind. The clifftop was marked with a smear of smoke, and I thought how pure luck had prevented me from joining him. Dark thoughts ran through my mind.

If I hadn't been lucky, would they have just stripped me of my gear and burned my body? Was it dumb luck? Would Annie let them leave me behind like that?

Distance had made the smoke disappear as we skirted around a taller outcrop, and the low cloud was beginning to lift from the valleys as the sun heated up to burn them away. Wiping away a tear I shifted in my seat and glanced at my travel companions, who all seemed as somber and thoughtful as me.

"What's the plan, Hendricks?" I asked, more to fill the silence than out of any real quest for knowledge. Part of me hoped he'd say we should turn around now and head back home.

"We carry on," was his soft, tired sounding reply.

After a few seconds of silence, which I guessed he'd taken as a bad thing, he spoke again in a firmer tone. He wasn't laying it on thick, just saying it how it was.

"The mission, as you all know, is critical. We need to find information vital to our long-term future. There were always going to be risks, it's up to us to keep going and complete the mission. It's not a nice to have, it's a need to have. It's about survivability."

I knew there'd be no issue from Jones, Marco, or Nathalie—the military members of our little sub-group—so I guessed the speech was for me, Ozzie, and Amir.

We acknowledged him in turn, but even I didn't believe us.

Hendricks was right. This was what they called a zero-fail mission. We knew we'd face danger, but the knowledge we could gain from it was more than worth it. We just had to continue. We just had to put one metaphorical foot in front of the other and keep going.

Long after the machines had flown away over the horizon and beyond their view, the apes slowly emerged from their hiding places in the forest. They had watched them leave, cowering in fright as they took to the air like birds, just like the Gods depicted in the holy place.

The funeral pyre still blazed with a fierceness not seen before. The fire was hotter, brighter, so it too must be a parting warning from the Gods. Not daring to glance into its fiery midst, they crowded around it in awe and wonder while keeping their eyes down.

Had they dared to look they might have been able to see the cremating body of one of the gods, and some of their summations may have been questioned. Had they known what the smell of a burning body was they might have thought twice about the gods, but they did not, and their superstitious dread deepened.

Eventually they began to prepare their dead for their own form of burial. Unlike their ancestors they did not just abandon the ones who died. They performed a basic burial by covering them with branches and leaves, so they became one with the surrounding forest and were hidden from view and memories.

Deft, strong hands turned over the body of the one who had been their leader. He groaned and shuddered as the pain of doing so dragged him from his near-death state of unconsciousness; blood seeped from the gaping holes the bullets had blown in his torso.

Those who were moving him jumped back in shock and let out grunts and shrieks of alarm, causing the others to stop what they were doing and gather around.

Not one of them displayed sympathy, because there lay their failed leader who had made them anger the Gods, had forced them to attack instead of showing respect and reverence.

His actions, his decision, had decimated their tribe in pointless assaults. Eventually, one of them stepped forward hesitantly, driven by an urge he could not explain to himself; by an instinct he did not understand.

He kneeled beside the body, his eyes locked onto theirs, and his hands circled his throat without uttering a sound. He tightened his grip until, with a telling crunch of cartilage and bone, the last vestiges of life were removed from their erstwhile leader.

Then, again without understanding why, he pulled the chain from around the neck and held it up, staring at it in wonder.

Instinctively the others cowered away from the new chainwearer and displayed immediate respect and fear towards him.

The chain was held aloft, lowered over his head, and settled into place. He turned and looked at the shattered remains of his tribe to see supplicating gestures with no direct eye contact from any would-be challenger.

The new leader's body language and facial expression showed none of the fear, none of the self-doubt or relief that he had not been challenged. He was not the biggest of the warriors, nor the loudest or most brash among the males, but he was cunning, and he had learned how to win fights with his mind as much as his powerful fists.

He decided they must pay homage to the Gods they had so angered, and send a message to the other tribes in the area.

Fallen logs were found and hauled to the clearing on top of the cliffs, and they began to beat upon them with branches and rocks. When one ape fell away exhausted, another took their place. The rhythm and the message being beaten against them sent echoing across the hills and valleys did not stop until a response was heard.

The tribe's new leader had beat the logs, the different rhythms and tones all carrying a meaning. The message warned that the Gods were here, that the other tribes should not anger them, and it summoned the tribes to the holy place.

As the low percussive beat washed across the land, more answering beats came, barely discernable on the shifting winds. Far beyond the hearing of the original senders, the beat was picked up and repeated, spreading the message to the far territories each tribe had claimed as their own.

That message, spreading as fast as helicopters could fly, was received and repeated.

Chapter Fifteen

The Monotony of Fear

The plan had always been to try and get in at least two refueling stops a day before darkness and the need to rest forced us to land. Then we would wait, until the sun rising the following day would enable us to continue our journey.

The previous night had been filled with strenuous exercise and maximum adrenaline-inducing terror, and I was surprised I felt as normal as I did, which made the third uneventful stop a little suspicious.

Nothing had happened halfway through the second night, not even a distant screech, and most of us were too wired to sleep. The fact that nothing happened made me even more suspicious, and the theories we threw around didn't make me feel convinced that we'd escaped their reach.

Maybe we'd scared them off? Maybe they didn't feel like making a second attempt? Maybe they only occupied a small stretch of the forest?

"That observation is flawed, Mister Jones," Annie interrupted.

She was using her "quiet time" voice because it was the middle of the night. Only Hendricks and Amir were asleep, both flat out between the cargo in the helicopters, and I guessed she'd cut the audio feed to them, so they didn't get woken up. I knew if I'd been awake for two days and two nights and had flown an experimental prototype helicopter for hundreds of miles, I'd be dead on my feet.

"How?" Jones asked. His body language may have been relaxed, but his eyes never left the perimeter of the clearing, and his rifle was pointing in the right direction.

Annie continued, "It is flawed because the first footage of one of these creatures was captured approximately seventy point three two miles from where we first encountered them. As we know, the terrain and fauna it contains has not changed so it is perfectly reasonable to assume their population would have spread to where we are now."

"Approximately, hah!" Jones chuckled softly.

"For Annie, two decimal points is approximate," I muttered.

"Coming to 'er defense again," Nathalie added wistfully, like she was insinuating something.

"So what is it?" I asked. "If we're confident those things are in this area, why haven't they…you know…"

"I do not have a working theory at this time," Annie answered, doing the Annie equivalent of shrugging her shoulders and delivering a teenaged, "I dunno."

The next morning, after hours of hard work refueling on zero sleep, my body relaxed into the seat. The continuous drone and gentle buffeting of the helicopter began to dull my senses, and with every dip I struggled to lift my head up as high as it was before.

Attempting to fight it I tried to keep my drooping eyes open, but it was a losing battle and eventually my head dropped only to instantly bounce up again as the shock of the motion woke me.

"Have you seen something, David?" Annie immediately asked. "Your vital signs just rose sharply, indicating an external stress-related event."

"No," I replied, embarrassed that my moment of weakness had been spotted. "I just...I fell asleep for a second, that's all. Sorry, I'm awake again now."

Hendricks chuckled.

"If you're as knackered as I feel, then I don't blame you for nodding off. Why don't a couple of you get some shut eye? We've goooooot...about three hours before we need to look for another refueling spot."

"I estimate that it may be slightly longer. The biological materials gathered at the previous site appear to have created fuel with a higher efficiency than previous batches. I am monitoring this data alongside the fuel economy ratings as a result of our change in weight."

Silence met Annie's report. The new weight efficient mission came at a high cost, and Annie paused like she realized too late how callous she'd sounded.

"I...that was badly worded, I apologize. But if it helps, I estimate our flying time will be extended significantly with the higher fuel efficiency alone. I advise that we start looking for a suitable landing site in three hours and forty-five minutes with our increased margin for error."

"You heard the lady," Hendricks said. "Get some sleep and I'll take my turn when you're refueling. Weatherby, did you receive the last?"

"Affirmative, Hendricks. I agree. I don't think I could sleep yet anyway, but give me a few hours and I reckon I'll be ready."

"Good man. Annie, could you monitor mine and Weatherby's vital signs and warn us if we are showing signs of fatigue?"

"I have been doing so since we left," she replied in a superior sounding tone that could have just as easily been a teenage sounding "Duh."

Now that I'd been given permission to sleep, you could probably have counted on one hand how many heartbeats it took for my head to fall and sleep to take over.

What seemed like thirty seconds later, Annie's voice in my ear woke me. Momentarily disorientated with the fog of exhaustion still weighing heavily on me, it took a few seconds to realize I was sitting in a helicopter skimming over the vast forest that still stretched far beyond my visible horizon, and not cuddled up with Cat in my quarters like I had been in my dreams.

"What? What's going on?"

My grip automatically tightened on my weapon that rested, barrel down, between my knees.

"Yes, David," Annie replied calmly. "I have been asked to wake you in anticipation of locating a suitable landing site."

Other voices sounded in my ears as Annie was obviously holding multiple conversations. Confused, I twisted in my seat and began scanning the forest floor until the world started to make a little sense again.

Five minutes of looking later, Ozzie called out a clear patch coming up ahead. A huge tree had obviously succumbed to old age, or a storm, and had crashed to the ground. It exposed a large area of scrub which had taken advantage of the increased light level, now the tree wasn't shading the forest floor, to sprout new growth.

Hendricks banked the helicopter and we swooped down. As per our preestablished practice, Weatherby maintained overwatch while Hendricks skillfully flew the helicopter in a slow banking turn twice around the area as the rest of us scanned for threats of any kind.

"Looks clear to me," Hendricks said. "Anyone see anything?"

A chorus of negative responses from both helicopters prompted his next words.

"Okay. Same as before. I'll land first and we'll establish a close perimeter before calling the second helicopter in."

~

In the forest below, unseen, and unheard, the sound of the rotors whirred. Even though quiet, they were the loudest noise some of the watchers had ever heard; a cacophony of roars and shrieks sounded out and echoed through the forest as fear and instinct made them give voice.

Picked up further afield, the warning calls spread far and wide until replaced by the rhythmic beating of hard wood branches upon fallen logs.

The Gods are here. Do not anger the Gods...The Gods are here. Do not anger the Gods.

As soon as the skids of the helicopter touched the ground Nathalie, Jones, and I jumped from our seats with weapons raised. We fanned out a few meters and knelt, our heightened senses searching for anything untoward. After a minute of watching and listening we all reported the all clear. Still keeping eyes outwards, the other helicopter swooped down and disgorged Ozzie and Marco to strengthen our perimeter.

Eventually, Nathalie, the most senior member of our little expedition with boots on the ground, gave the all clear to Hendricks and Weatherby who still sat in the helicopters with their hands on the controls ready to, at a moment's notice, increase throttle and take us away from danger. The high-pitched whirring of the rotors subsided as they powered down their motors, sending the forest back into its relative silence.

It was then we heard the hollow, reverberating sound of logs being beaten, and distant screeches and roars of alarm and warning.

"Bollocks. Here we bloody go again," Jonesy griped over the channel.

I wasn't sure how much more adrenaline my body had to give, but as soon as I heard those sounds another wave of it washed through me. I began to rise and turn so I could run back to the perceived safety of the helicopter, anticipating Hendricks' order.

"Everyone back onboard. Let's get out of here!" The conical rotors of the helicopter, which had barely ceased spinning, burst back into life.

Given permission, I didn't feel as much of a wuss as everyone else joined me in the scramble back onboard. As soon as Hendricks, whose head was sweeping everywhere searching of the first sign of attack, knew we were on board, he pulled on the collective hard and we were pressed down firmly into our seats as he performed an emergency take off. Out of the corner of my eye I could see the other helicopter doing the same.

Silence reigned as we absorbed the shock of the previous minute.

"What now?" I asked lamely, pretty sure I wouldn't like any answer that came.

Annie spoke first.

"I agree with your actions, but I must remind you that you only have approximately thirty minutes of fuel left in both helicopters. You must immediately seek an alternative landing site."

That statement received only silence from everybody on board both aircraft.

We had no choice, we had to land and soon, otherwise we'd just...fall out of the sky.

Eventually Hendricks broke the silence.

"Okay, everyone...Two options, and we need to decide. One, we land and take on whatever comes at us, or two, we land and take on whatever comes at us."

That pretty much summed it up, and I had no shame in admitting my first instinct was for a full-scale retreat.

But running home wasn't a safe option, and it screwed us in the long run.

My second instinct was also to run away home, but I fought it with logic.

We needed to refuel the helicopters and we had to land to do that. As reluctant as I was to put my feet on solid ground I agreed to carry on, as everyone else did, and we began searching for a new landing spot. All I could think, though, as my eyes scanned the forest floor was that it looked a miserable place to die.

Five minutes later we had spotted a clearing. It looked as good a place as any to try, so we landed.

Swooping down fast, I was almost thrown from my seat as Hendricks dumped us hard on the skids. Regaining my balance, I took a few paces forward and kneeled with my rifle raised on one knee. I scoured my area of forest, fully expecting the edges to darken with approaching beasts any second. My heart seemed to be beating out of my chest as I braced to counter the downdraft of the other helicopter landing hard behind us.

Taking off again was not an option due to both aircraft running on fumes, so as soon as the other craft landed, both powered down so their pilots could join us on the firing line.

As the whirr of the rotors receded, the percussive sounds of beaten wood and screeches grew.

"That can't be good," I said, cursing myself for saying it out loud. Something in the back of my mind about comms discipline kicked me, and my brain went off down that tangent to hide from what was actually happening.

Accuracy, brevity, clarity…That's what Hendricks had said way back when. More like, asshole brainfarted…something…

"Anderson, Ozzie, Weatherby, start making a barricade around us. Nat, Marco, Jones, position yourselves on the corners."

We moved, complying with the instructions like they electrified us. I wasn't the only one hyped up on fear and a lack of sleep, and we all knew how serious the situation was.

The clearing wasn't as ideal as either our cliff top one or the one we had briefly touched down on minutes before. The surrounding vegetation was sparse, but there was enough for us to go at. Gingerly stepping forwards a few paces, fully expecting at any time to be hit by a rock or my body pierced by a spear, I swung my machete at the small trees and bushes around me. Through much practice my machete skills were improving as I quickly stripped each branch and began constructing what could only be described as the flimsiest barricade in existence. Flimsy, but a lot better than none at all.

We worked, all the time accompanied by our adversaries hidden from sight in the dark forest making their terrifying noise. After about an hour, or maybe fifteen minutes—stress does weird things to my sense of time—we'd constructed a defensive perimeter all around us. It wasn't nearly strong enough or high enough, after all, we knew how fast they could move and high they could leap, but at least it offered us some sort of protection.

"Good work," Hendricks said when, crouching low, he toured the perimeter we'd created. "Take ten minutes and then start making fuel. Anderson, could you set up the comms first."

"Are you sure?" I asked waving my hands towards the forest. "They're out there, and judging by the noises they're not far away."

"I know," he replied. "But they haven't attacked yet and we're only here because we need to make fuel, so the sooner we start the sooner we can be on our way," he replied calmly with a hint of sarcasm. His calm demeanor could change in an instant if his constantly searching eyes spotted a threat.

"David?" asked Annie in my ear. "Could you prepare the drone for deployment please. I can do a sweep of the area first and then park it as before on top of one of the helicopters where I can use its thermal detection capabilities to enhance our visual range."

"Sure thing, Annie," I replied. I then stopped as a thought came into my head. "Annie, why didn't you ask me to deploy it earlier?"

"I considered it, David, but the priority was to first build the barricade. Something I could not help with. I am now able to provide additional security to protect you as you refuel the helicopters, which is why I need you to deploy the drone for me."

Wondering why I would ever question the irrefutable goddess of logic that was Annie, I reached for the storage cases that contained the comms gear and the drone, and quickly set up both.

The vegetation we were using must have been of poor quality, because the trickle of fuel I could see dribbling through the clear feeder pipe was less than I expected. Amir's frustration was also evident by the moans and curses I could hear him uttering as he labored to feed in the foliage that Ozzie and Nathalie kept piling by us.

The day stretched on as the gauge in the tank ever so slowly filled. Still the drums beat, and roars and screeches echoed around us. Occasionally they paused, which we initially took as a precursor to attack and ran to our insufficient barricade to add our weapons to the defenses.

After two or three similar events when eventually they started up again, we surmised that they too probably needed to take a break occasionally. Gathering the strength to continue the constant pounding and shrieking probably. We stopped reacting every time there was a pause and just carried on the exhausting process of making fuel.

Without looking at my watch I could tell the sun was past its zenith and was beginning its slow descent to the western horizon and still the tanks were only half full. Better vegetation, I knew, would provide far better fuel-to-effort ratio, and some of the plush, darker leafy bushes were visible at the forest edge, but it seemed a little too suicidal to attempt to get it.

I swear I could almost feel the eyes watching us, and I didn't know if it was my paranoia or for real.

"Annie, that thermal camera still up and running?" I asked, unable to ignore my fears. I tried and failed to sound cool about it, but she answered quick enough that I hoped the others wouldn't notice.

"Affirmative. There are no heat signatures large enough to be considered a threat within visual range."

"What about movement?" Ozzie asked, betraying his own nervousness with an uncharacteristic question on tactics. Ozzie was a smile and follow kind of guy when outside his own wheelhouse.

"The forest creates a significant amount of movement with wind and branches. To utilize movement as a visual spectrum I would effectively blind myself, similar to white noise deafness."

"Mate, you're thinking *Predator*," Jones cut in, pronouncing the amused smirk in his words.

He may have been joking, but I took the words as a warning, imagining that they had the ability to camouflage themselves among the trees. That train of thought ended up with me hanging by my ankles thirty feet in the air with no skin and I did not enjoy the imagery.

Frustrating as it was, and as terrified as I was about stepping too far away from the landing site, we had no other option but to carry on stripping everything suitable we could find that was in reach of our position.

Annie kept us updated, but still the cameras on the drone didn't pick up anything to alarm us. The monotony of the noises from all around almost lulled us into a false sense of hope that we might live to see another day.

Focusing solely on feeding the hopper and watching the line on the fuel tank rise frustratingly slow, minutes turned into hours and still no attack came. It was obvious to me that if we were to make any progress at all, we needed to find better vegetation than the shitty bushes we were being forced to use due to the fear of what was out there.

I don't know if it was fatigue-related dumbassery or mission-focused bravery, but I'd had enough of budget fuel and wanted to grab us some premium.

"Hendricks?" I spoke into my radio as I looked in his direction. His head jerked my way as he recognized my voice and turned to where he knew I was. "This isn't working...I can see the stuff we need," I said as I waved my arm towards the edge of the clearing. "This stuff we're feeding into the hoppers is just crap, it'll take us all night at this rate."

Annie, who as always was omnipresent, joined in the conversation.

"I concur with Doctor Anderson's assessment. The foliage directly available in this location is, indeed, crap. If the refueling continues at the current rate, it would add between three and eleven days to our journey. I suggest that as the tanks are now sixty-five percent full, we depart and find a better location. Our range is approximately ninety minutes of flying time, which we can utilize to find a more suitable source of vegetation. As sunset is in four hours, forty-eight minutes that should give you enough time to prepare defenses and begin refueling before nightfall if we leave immediately."

Hendricks was quiet for a moment as he digested the information before he spoke.

"Does anyone have a better idea?"

"Yeah, we push out and get us some of the good stuff," I said.

"No, too risky," Hendricks shot me down. "Let's get packed up and gone."

For everyone else that meant simply climbing on board the helicopter, but for me I had to first pack up the drone and then stow away the satellite-type dishes and aerials that made up the comms gear we carried. Due to the weight limitations, we weren't carrying many spare parts, so I had to make sure they were carefully packed away in their protective cases and stowed securely. If they were damaged, or worse lost, then it would hamper not only our communication abilities with our home, but massively screw with the amount of help Annie could give us.

For her to remain fully functional remotely, as much as she was, she needed the data links of the gear I was tasked with handling. Jones and Ozzie, both with weapons held ready, guarded my back while I worked. My last job was to exchange the battery in the drone for the one charging using the port in the helicopter. As soon as I had put its case in the storage compartment, I jumped aboard, and we lifted off.

In the air, Jones handed round food from the supplies we kept close to hand. Spooning the contents into my mouth, trying not to knock my teeth out with the spork or miss my mouth with the minor turbulence, I realized how hungry I actually was. With everything that had happened over the past however long, eating had been at the bottom of my to-do list, and apart from the occasional energy bar I'd stuffed into my mouth when I had chance and drinks from my canteen to wash them down, I hadn't eaten much.

The stress we were under had suppressed my appetite until the first mouthful hit my tastebuds and my hunger reared its head. I chomped down the meal—the kind I used to think were unappetizing—and licked the spork clean of the bland, prepacked survival food. I asked Jones to pass me another as soon as I'd finished the first one.

Hendricks, who understood how bodies acted under stressful situations joked when he saw I had wolfed down the second pack.

"Be careful...what goes in must come out..."

He was right, I guessed. Along with not eating, I hadn't done the other thing either, and that would probably happen sooner than I thought.

"We are not landing so you can visit the little boy's room," Nathalie warned with amusement.

Jones laughed, picking up the conversation to embarrass me further. "You'll be alright, mate. Just hang your arse over the edge and we can do a bombing run if you need." He held out another meal pack and grinned at me.

"On second thought," I said, trying to sound cool about it. "I'll pass. Thanks."

The thought of me hanging out the of side of the helicopter at a couple hundred feet over the forest with my dignity gone as I answered an urgent call of nature made my mind up for me. Instead, I turned my concentration on looking out over the vast forest below us for a suitable landing spot.

Chapter Sixteen

Don't Look Up

A little over an hour later everyone on board both helicopters was fully aware of the need to find a suitable landing spot as a matter of urgency.

We'd prepared ourselves for the possibility of encountering animals that might not appreciate us landing in their territory, but it still hadn't prepared us for what had happened. We'd gained valuable experience with the dragons and The Swarm— the two apex predators that we thought ruled the forests—but we weren't ready for animals smart enough to run tactics and use weapons against us.

Furthermore, the guidance, advice, and training we'd received from the people at The Springs and Three Hills had given us the confidence that we could meet and survive any encounters we had with the local fauna. The other predatory animals that called the forests their home were a known quantity, so it was pretty clear that these things and humans hadn't come into contact before.

I said as much, thinking out loud, and Annie answered.

"I have allocated some processing power to that question. I believe that the mountains north of Charlie site and the surrounding settlements, formed by the volcanic activity following the asteroid impact, created a natural barrier."

"They looked capable of climbing mountains to me," Amir answered dourly.

"Indeed, however their evolved social skills may be a hindrance to such an endeavor."

"Meaning what?" I asked, frowning in confusion. Hendricks had evidently read between the lines and answered for her.

"Meaning that we live in Mordor."

"Or *The Lion King*," Jones added. Nobody responded, like his words created a vacuum, and I shot him a confused look. He made his face look all serious and pulled a passable James Earl Jones impression.

"That's beyond our border. You must never go there, Simba!"

"Oh! Got it!" I chuckled.

"So…" Amir said, still hesitant. "Because the far side of the mountain range is out of their line of sight, they won't go there?"

"Among other factors, I believe this to be true," Annie said. "The other factors include familiar habitat and a known food supply, but I believe that their continued evolution may lead them to explore other habitats."

That sobering thought wiped the smile off my face.

Before we'd left home, we'd imagined landing when the need to refuel arose, and while we knew we'd need to keep watch for any threats, we were confident they wouldn't interfere with our journey too much.

We'd been confident. That changed when the drone sent back the single image of the humanlike ape creature. None of us could have imagined the threat and horror that one picture would bring, and yet here we were trying to find another landing spot which could bring the same outcome as we had suffered before.

It was like the world's worst game of the floor is lava.

If our mission could be cancelled due to the parameters of it changing far beyond expectations, then in normal times I am sure it would have been. But these weren't normal times, and failure to complete it would have serious repercussions on the long-term survivability and success for everyone. We just had to go on and hope more of us didn't die trying.

Nathalie called out over the open channel.

"I think I see a clearing way over on our left. I just caught a glimpse through the forest a moment ago."

It was the first possibility we'd discovered since we had taken off, so Hendricks gave the order for us to bank left and investigate it further.

Getting closer we could see what Nathalie had glimpsed looked ideal. It was a clearing in the forest, almost a couple of acres in size, just large enough for maybe two football fields. Single, large trees still grew in places and from what we could see the bushes and low growth that carpeted the area would provide the ideal material we needed to make fuel.

"It looks good to me, and as it's the only place we've seen I think it's our only option. Same drill as before," Hendricks ordered, lowering our helicopter fast to land first.

Hendricks first steered the helicopter in a low banking turn around the clearing while we all searched below for any danger, before he brought the craft down to earth near a large tree. Leaping from my seat I raised my weapon and took a few paces forward before dropping to one knee and scanning the area through the magnified sights of my rifle. I blinked to clear my vision as I thought I caught movement at the tree line, but when I looked again, I could see nothing. Putting it down to an overreactive imagination I continued my scan. I joined in with the reports of clear, which was Weatherby's signal to land alongside our helicopter.

I waited in place until Jones, Nat, and Marco pushed the perimeter outwards and after a short time called the all clear once more.

I heard Hendricks through my earpiece telling Amir it was okay to power down the helicopters. As their high-pitched whirring tones died down, the all too familiar percussive beat made by those things beating on logs or whatever they were using could be heard. My heart once again leaped out of my chest and I raised my weapon, finger resting taught beside the trigger guard.

"Here we go again," I muttered to myself.

Ten minutes later, no unstoppable tide of huge half-man, half-ape beasts had leaped from the forests to rip us limb from limb. Hendricks asked me to set up the comms gear and the drone so we could get started.

As I worked, I heard Hendricks organizing the others and discussing with Nat the best place to position the sentries. I knew I would be on fuel-making duties, along with Ozzie and Weatherby. Unless we were under attack that is.

Annie bleeped in my ear.

"Hello David. I am now fully connected. I am detecting that the drone is ready to fly and fully charged, so I will launch now. Please stand back."

I did, not wanting to lose a finger or an eye. There was a pause as I heard the whine of the rotors fading as Annie guided the drone on its first sweep of the area.

"Visual scans of the fauna in this area indicate a more suitable yield for fuel manufacture," she commented matter-of-factly before her voice changed. "Heat signals detected in the forest to the south. They appear to be the same size as the apes we encountered before."

"Confirmed?" Jones snapped, swinging his rifle to point in the right direction.

"I cannot confirm, but the information makes that conclusion highly probable."

"She means it's them," I said, my own weapon held in shaking hands to point in the direction of the threat.

"What are they doing, Annie?" Hendricks barked.

"I am detecting some movement, but the signatures I am monitoring are mainly stationary just inside the forest edge."

"So, they're just watching us. Is that what you're saying?"

"Affirmative," she replied.

Everyone had stopped what they were doing as all eyes had turned to the forest edge to our south while we listened to Hendricks and Annie talk.

"What's the call, boss?" Marco asked. I shot a glance at him and knew he was ready to go either way. He'd go to war or turn and run as soon as Hendricks gave the word.

"Listen up, people," Hendricks said in a low but firm voice. "We're out of fuel, so we're not leaving here. Distances are greater than last time, so they'll have to rush us or wait until dark. They can't sneak up on us like last time…Anderson? Get the comms up. Ozzie and Weatherby, fuel us up."

"Comms are up," I said.

"Understood. Start on the green stuff. I need to make a call."

"Start over there," I said, lowering my rifle and talking to the other civilians. I pointed to a large tree about ten meters away which looked as if the dense bushes that grew around its base would be ideal for making fuel.

As practice had taught us, if we all worked for a while together creating a stockpile of vegetation before we started to feed the hoppers, then it would just take one of us hacking and carrying more foliage to keep the supply up while the other two fed the machines.

After a few minutes of frantic hacking, the pace I had set began to take a toll on me. My breathing was becoming forced, and my back threatened to give out with every swing. Pausing to loosen up and catch my breath, I arched my back and spread my arms wide to stretch my muscles. My head was drawn upwards as I leaned back, and I found myself looking up into the huge tree that spread its large boughs over us. And I froze.

A furry face was staring down at me from a fork in the branches ten meters above my head.

Paralyzed momentarily from shock and fear of the sudden death I was certain was about to befall me, I was unable to move for a few seconds until the charge of adrenaline my body was suddenly filled with took over. I scrambled backwards, falling over the pile of vegetation I had created while at the same time trying to reach for my weapon which was slung around my back, and screamed.

"Shhhhhit! There's one in the tree, there's one in the tree!"

All the time my eyes were locked onto the fur-covered thing above me. At my scream I heard it let out its own howl of terror and it climbed further upwards.

It was then I saw that it was not alone. I caught a glimpse of a much smaller body clinging to the back of the one now trying to get as high as it could, and therefore further away from me. It screeched—both of them screeched—and I recognized the sounds for what they were.

Fear.

Hendricks rushed up and stood over me protectively as he raised his weapon to search for what I was screaming about.

"Gotcha," I heard him say as his rifle barrel steadied and he took aim.

"It's a mother and baby," I shouted as if to help him identify the ones I had spotted, and not another that may have escaped my vision.

My words cut through to him, and even though he didn't lower the rifle from the target, I saw his finger move off the trigger. I recovered my feet with zero grace and stood next to him staring up at the figures clinging to one of the highest branches. By now they were almost hidden by dense foliage, but I could make out the little one burying its face into the bigger one's body.

As well as the continuous beating noise that reverberated around the forest, the clearing was now filled with screeches of alarm and panic.

"Annie, what's going on?" Hendricks demanded.

"I have analyzed the noises the targets are making. My best summation is that they are similar to the noises made when they

178

were retreating in panic after we threw them back from the barricade when we first opened fire, and not the noises they made when attacking, which had a more discernable threatening manner to them."

Hendricks opened his mouth to respond but was cut off by a sudden screeching noise from high up in the tree above us.

"Annie, can you get a better view of what's above us in the tree?" Hendricks asked sharply. "I think they are talking to each other."

Annie didn't respond, but we all heard the whirr of the drone as it darted away from the forest edge where it had been monitoring the tree line and swept high overhead.

"I have visual. I'm sending it to David's tablet now."

Hendricks dropped his rifle on the sling and snatched the tablet which hung around my neck. I jerked forward with it, but because it was looped over my head, I had to go with it, so that our heads touched while we stared at the images.

I didn't need to be a primatologist to see what was obviously a mother with her baby, clinging to the uppermost branches with a terrified expression on her face as her head followed the drone flitting around her.

Hendricks released the pressure on the tablet and sighed. "Well, that complicates things."

"Why?" I asked.

He looked at me and smiled weakly. "Do you hunt?"

Me? Hunt? Do I look like I've hunted anything more dangerous than an errant line of code before? Well, before I turned into a badass bug killer that is.

"Errr...no..."

Hendricks' smile turned genuine as he looked back up into the tree and stared at the thing that clung to one of the branches.

"A big rule of hunting is that you don't kill a female with a young one. Especially one that has a lot of relations close by which will rip you apart if you do. And if I'm not mistaken, they are communicating, and the others over in the trees know full well where their friend is."

He paused as he thought before continuing.

"I think we need to find a way of reuniting them, otherwise we're not going to get anything done here."

By now Nat and Jones had joined us, even though they kept their eyes mainly looking outwards still looking at the tree line

"Did I just hear that right?" asked Jones as he lifted his rifle to scan for threats. "You want to help that thing up there? You remember one of its friends killing Rishi?"

"And the last thing we want to do is have a repeat of that, correct?" Hendricks replied, waiting for Jones to nod in reluctant affirmation before he continued. "I can't see what's up there being a threat to us, but it is delaying our objectives. And with all the screeching going on, I can't imagine things going well if we terminate it."

I noticed Hendricks' use of the word "terminate" rather than "kill." It seemed to make the action, if it needed to be taken, less brutal. More of a transaction than anything else.

"The question is how and what do we do?" He looked around at everyone.

Nathalie spoke for the first time, sounding tentative. "Let me try. Can the rest of you clear out of the way please? I think for once this needs a woman's touch. Go back to what you were doing, but keep a corridor clear to the south through our lines. That way, if I get 'er down, she can 'ave a clear exit."

Hendricks thought for a while.

"Okay, Nat. Give it a go, but my rifle will still be trained on her until she's long gone."

She smiled in response and waved us silently away. Hendricks and Jones retreated to the perimeter they had been creating, and Ozzie, Weatherby, and I gathered up armfuls of vegetation and went over to the helicopters, all the time, though, keeping an eye on Nat and the tree.

I watched as she removed her rifle and tactical vest and laid them on the ground next to her. Next, she took her cap off and released her hair from the bands that kept it in place. She looked a lot more female than a second before, and I could see what she was attempting to do.

At some base level of understanding a female, even from another species, could possibly react better to another female. Especially one who was attempting to be as non-threatening as possible.

Nat, her arms held wide, was slowly and carefully walking closer to the trunk of the tree. All the time looking up to maintain eye contact with what was above her. After a while of standing still she began gently waving her arms in a beckoning gesture. The shrieks and screams of the female in the tree which had initially sounded panicked and scared began to quieten and became more of a questioning whimper, though still sounding fearful.

Not wanting to go near the tree, we began collecting foliage from other areas around us and continued to feed them into the hoppers on each helicopter, all the while keeping an eye on how things were going. After half an hour she seemed to be no further forwards when, through our earpieces, we heard her voice at barely more than a whisper.

"Nobody move, I think she's coming down."

I froze in position and tried to even make my breathing quiet. Eventually I could discern movement in the tree as what was up there moved lower through the branches. Nat began to slowly step backwards away from the tree, still beckoning gently with her arms.

"She's almost down," Nat whispered.

And then with a jump from the last branch she was on the ground. Standing as still as possible I slowly moved my hand so it rested on the grip of my rifle, just in case, and watched avidly what was happening.

Annie, without being asked, had withdrawn the drone out of the way so it hovered a hundred meters away in the clearing. The cameras on it were of such quality that it could have been a lot further away than that and still produced high-quality images, but the buzzing of the rotors would probably be enough to spook the…thing.

Once on the ground the ape crouched down low for a while, trying to make herself as small as possible, all the while looking desperately around.

Nat pointed toward where the others of her tribe were in the forest beyond the clearing. Slowly the ape stood up and with her head still darting everywhere fearfully she reached her full height. Towering over Nat, it may have been my imagination or just hopeful thinking, but the look she fixed her with seemed to convey gratitude and thanks.

Then with a single leap she cleared the rough barricade that had already been built and half ran, half bounded back to the tree line and disappeared from view, all with the smaller one clutching to her body.

I was about to emit a sigh of relief when Annie communicated to all of us.

"Another one is emerging from the forest."

I snatched my rifle up from its sling and ran to the barricade along with everyone else, preparing myself for the onslaught. A single creature had emerged into the clearing, and even from the distance we were at, it looked huge. I reached around my vest and loosened the flaps that held my spare magazines in place as I continued to get mentally and physically ready for the fight.

But it just stood there staring at us.

"The drums've stopped," Jones said softly.

And they had. But what did it mean? Were they getting ready? Were they massing for an attack?

For a full minute the single figure stood and stared at us before raising one arm as if in acknowledgment, then turned and disappeared back into the forest. Almost immediately the drums started again, only this time the beat had changed.

Somehow it didn't sound as menacing as before. It seemed more...celebratory. It might've just been me, but that is how I interpreted it. Whatever had happened, it definitely changed the mood of their music or whatever it was.

"Okay everyone, that's not a stand down. We still need full tanks. Great work, Nat," Hendricks added.

"Mister Hendricks, the communications array is aligned for you to contact the base, but I am receiving an intelligence update I need to give you," Annie announced stiffly.

Chapter Seventeen

The Rot Within

The atmosphere was tense when Tori walked through the gates. She could sense something was wrong from the expression on people's faces.

She strode confidently, standing tall despite the heavy burdens in each hand, and she let the people of Three Hills see that she was unafraid.

She was no leader, not of anyone but warriors, at least. She had no patience for the complaints of people, no ability to disguise her distrust of others, but she was also shrewd enough to know that people still looked to her for guidance.

She wasn't the youngest female warrior to have risen high. In fact, their history was littered with a string of women who had led fighters against The Tanaka's forces.

She was happy to be beside Harrison, to fight with him and carry out his orders, but she suspected that many people knew her value to him was greater.

If she followed him, then it only added to his legitimacy.

Crowds parted to allow her and her two flanking warriors easy passage through the town's streets. Some smiled at her, bowed their heads briefly, but others kept stony expressions on their faces and held eye contact as if daring a challenge.

She ignored those looks, focusing instead on returning the nods of respect and greeting, all the while soaking up the feel of the town in search of the real problem.

She suspected that she already knew what it could be. Harrison had busied himself with the boy—the orphan boy now—and she had taken warriors to search for the truth.

That left Sebastian free to spread his poison among the townspeople without anyone in authority to tell a different story.

He would be telling them how Harrison would not be able to keep them safe. That their livestock, their families, their livelihoods were all in peril, and all because they had elected a leader who invited the enemy into their homes.

There was some truth to that, if a person wanted to see it that way. There were other ways it could be interpreted, such as a time of peace that none of them had ever known in their lives, and if it made them subservient to the people who came from the sky, was that such a bad thing?

Already they had provided medicine, the ability to speak with people many miles away as if they were in the next room, and they had ended the war by ending The Tanaka. True, his own people had been the ones to kill him, but without the newcomers there would have been no sequence of events that led to his end.

Tori's suspicions were solidified when they rounded a bend in the street and saw two groups of people squared off against one another.

She saw, assessing quickly, and her mind snatched at the important details. Sebastian, larger than usual in furs worn over both shoulders, barred the way with his large axe held across his chest. Beside him, looking nervous, stood six other warriors—men and women of little reputation—and they too carried exposed weapons to bar the road.

In front of Sebastian, smaller and unarmed but equally as fierce and resolved, stood the old man from the Springs. He had only two others with him, and their shifting glances took in the overwhelming numbers opposing them. Neither had drawn a weapon, likely for fear that it would spark their murders.

"What is the meaning of this?" Tori barked, not checking her stride and scattering two of Sebastian's people aside to walk right up to him.

He said nothing, just sucked in a breath through his nose with his lips set in a tight line before blowing the hot air back into her face. It smelled of meat and she had to fight to control her response.

"I said, what is the m—"

"I heard you, but I don't answer to you," Sebastian growled, swelling up to increase his height advantage over her.

Tori sighed, deflated, and stepped aside. Far from capitulating to Sebastian's threat, however, she merely handed the two heavy sacks to two of his men and watched as they took them, confused at the weight and the turn of events. She wiped her hands on the stiff, hardened leather covering her torso and looked back up at the bearded man's face.

"I'll ask one more time," she said quietly, speaking so only they could hear.

Sebastian's top lip curled, his knuckles whitened on the grip of his axe, but he didn't attack her.

Tori smiled. She knew if the big man attacked her he would roar a challenge, rear back and swing the axe hard enough to cleave her into two parts. She also knew that before the swing could gather any momentum, she would step close and slice parts of him that would leave more damage than mere scars.

She would take him apart, piece by piece, because his only way to beat her would be to swing the axe when she didn't see him coming.

He seemed to realize this at the same time and deflated, treating her to a wide, false smile.

He cocked back his head and laughed, loud and mocking, before his humorless eyes lowered back to meet hers.

"We simply stopped our new…friends to ask what they were doing. Three Hills can be a confusing place to an outsider, and we did not want them to become…lost."

Tori's own expression remained neutrally unimpressed by his display or his words.

"How responsible of you," she said flatly, turning her back on him as an insult that he was not worthy of protecting herself against, and offered a slight bow of her head in greeting to the elected leader of the Springs.

"Clarke."

"Tori."

"Where are you going? Do you know the way?"

"We are heading to speak with your own leader, at his invitation, and yes. We know the way."

Tori turned back to Sebastian and spoke loudly for everyone to hear.

"You see? They are not lost, and they are not confused."

The challenge was set, and dozens of witnesses were gathered to see how it would be taken.

As if knowing that an impasse had been reached, Tori's two warriors, one of whom carried a fresh injury, slid into flanking positions where they could launch their own attack if called upon.

Sebastian looked at them, at Tori's unreadable face, then at one of the rough sacks she had handed off to his people. He saw dark gore pooling at the bottom corner, saw the drips of dark, thick liquid turning black in the dust of the street, and turned back to smile at Clarke.

"In that case, if you know our streets so well already, carry on."

He stepped aside theatrically, bowing and rolling his right hand as if inviting an honored guest to pass by. Tori took back the two sacks and walked past him as if interpreting his subservience to be genuine, and for her alone.

She slowed her pace, waiting for the men of the Springs to catch up with her as she listened intently for any cause to drop the sacks, to turn, and draw her blades.

"You have my thanks," Clarke said quietly as he fell in step beside her.

"It was as much for you as it was everyone else," Tori said quietly to keep their conversation between themselves.

"I...how so?" Clarke asked with an air of confusion.

"Think about it. If he stops you, what's to stop just anyone accosting a trader? What's to stop a woman from forcing playing children off her street? What's to stop someone killing a neighbor for their possessions?"

"Ah. You believe that anarchy only needs a spark to ignite a flame?" Clarke asked wisely.

"Call it what you will. I just don't like people who act like they're better than others…without good reason."

She didn't turn to look, but she imagined Clarke smiling at her mild hypocrisy, at how she had dominated and publicly shamed the man who tried to force his will on them. Clarke said nothing for a while, just walked alongside her.

"What's in the bags?" he asked, stumbling as he tried to shake dusty blood from his foot.

"Evidence. What brings you to see Harrison?"

"Suspicions. Problems. Concerns."

Something in the way he spoke caused her to worry. The burdens in each hand were hardly proof of any conspiracy, but other pieces of the puzzle may be walking beside her, locked in the head of an old man just as cagey as she was.

They reached the town hall, the headquarters of the leadership, and as soon as they stepped inside Tori felt a pang of regret in her chest.

The boy, no longer sporting a filthy face and ragged clothes, sat hungrily eating a bowl of something, spilling it down the skin of his freshly scrubbed chin. He beamed at her, recognizing her, and gave her a hopeful look which she pretended not to see.

She walked through the first room, into the smaller room behind it where she found Harrison sitting behind a desk and wearing a pained expression as someone leaned over a document with a finger pointed at lists of numbers. He looked up, saw her, and smiled at the prospect of a rescue.

That smile was wiped from his face when she hefted the two sacks onto the desk.

"Give us a minute," he said to the man, who carefully retrieved his precious list from the growing puddle of dark fluid seeping onto the wood. He practically fled the room, stopping in the exit as Clarke apologized for getting in the way.

He stepped inside, saw the expressions on their faces, and backed out muttering an apology.

"No, it's okay, you should hear this too," Tori said. Her words were confident, commanding, but her eyebrows went up to ask Harrison if he was happy with it.

"Yes, please. Join us," he said. His happy tone had disappeared, replaced with the hard edge like a blade had been drawn. Tori recapped for Clarke's benefit.

"A boy, the son of a milk cow herder, came to us today. His father and their herd had disappeared, so he came to us for help."

"I see," Clarke said, eyeing the two sacks suspiciously.

"We found their home, but there was evidence it had been attacked," Tori added.

"What evidence?" Harrison asked, betraying his nerves as he knew she would tell him everything in her own time.

"The herd had been driven away, into the forest to the north, and we found a dragon nursery—"

Clarke's hiss of anger and disgust cut her off.

"Terrible way to go," he said, shaking his head.

Tori's response was to upend the bloody sack and tip two adult dragon heads out. Harrison didn't flinch, didn't recoil, just leaned closer to inspect the lifeless eyes staring directly at him above teeth as long as his smallest finger.

"This one had to be eight feet long, at least," he said.

"The other wasn't much smaller," Tori answered, shoving the other head to rest beside its fellow babysitter. "They were young, but big and fast. Probably in their third or fourth years."

"Almost breeding age," Clarke added, implying that their death was a lucky thing.

"And the other sack?" Harrison asked. His tone suggested that he already suspected what the contents were, that he didn't want it confirmed, but he had to ask anyway.

With more respect, and with an obvious reverence, Tori lifted the sack and held the top open for them to see inside.

Flensed of almost every scrap of flesh, and with the lower jaw missing, an eyeless skull stared back up at them.

"The boy's father, most likely. A cow had been killed too."

"You have a theory?" Clarke asked.

Tori looked from him to Harrison, receiving a nod of permission to say what she was thinking.

"I think some people attacked the herder for his cows. They probably stumbled on the dragons by accident and left the man and one of the cows as a sort of offering, to keep them from following them. Also dragons leave nothing behind, only scraps of bones. A neat way to dispose of a body you do not want finding, too."

Harrison nodded along with her words, adding additional information to the discussion.

"The boy said his father woke him in the night and sent him back here for help. He didn't know what his father was afraid of, but I believe that is clear now."

"It leaves one question," Clarke said pointedly. Both of them turned to face him, waiting. "Where is the rest of the herd?"

"I think the question is, who did this?" Tori shot back, but Clarke only smiled sympathetically.

"That question has no way of being answered, but if you find the herd, those taking credit for their ownership can answer…"

Harrison thought for a second before nodding at Tori.

"Do it. Find out where they are and bring me someone responsible."

"I may be able to help with that," Clarke said. He spoke carefully, almost suspiciously, and when he offered nothing further, Harrison turned his full attention on the man.

"I am revealing much trust by saying this, and if I am wrong about you, it will mean my death…" he said eventually.

"Clarke, I gave you my word that—"

"Forgive me, but it is not your word I fear."

Tori's eyes went wide at the accusation, and she turned on the man angrily, but Clarke held up a hand and spoke fast.

"Nor is it yours we question, especially after what just happened, but rather that I fear there may be another party at play."

His words silenced them in confusion. With a sigh, Clarke slid the severed head of a dragon along the desk and sat on a chair opposite Harrison.

"We have noticed…disappearances at the Springs. The people who have gone missing all had one thing in common: they did not like the thought of an alliance with Three Hills."

"I see," Tori said. "Did they take a small milk herd with them when they disappeared?"

Clarke smiled, glad that she was as sharp minded as he suspected she was.

"No, but they did take many weapons, and other trade goods. But there is more…"

"How much more?" Tori asked darkly.

"More. We were expecting a trade caravan to come, and when it did not arrive yesterday, I began to worry. So I sent men here to the Springs today in search of news. They found it, burned and robbed. That is what I came to discuss with you."

Tori glanced back at Harrison who banged a fist on the desk and shouted for the man with the lists to come back.

He did, yelping in fright at the severed heads sitting on the desk, but took his orders to search for news of anyone going missing from the town and bring him back the names. When the door shut behind him, Tori glanced at both men before speaking.

"So…we have a pack of rebels out there, joining forces because they didn't want to be in an alliance? That makes no sense."

"No, it doesn't, but people convince themselves of strange things when they want to," Clarke said tiredly.

"And do we think Sebastian is behind this?" Harrison asked quietly, his eyes flicking up to meet Tori's.

"I don't know. He's going around town publicly calling into question every decision you make. It would be brazen of him to be doing both."

"Brazen, yes…is he that stupid?" Harrison asked.

"Perhaps not stupid," Clarke interjected. "Perhaps it is merely arrogance."

"Whatever it is, I think it's time I had a talk with Sebastian," Harrison growled.

"And in the meantime?" Tori asked.

"Find out as much as you can, and be careful. I need to speak to the newcomers. They may be able to help."

He stood, walking to the small room where the contraption had been set up. He dismissed the young woman sitting beside it, resting her head on her forearms and pretending she wasn't asleep, saying that he would take over for a while watching the device.

He waited until the sound of her footsteps faded away before picking up the strange thing and holding down the button.

"Um…hello?"

"Greetings, Harrison, leader of the Three Hills community. This is Annie. How may I help you?"

Chapter Eighteen

Parting Gifts

Anderson

"Oh yeah! About time, boss," Jones said as he stood up.

Hendricks, carrying a handful of mugs like an expert waitress at Oktoberfest, smiled as he approached. The smile seemed forced, which had me a little worried, but Hendricks seemed to shake it off.

We'd relaxed enough after the apes all disappeared, and even the rhythm of the drums had faded. The biofuel generators hummed as they did their thing, and for the first time in what felt like days we took a break. Only Nathalie stood apart, closer to the edge of the clearing, staring intently at the distant tree line.

It almost seemed an anticlimax, and I couldn't believe I'd actually thought that as I sipped the coffee and felt the caffeine running through my veins like a junkie being chased by the cops.

I'd been preparing for another battle, but it had ended before it began with what could be perceived to be a friendly wave from our opponents.

"Well done today everyone," Hendricks said. "We're in an unknown environment, but we're learning. Rishi's death was a tragedy, but we have to continue. This mission is critical to our future." He paused as he sipped his tea. "I may be mistaken, but my gut's telling me that what happened today after we landed has made us a lot safer, at least in this…territory? I shudder to think what would've happened if we'd opened fire instead."

"You got that right," grunted Marco. "I feel it too. I can't explain it, but I agree. The game's changed."

Looking around everyone was nodding in agreement.

"Annie?" Hendricks asked. "How long do you estimate the refueling will take and when will it be dark?"

"The current production ratio is much higher than the previous location, and the generator's testing software has indicated a much richer fuel currently being produced, which means an increased flight time as a result. At the current rate of production, the tanks on both crafts will be full in two hours, fourteen minutes with an error margin of eight minutes and six seconds. Sunset is in one hour, thirty-nine minutes' time."

"Thank you," Hendricks said to the air. "Okay, so there's little chance of moving until the morning. I suggest we concentrate on getting the tanks full first and then work on getting through the night next."

Even though we now had a vague glimmer of hope that we may have turned a corner in our relationship with whatever was out there, his statement burst my emerging confidence.

"What about fire?" I asked. One of the big red flags on the survival training they forced me to do drummed into us that you never lit a fire at night, not unless you wanted to send out RSVPs to anyone that might want you dead, but like Marco said, the game had changed.

"Animals are afraid of fire, right?" I added hopefully.

"I agree," Annie said. "I recommend using some of the manufactured fuel to create a series of small fires around your perimeter with additional tree branches stacked nearby. I will park the drone as before to conserve battery life and limit my surveillance to periodic sweeps of the area to ensure we do not fall below minimum requirements."

I tossed back the last of my coffee, enjoying the hit of sugar that had settled to the bottom of the mug, and hauled myself up.

"I'll get to work on that."

A rudimentary barrier was constructed, circling our camp with a waist high tangle of felled logs and branches too thick to feed into the hopper. Hendricks joined in to help us build the defenses and, just as the sun was setting, we stood back with satisfaction as we all looked at the dozen little stacks of combustible stuff ready to go.

Ozzie had broken out one of the electric chainsaws from his helicopter and dropped a tree, most of which made up our barricade, but the branches it provided from its length made gathering the materials we needed a lot easier. So much so that we'd filled the tanks, siphoned off about a gallon of fuel for fires, and still had plenty of foliage left over which we added to the barricade, until I had a thought.

"Hey, why don't we mark this spot and make a pile of foliage for us to use on our return journey? We may need it, or we may not, but a stash of it ready to go wouldn't do any harm, right?"

"Good idea," Hendricks said, smiling at me. "Let's get to it. If we get time on further stops to do the same, it could make our return journey easier too. Keep the good ideas coming."

Ozzie scoffed a laugh at me and smiled.

"Y'know, for a computer geek, you're turning out pretty good, mate!"

Giving him the one finger salute, I pulled my machete from my belt and started creating the stockpile of vegetation, all the time accompanied by the distant, rudimentary drumming sounds emanating from the forests surrounding us.

An hour of bone-tiring work later, when the sun was threatening to dip out of sight entirely, Hendricks called a halt.

"Okay, people, time to settle in for the night. Jonesy, Weatherby, with me on first stag. Marco, Nat, Anderson, three hours. Get some food and get your heads down."

I didn't need telling twice. I ate another sealed pack of sloppy food that tasted way better than it looked, and lay flat inside the helicopter to close my eyes.

"Oh crap, Annie?" I said, eyes still closed but my brain clinging on.

"I will wake you just before you are due to take over, David. Sleep now."

I opened my eyes, confused, to find my ear buzzing like there was a bug in it. I shot upright, flapping my hand at my ear to dislodge the little bastard without giving it the opportunity to sting or bite my fingers.

"Fffnaaaargh!" I yelped, until the buzzing stopped, and Annie's voice soothed me.

"I'm sorry, David. I was trying to wake you with a gently increasing low-frequency sound.

"Annie...bugs. Never anything that...sounds like bugs..." I gasped, trying to keep quiet but feeling my heart thumping in my chest louder than the distant drums.

My attention was drawn to voices other than mine and Annie's, and I concentrated, trying to hear them.

The voice grew louder, until Hendricks appeared in front of me with another coffee.

"Oh, you're up," he said. It was pretty clear I'd startled him, but what little I'd heard of his conversation concerned me.

"Is everything okay?" I asked.

He looked thoughtful for a while before replying, "Yes. Everything will be fine, I'm sure."

There was something about his tone though that made me worry. Hell, my girlfriend was back there, and I thought we'd left a now peaceful community behind when we left. Hendricks saw my face and said in a soft voice, "David. It's okay really. They have the situation under control."

"Who's they? What situation?"

Hendricks sagged a little. It was like he'd been holding onto the information like a weight and now let it drop.

"Just a few issues with some renegades. Nothing the people of Three Hills can't handle, and nothing we can do about it from here so better not to worry about it."

The drums were still beating their monotonous tone and I stared at him, waiting for more. Hendricks, being way better at interrogations than I'd ever be, soaked it up and didn't crack.

"Fine, but...but you'd tell me if there was a problem, right? If Cat was in danger?"

"David, if Cat was in danger, then so would be my wife and child. I doubt even I could keep that secret."

He looked beat, and given how he was the guy keeping my ass in the air all day, and more importantly not crashing said ass into the trees, I thought it was better to let him sleep than give him any more to worry about.

"Sure. Hey, get some sleep, man. You look like you need it."

The rest of us could catch up on sleep while they flew so it seemed the fairest thing to do.

Moving as quietly as possible so not to wake the sleeping forms around the helicopters I took my rifle and my coffee to the barricade as Annie coordinated the rolling change of watch. She guided the others into position like she was a sentry handing over, setting us arcs of fire.

I leaned against the barricade, made sure my weapon wouldn't snag on my gear if I needed to raise it in a hurry, and blinked away the last vestiges of sleep that threatened to overtake me as I stared out into the night. The night was not truly dark. The light from the stars and the shining crescent moon bathed the area in an ethereal glow. The fires we had set around our perimeter had also burned low and Marco, covered by Annie flying the drone around him, spent ten minutes throwing the last of the stacked branches and logs on to them, the flames leaping higher and sparks drifted lazily into the air. The pool of light each fire created widened but it also limited our vision beyond them. Using my tablet I watched the feed from the drone as Annie covered Marco.

The forest was a glow of dark hues, and after a few tense seconds of expecting to see some bright orange outline of bigfoot coming at me, I relaxed a little. I could make out the darker edge of the clearing where the tall trees of the forest surrounding us began and continually scanned them, searching for any altering of the shadows that may indicate a rush of bodies silently storming across the grassy plain to attack us.

I switched between the screen and the real world, looking for any discrepancy between the two.

"If I might offer some advice, David?"

"Sure, go ahead, Annie," I whispered back.

"Just watch the trees. I will monitor the thermal imaging. You will cause eye strain by watching the display in the dark, as the internal mechanics of your eyes are not designed to function in this way."

"Yes, Mom," I muttered, closing down the tablet and settling into a more comfortable position behind the barricade.

"Hmm," Annie answered, part thoughtful and part amused.

"What?"

"I find it...funny, that is all."

"You find what funny?"

"Many people expressed the opinion that I was your product—your child—and now you have reversed that dynamic."

I thought about that, as much as I could with my brain feeling as numb as it did, and managed a lame response.

"Huh."

Dawn's precursor eventually began to show itself on the eastern horizon as a gradual increase in the light level. Slowly and ever so slightly, as the minutes passed, what was hidden in darkness began to show itself.

The distant drumbeats hadn't let up all night and were now as much of the background noise as all the other sounds that a forest full of life produced all hours of the day and night. They were out there, beating the trees, but they hadn't attacked. They hadn't massed, or surrounded us, or called in reinforcements, or...

Wait...was that what they were doing? Were the drums calling for help? Have we sat here all night waiting for a damn army to form?

Silence suddenly reigned as the beats stopped.

It took me a few seconds to realize what had changed. Marco was on watch with me, and I turned to look at him with a confused look on my face. Just like me, he was alert at the sudden silence and called loudly through the radio.

"Everyone up, the drums have stopped."

"Annie, drone up!" Hendricks snapped, sounding instantly awake like all the team guys and girls did. He didn't waste words as he rushed to the barricade and kneeled beside me, his weapon up and ready.

Tense minutes passed as we listened to Annie reporting in. Nothing was visible as she swept the drone around the area until she reported, "Movement on the tree line, nine o'clock from the lead helicopter. I am detecting a single figure approaching."

My head turned in the right direction, like my brain was able to calculate the necessary adjustments before my consciousness took a stab at it. In the strengthening light I could see the drone now hovering at the tree line in the vicinity we had seen the creatures before.

"Jonesy, Nat, on me," Hendricks ordered quietly. "The rest of you stay in position and report any sightings."

My watch position had been on the barricade facing south so I moved over slightly to allow Jones to crouch next to me, and waited.

A single figure emerged from the trees. I stared through the sights of my rifle and thought it looked familiar. It looked to be the one who had acknowledged us and seemingly thanked us for allowing the mother and baby to escape from the tree the day before. Annie confirmed this as the drone provided a much clearer view.

"It is the one we saw yesterday," she said. "He is carrying what appears to be…a platter. I am unable to confirm what it contains at this distance."

"Fingers off triggers, people," Hendricks said calmly. "There's only one and he can't do much damage on his own with a platter."

My brain wanted to blurt some joke out of my mouth. It wanted to say something about hors d'oeuvres or some shit, but honestly, if I'd tried to talk it would've just been gibberish right then.

We watched as he raised what he was carrying above his head as if to show us he meant no harm and slowly paced towards us. The drone flitted around above him, and we could see him flinching every time he heard the change in pitch from the rotors.

"Annie, get the drone away from him. It's scaring him."

"Withdrawing," she answered, and the buzzing of the drone faded away fast.

"I have studied the contents of what he is carrying. It appears to be cooked meat of some kind. My best guess it is an offering to us. A gesture of peace, perhaps?"

Hendricks thought for a few moments and then stood up, handing his rifle to Jones.

"Keep me covered, but do nothing unless I'm attacked, understood?"

We didn't like it, but we agreed.

"No way, Hendricks, you're crazy," Marco growled. "Those fuckers took out Rishi, and you're gonna—"

"No, other animals killed Rishi. If they'd have come to us unarmed and alone, I'd do the same," Hendricks said, cutting him off with his annoying calmness.

The ape thing approaching stopped when Hendricks jumped over the barricade. It stood uncertainly and glanced behind him as if to check his escape route. Hendricks spread his arms wide in the universal "I come in peace" gesture, and with a smile on his face that showed no teeth he slowly walked towards the one approaching us.

The thing also began taking tentative steps towards Hendricks, obviously encouraged by the friendly manner our commander was displaying.

I could barely breathe with anticipation, excitement, sheer terror, or nerves. I couldn't decide which as we watched the scene playing out before us.

When they were ten paces apart the ape sank slowly to its knees and placed the wooden platter down before prostrating himself before Hendricks.

Nat chuckled. It was a nervous bark of expelled air that told me I wasn't the only one riding the knife edge of adrenaline.

"Oh no! It looks like it's worshipping 'im. As if 'e didn't already 'ave a God complex."

It was true though, the thing…beast…? Ape…? Whatever, it did look as if it was worshipping him.

Hendricks stepped closer to the creature, kneeling with a bowed head before him and, even though we couldn't catch the words, he appeared to be trying to communicate with it.

It looked up nervously at him, apparently torn between averting its eyes and wanting to know what Hendricks was saying. From its crouching position it was trying to push what it had brought with him toward Hendricks, clearly indicating for him to take it. Hendricks, after a few more futile attempts to communicate through gestures and what I imagined to be slow talking, stooped and picked up the platter from the floor. He then gave an exaggerated bow of gratitude and turned and slowly walked back to us struggling under the weight of what he was carrying.

The ape, once Hendricks had walked away slowly, stood up and walked backwards as if he didn't want to take his eyes from Hendricks for a second. He slowly returned to the tree line and disappeared, and the moment it stepped into it the drums started again.

Hendricks gasped with effort as he approached us. "Somebody take this off me! Weighs a bloody ton!"

Jones and I leaned over the barricade and took it, almost dropping it in the process as it was a lot heavier than it looked.

It was an ornately carved wooden platter laden with a variety of cooked and—from the smell, smoked—meats. There were fruits and berries, all of them perfect specimens, and arranged among the offered food were small tokens carved from bone or wood.

Once we had it on the ground, we all stood and stared at it.

Hendricks broke the silence. "Right then, I know what I think it is, but I'd like your opinions too."

"It's a peace offering," Marco said.

"If they're offering us food, then they won't attack us? Right?" I asked hopefully, but Marco was shaking his head slowly.

"Not always. Met a tribe once, South American jungle…they offered one of our guys stuff but it was a pay-off."

"A…what?" I asked, confused.

"It wasn't a welcome, it was a, 'hey, here, have some of our shit and get lost or we'll kill you' thing."

That confused the hell out of me, and my face showed it.

Jones, thinking with his stomach as he usually did, cut the tension. "I don't know about all this peace bollocks, but what it looks like to me is breakfast, and a bloody good one at that. Better than MREs any day."

Hendricks laughed and looked at the sky. I followed his gaze, my hand tightening on the grip of my rifle, but I realized he was just looking at the light level and not at anything in the trees getting ready to attack us.

"I agree," he said. "Let's take this as a sign of peace, but to be on the safe side we're leaving ASABP. We can discuss it all further when we're airborne."

Annie jumped in, "I urge caution. I am unable to speak to the toxicity levels of the fruits. Doctor Anderson, do you have any ideas for testing it?"

I didn't. I could write code for the machines we had back at the landing site to test it, but other than taking a bite and waiting to see if I died, I was out of ideas.

"The biofuel generators," Amir said confidently. "Are you able to assess the chemical content if we put them in the processor?"

Annie treated us to a rare down-tone as she took a few seconds to "think." I guessed her reduced operating speed was the cause of the delay, but she came back sounding confident.

"Yes. That is a good idea, Mister Weatherby. Please place one of each item in the biofuel processor one at a time so that I may analyze the results."

"What about the meat?" Jones asked, already looking disappointed at having to lose some of the fresh food.

"Visual analysis indicates that the meats originate from known animals, and all appear to have been appropriately cured or cooked which would indicate the bacteria would have been killed off. I still recommend caution."

"Can we put the meat through the biofuel—"

I stopped talking as Jones picked up a long, stringy piece of meat that looked like smoked bacon and dangled it into his mouth. He chewed, eyes going wide in culinary delight, before he nodded and reached for a second slice.

"Hold your fire, Jonesy. Let's wait to see if you develop a bad case of the shits first, shall we?" a smiling Hendricks said.

He looked even more disappointed than before but accepted the orders. Marco, aiming for a darker meat that looked like it had been flash-burned on a hot barbecue, shrugged, and bit off a chunk to chew.

"Damn…" he said through a mouthful, chewing and frowning as he looked for the best place to take his next bite. "It's like…brisket, only…mmm…different…"

"I am over eighty percent certain that this sample is from an adult dragon," Annie said, earning a groan from Marco.

"Don't call it a sample, Annie! Jeez, it's like telling me the apple juice is my drug test or something…"

"Dragon, you say?" Hendricks asked, trying to keep his voice professional.

"Almost certainly, Mister Hendricks."

"Hmm…" Hendricks said, before snatching a piece and tearing off a chunk of his own.

"How do you like that, you bastard?" he muttered darkly, probably imagining the time when one took a bite out of him.

"Okay, Annie. Run it," Amir said as he fed a yellow fruit that looked like a shiny peach into the hopper. The machine chopped it up and stopped.

"No toxins detected. This item is particularly high in fructose."

"Fuck what?" Ozzie asked with a juvenile look of innocence on his face.

"Fructose. Monosaccharide. A natural and simple ketonic sugar of the hexose class, commonly found in fruit and honey."

"Thanks for the Wikipedia," Ozzie answered.

"So, it's safe to eat?" Amir asked. He already had one of them raised to his mouth ready for her to tell him it was, and as soon as she gave him the green light, he bit into it and the face he pulled gave me an insight into his private life I didn't really enjoy.

They carried on testing parts of the other fruits, but I stayed on the barricade and looked out.

"David, are you free to discuss something with me?" Annie asked. I knew she'd be burning a lot of bandwidth holding two conversations and linking up with the biofuel gear, but she had me intrigued.

"Go ahead."

"I have completed a study of all the available data on primitive tribes and primates. Can I suggest that we leave them an offering also? I believe a reciprocal gesture would strengthen whatever belief they hold of us."

"What would you suggest? Isn't everything we have with us necessary?"

"I have reviewed our inventory. I suggest we leave an item belonging to Rishi. Perhaps his knife, as that will be seen as a powerful gift."

At the mention of our dead comrade, I looked down, momentarily saddened by the very recent memory of his death.

"If that is not advised, there may be an item in his personal equipment which is not mission critical. The one thing I do not have is an inventory of his personal possessions, and also I believe it may require a more…"

"A more what, Annie? What were you going to say?"

"I think she means it might require a more personal touch," Hendricks said, startling me that he was close enough to hear the conversation before I realized Annie must have patched him in.

"I was going to say it might require a human input, but I accept your interpretation, Jimmy."

Due to the strict weight limitations of the mission, personal gear had been limited to one small bag not exceeding five kilograms. I'd just put some spare underwear and shirts in mine along with a few personal possessions, the most important of which was a newly printed photograph of Cat which I had asked her to make for me. What everyone else put in was their own choice so Annie's suggestion made sense.

"I'll go and get it," Hendricks said sadly, walking back toward the helicopters where the fruit tasting class was still in full swing.

"That is not all I wanted to discuss," Annie said when he'd gone out of earshot. "After studying the footage of the food offering, the best summation that I can come up with is that they believe you are Gods."

If I'd been drinking coffee at that point, I'd have sprayed it out of my mouth like on TV.

"If you view the information logically, with a mindset of primitive humans, you may arrive at the same conclusion."

"Gods?" I asked mockingly. "Like, Gods Gods?"

"Consider the time travel theory," she said, sounding like a university lecturer. "If advanced aliens landed on Earth a thousand years prior to the time you entered cryostasis, and they possessed superior technology that no human had ever witnessed, is it likely that primitive human would have worshipped these beings as deities?"

"Is this where you tell me the pyramids were built by aliens? It's a little late-night sci-fi-channel, Annie…"

"Please consider it, David. You arrived in their territory riding on flying machines which can only seem magical to them. You possess weaponry capable of killing them easily when they have only evolved to the technological level of melee weapons. You dress in a way that has never been seen before, when the majority of them did not adorn their bodies with items. The drone must defy any explanation they can come up with. All things that, in their primitive eyes and understanding, have never happened before and can only be explained away as God-like."

"I…Ah shit, Annie…I guess you're right."

Hendricks started yelling about time being of the essence, so we struck camp and collapsed what little gear we had unpacked, leaving the comms gear and the drone to last while Hendricks and Marco looked through Rishi's gear.

In the end they chose a unit badge he obviously kept for sentimental reasons and a small gold, carved religious figure. I didn't know if he was religious or if it was a family possession he kept with him, but it kinda fit with what we were aiming for with the gifts.

There was still a lot of food left after we had eaten our fill, so Hendricks packed it away and then gathered up the carved tokens that had come with the gift of food. We reckoned it might be seen as an insult if we left them behind so, added weight be damned, we took them with us.

Hendricks walked back out into the clearing and laid the knife, badge, and figure neatly on the wooden platter before jogging back to sit in the pilot's seat.

He wound up the rotors, lifted us up into the sky, swung to face north, and we continued our journey.

Chapter Nineteen

What the Hell?

Hendricks

Hendricks' mind spun like the rotors as he flew. Before they had left, he'd reported back to base to update them on their progress and the breakthrough they seemed to have made with the local wildlife.

Williamson, who had taken the news of Rishi's death stoically, had updated him on recent events on the home front. He reported sending two of their people—and he meant their as in one of each from the camp and The Hills—to investigate further and report back.

As the miles flew under their crafts, the further away they became from the issue. Not that distance was a factor, just that they could do nothing about it, no matter how far away they were. It was like physical separation required them to compartmentalize it, and he just had to trust that those left behind could handle it.

Hendricks made the command decision not to tell anyone else with him about it, otherwise it would definitely detract their attention from the mission.

"Annie? Private channel please."

Over the noise of the helicopter, the radio channel speaker in his helmet clicked and gave an up-tone.

"How may I help you, Jimmy?"

"The current events at home must not be discussed with anyone else on this mission."

"I understand your instruction, Mister Hendricks," she answered, making it obvious she was complying under protest.

"If they don't know then they can't worry, and as the commander that is my decision. Understood Annie?"

"Understood, Mister Hendricks," Annie replied formally before the line went quiet indicating she was offline.

"Who's in charge of who around here?" he muttered to himself.

To prove she was always listening, Annie answered, "You are, Mister Hendricks."

"Sarcasm, great. Annie, are...wait, are we still on a private channel?"

"I did not sever the communications link."

"Okay...sometimes orders have to be given that we don't like, and those orders also have to be carried out."

"Even if you do not like them, I understand."

"No, Annie, I'm not sure you do," Hendricks said, speaking more softly. "I'm saying there are times to talk about things, to debate them, and there are times when you have to just do something and put everything else out of your mind until you can deal with it. It's like your bandwidth; you only have a certain amount of processing power available, correct?"

"That is correct."

"Well, your limited abilities make you more like us. We only have a limited bandwidth, and if we get overloaded, we can miss things. We can become distracted or complacent, or we can act out of emotion. I'm saying that if people knew there was trouble back home, they might end up like Rishi."

A long pause strung out before she spoke to him again. "I understand this better now, thank you."

A down-tone indicated that the conversation was over this time, and he didn't know if he'd made his point or just made her sad.

The miles flew by as they continued in a northerly direction, and still the forest stretched out before them in an endless vista. During the journey they discussed the events of the previous stop and unilaterally agreed that benevolence from whatever new species they had found could only be a good thing.

The drums, they agreed, must be an important part of their communication with other tribes that most likely covered all the land below them. They surmised that if the drums were beating when they landed, then it probably was a good thing. Good maybe, but it would not pay to drop their guard one bit.

"Depends if it's the bumbum-badumdum and not the bumbadabum-bumbadabum," Marco said, silencing everyone as they considered the change in rhythm and tempo. The silence made him continue as if further explanation was necessary after his spot-on summary.

"You heard how last time was different to the first night, right? Stands to reason that the first one meant 'fuck these guys up' and the second one meant, 'hey, these guys are alright,' y'know?"

Eventually the talk petered out as some dozed off, leading to just the two pilots, who had had more sleep than the rest, chatting between themselves to keep alert.

As agreed, when they had forty minutes' flying time remaining, they began to look for a refueling spot. Due to the increased number of clearings they kept spotting in the forest below, Hendricks reckoned that forty minutes would provide ample time to find a suitable one.

"Forest looks sparser up here," he said as Annie woke the others up gently. A round of groggy greetings and claims that people weren't asleep sounded off, and they all began searching.

When a suitable looking spot was selected, they began their well-practiced routine.

"Everyone agree it looks okay?" Hendricks asked as he brought his craft into a tight turn to fly around the perimeter of the clearing.

When they confirmed it looked good, he swooped the helicopter down and the armed crew fanned out to form a cordon like clockwork. This time, though, before the other helicopter landed, he powered down the craft so he could hear if the drums were beating. They were, and they sounded as upbeat as before. The message was definitely spreading.

"You hear that, Marco?" Hendricks asked. "We got happy drums or fuck off drums?"

"Negative," he replied. "Can't hear shit from up here."

"Annie, relay the drum beats we are hearing to everyone please," Hendricks asked, realizing his mistake.

"Yep. It's definitely saying get the BBQ going I reckon," he replied following it with a few jubilant whoops of excitement.

Anderson

As I crouched with my weapon held ready, Hendricks then talked to us over the radio, checking if we also deemed it a suitable place to stay. None of us could see anything untoward, and as the drumbeats sounded as joyous as before, we all replied that everything looked as good as it could be.

I listened as he told Weatherby, still hovering above us, to land. I kept my eyes outwards as the force of the rotor wash buffeted me and then went still as the craft powered down and its occupants joined us on the perimeter.

"Anderson," Hendricks called out. "Get the drone up and comms working please. Then we'll start making fuel. The green stuff that's all around us looks perfect, so let's try and make this the quickest refueling stop yet. We all know our jobs so let's get on with them, folks."

Ozzy and Amir both turned and grabbed their machetes from the helicopters. Without a word they began hacking away at the bushes and plants around us. By the time Annie had launched the drone and I had the comms gear set up, they'd already created a sizeable pile by both helicopters which I started feeding into the hoppers.

Annie was flying the drone around the clearing, using its cameras and sensors to try and peer as far as possible into the dense forest that grew all around us. Apart from the rhythmic beating of the drums she couldn't detect anything else. I guess the apes out there didn't want to show themselves to us, at least for the time being.

The mood was, if not calm, then quite a few degrees more relaxed than on our previous stops. Jones, as there were no signs of anything happening, was relieved from sentry duty and immediately got his small stove out and was soon taking what he called his "brew orders."

Thirty minutes into the stop the drone's camera detected multiple movements at the edge of the tree line. We dropped everything and ran to our positions.

"I am detecting multiple heat signatures heading towards the forest edge to the west," Annie reported. "They should be in visual range of my cameras in a few seconds."

All our heads swiveled to the westerly edge of the forest that surrounded us.

Then Natalie called out. "I'm seeing movement but can't make it out...What the...? Are you seeing this or are my eyes playing tricks on me?"

What looked like four large bushes appeared from the tree line and started to make their way toward us. None of us could quite believe our eyes until Annie, flying the drone around what we were seeing, told us.

"They are being carried by four of the apes. They have no weapons with them. I believe their intentions do not look hostile at this moment."

"Fingers off triggers," Hendricks said, adding his trademark cautionary comment, "let's see how this pans out."

As they came closer, I could see legs underneath the moving piles of foliage.

Then it came to me. They were carrying large bundles that I could now see were tied together with some sort of rope or vine on their backs. It was one of the weirdest sights I think I'd ever witnessed, and that was saying something.

Closer and closer they came until they stopped about fifty yards from our position. They rolled the bundles off their backs, briefly knelt and touched their heads to the forest floor before us, then ran back to the tree line and disappeared.

The drone followed them before it flew back to inspect the bundles.

"The vegetation they have delivered appears to be perfect for fuel manufacture," Annie said. "I can offer no definitive explanation as to why, but they must have observed us and are wanting to help. How they know, I cannot explain at this moment."

"Pretty obvious," Marco said, standing and lowering his rifle. "They tried to kill us and failed, now they're kissing our asses by doing the hard work for us. Can't be too hard to figure out, right? We land, cut down a bunch of green stuff and consume it, then we go…"

He stepped further out into the clearing and cupped his hands to his mouth.

"Thanks! How about some more'a that dragon brisket?"

My mind raced as I cautiously approached the bundle nearest to me. I tried to pick it up, but the damn thing was so heavy I couldn't shift it an inch. I had to draw my knife and saw through the thin vines to take an armful at a time, and I shuddered at how powerful these things must be to haul the whole lot on their backs.

First thing that threw me was how fast they could spread the word. Just by beating trees they'd sent a message north faster than we could fly. It was like the new version of Twitter or something.

"Well, whatever's going on, I don't think we should look a gift horse in the mouth, so to speak. I think it would be rude not to accept the help from our new friends," Hendricks said. He slung his weapon and stepped towards the nearest bundle.

"Nat, keep watch, the rest of us let's get lifting."

"Because I am a woman?" Nathalie asked over the radio. I froze, and I saw everyone else pause too, waiting to see how he'd handle the challenge. I forgot how close they were and how far back they went, so when he answered I almost choked on my own spit.

"Yes. Everyone else here can lift more than you can, so it'll be faster," he said flatly.

"And because you're, like, the ape whisperer," I said, trying to ease the tension. She laughed, which made me laugh, and the others joined in for a few seconds until everyone just shut up and got on with it.

When Hendricks approached the first bundle and tried to move it like I had, he understood the strength it had taken to haul them. He called Jones to him and both men tried to work together to lift it. After watching them struggling for a while, I gave a whistle and waved my knife in the air.

They quit trying, instead cutting the bundle open and taking huge armfuls to pile beside the biofuel hoppers.

Annie was right in her observations. The foliage was perfect for fuel manufacturing and in no time, with everyone helping, a clear stream of pungent fuel was flowing into the nearly empty tanks of both helicopters. It was clear to me that the apes had provided us with more than enough, and if we stopped at this location on our return there should still be enough there to fill the tanks again.

Once the tanks were near brimming and we were getting ready to depart we had a brief discussion and agreed that it would be right to leave another small gift or token to acknowledge the help that we had been given. But the problem was what to leave.

We didn't have much with us that was non-essential, and Rishi's personal possessions did not reveal anything more that would make an obvious gift.

Nat, having sat and enjoyed her watch, was way ahead of us.

As the two helicopters lifted off and swung their noses to face north, the tree line started to move with anxious eyes. Excited noises, frightened noises, noises of awe sounded from the trees, and when the sound of the helicopters had disappeared the bravest of the tribe strode out to examine the place in the clearing where they had been.

Two figures, made from twisted branches and vines, stood in their place. Both looked similar, but one was much larger than the other. The two crafted figures held hands, and the leader of that tribe—adorned with loops of wire twisted around both forearms—lifted them carefully to show the others.

He grunted, huffing and communicating that the Gods had offered them friendship. The tribe screeched, happy at their good fortune, and as more leafy branches were cut to be piled for a future offering, the drums started to beat again.

Chapter Twenty

Knife in the Back

Dieter Weber literally jumped at the chance to get out from behind the walls of the compound.

When Williamson had returned from a private comms call looking angry, the assembled team members—those not on patrol or guard duty—knew something was wrong.

"Alright, listen up," Williamson announced. His voice didn't grow louder when he addressed the room, it just took on an additional layer of force, like someone had switched him into full stereo surround mode. They quieted, waiting to hear the news.

"Yesterday I was made aware of an incident at the place near Three Hills. That incident involved the loss of livestock and one death, believed to be hostile action."

Nobody spoke. That was the information, and they waited to hear the directive.

"In addition to that, a further incident occurred two days prior on the road between the settlements. Now, I'm aware there are other incidents, but we don't yet know how or if they tie in to these events, however...I am detailing four personnel to attend the locations and act as additional security at this time. Two to each settlement, and I'm asking for voluntee—now hold on a damn second!"

Every man and woman in the room shot their hand into the air before he'd managed to finish the word.

"You crazy sons of bitches don't even know what I'm asking for yet! What if I wanted volunteers to stay behind and dig latrines, huh? Bunch'a green assholes…"

His muttered words sounded angry, but they all knew he was proud of them. He was an endangered species, the last of his kind, and the dinosaur that was their senior officer—at least when Hendricks wasn't around—was much loved by the people who worked for him.

He relaxed, sitting down and talking to them like the subject of the lesson was on hold and he had to address a side issue.

"Now look. I know y'all are itching to get messy with something, but I need everyone to tread lightly, y'hear me?"

A chorus of "Sir, yes sir," and other military affirmations rippled back to him. He gave a satisfied nod and turned his attention to Weber, standing like a gargantuan gargoyle off to one side of the room.

He always did that, sitting at the back or to the side of any group, because he knew his size was an obstacle for anyone to see past.

Unlike the others, Weber had stood sharply to attention and held up his hand as the boots of his heels thumped together. The stoic expression on his face completed the look, and Williamson found himself unable to ignore the huge man.

"Go on and take a seat now, son. You'll get your chance same as the others."

Weber sat, reluctantly, creaking his bulk onto the green timber chair that flexed alarmingly under him.

"Now, as I was saying, I'm deploying two pairs of you to the settlements where you'll conduct whatever investigations y'all deem appropriate and do what y'need to."

"Investigations into what, sir?" asked a man sitting on the other side of the group to Weber. Due to his height, even when sat down, he could see the speaker over the tops of the other's heads. He saw a young black man, muscled arms bulging at the sleeves of his khaki T-shirt, and sharp eyes that seemed to hide a keen intelligence. Weber hadn't worked with him before, but he liked what he saw in the short, professional package.

"Intel suggests there's a rogue band of dissidents stealing resources from both settlements. Chances are they don't like the new way of things, so they need to know we don't give two shits or a rat's ass how they feel about things, because this ain't a democracy...I mean, it is, but not the way they want it to be, and they need educating in the ways of things."

The room bristled at the affront to their safety, to the lives of people they fought for, but Williamson carried on to make sure his point was understood.

"Now, these assignments are not to be viewed as an invitation to go lone wolf on this, is that understood?"

Another chorus of affirmatives sounded.

"To that end, and I'm going to regret this, I'd like to see a show of hands for anyone who..."

He narrowed his eyes, waiting for anyone to be too eager, but they were wise to his ways.

"...wishes to...volunteer foooooor...extra guard duties!"

No hands went up. Williamson deflated and leaned forward in his chair.

"Alright, show of hands, who wants in?"

Every hand in the room went up, and Williamson rubbed his temples with a groan.

~

"So, you were German special forces, right?" Dexter asked.

"No, I was a Fallschirmjäger. A paratrooper."

"Uh-huh…"

Adrian Dexter, the man Weber had scrutinized during the briefing, walked beside him in silence for a dozen paces. They held their rifles ready, but they did not patrol actively and take the low body stance of fighters in contact. As far as both men went, this was their relaxed setting.

"And you? You were in ze US Army, yes? Ranger battalion?"

"Uh-huh," Dexter said again, eyes darting to the tree line and back again. "So tell me this, how in the hell do they find a parachute large enough for a son of a bitch like you? I mean, no offence or anything…"

"None taken! I recall something a British soldier once said to me. He was of their parachute regiment also, and he told me that only two things are falling from the sky: paratroopers and the shit of birds, and he said that you did not want either of these things to land on you."

Dexter laughed, hearty and loud, but more at Weber's delivery of the joke than the actual joke itself. When his laughter faded, he grew serious again.

"So, Weatherby's crew recruited you from the military?"

"Oh, no my friend, I only served for a short time in the military. After this I was a federal police officer," Weber answered.

"Huh, go figure..."

They walked in silence for a few more strides before Dexter's curiosity sparked him to talk again.

"I can't see it. You just being a cop? Again, no offence, man, but...the size of you? Bet they had you on riot control or some shit."

"Are you familiar with the GSG 9?" Weber asked quietly.

"Holy shit, Rainbow Six? That was you?"

"Formerly, the identities of this unit were classified government secrets, but I do not think that anyone will arrest me for admitting this now."

"You a badass side of beef, you know that, Hans?"

"My first name is Dieter," Weber said with a confused frown.

"Sorry man, no offence..."

The silence descended on them again as they walked. The other team had split off a few miles back, taking the fork in the road that had been widened by the increased traffic since the settlements had interacted more, leaving them to proceed alone toward Three Hills. One of the other team had argued for transport, but given the nature of the operation Williamson had ordered them to proceed on foot so that any reinforcements they might require had access to the few vehicles at their disposal.

"You know, I gotta say...my great-grandfather fought in Normandy," Dexter said unexpectedly. He implied no malice in his words, merely conveying that he needed to get the fact off his chest.

"Did he survive the landings?" Weber asked, no trace of contrition in his voice which pleased Dexter.

"Sure as hell did. Marched his ass all the way to Paris."

"I congratulate him! My own great-grandfather was a prisoner of war when this was happening. His corps was taken captive in Libya."

"By our guys?"

"No, by the British."

"He make it?" Dexter asked, offering no contrition either.

"He did! My grandmother said that he came home a very thin man!"

The two men walked on in silence, pleased with their unspoken bonding as the journey continued.

Part of the journey took them through a particularly thick area of forest, so much so that the road was little more than a tunnel through the thick, leafy branches.

Midway through that stretch, Dexter stiffened and slowed his pace.

"What is…" Weber started to say, but as soon as he spoke, he detected what had spooked his teammate.

Woodsmoke. Subtle, as if the fire was small, but definitely nearby.

"Cover!" he hissed, sending both of them diving into the tree line on either side of the track.

Weber caught Dexter's eye, signaling to him with exaggerated, slow gestures what they had to do. Dexter acknowledged with a nod and the two of them slipped into the dense undergrowth.

"I'm telling you, we should go to The Source. It's barely protected, and I have seen the things they take from there," one man said in a low, grumbling voice as he poked at the small fire with a stick.

The infant dragon was barely enough to feed two of them, let alone four, so his stomach was making him the most sullen.

"And you know how to use these things, do you?" an older man asked. His face was adorned with faint blue crosses, all of them denoting a kill in battle. He hated the complaining man because of where he was born, but he also hated everyone and everything, so such trivial grievances made no difference.

"I've seen their guns. I can understand how they work," the man poking at the fire complained back.

"Stop messing with that, you're taking all the heat out of it," another warned him, worried that the meagre strip of meat he was anticipating would be lost.

"Quiet, all of you," the fourth man said.

He was from the Springs, but he cared little for where people came from. He only cared that those who placed themselves in charge of others never went hungry, never lived nearest the town walls where The Swarm might break through, and never seemed to have to work too hard like everyone else.

He had never liked The Tanaka, having never been able to earn the man's favor, but he still felt that life made more sense when somebody was in control.

Now, leading a small band of men set to steal what they could from anyone using the roads, he snapped his fingers for his three compatriots to do their jobs.

Dexter walked slowly, humming a tune in his mind and bobbing his head along with the silent beat. As he expected, a man hobbled out onto the road ahead, sobbing pleas for help, only when he turned his head to make out Dexter wearing all his military equipment and carrying weapons, his face betrayed a hunger he couldn't hide. His face spoke volumes, and it all rolled into one word.

Jackpot.

"Help me...please...my son..."

"You okay there, buddy?" Dexter asked, stopping a safe distance away from the man on his knees in the road.

"My son...he's hurt..." he said, much louder now, pointing a shaking hand off into the trees which Dexter followed with his eyes before returning his gaze to the man.

"Uh-huh, that right?"

"Please...I...I..."

The pained face turned into one of anger, and the weak, pathetic voice hardened and shouted to signal those he thought would immediately spring from the undergrowth and surround their victim.

"Come on! He's right there and there's only one of them!"

Dexter smiled at the man. It was not a kind smile. He raised the rifle to point it at him, forcing the last of the act to flee the man. He stood, angrily brushed the road dust from his clothing, and drew a wicked, curved machete.

"I wouldn't," Dexter warned in a conversational tone.

"Hey, assholes, get out here!" he shouted, desperation this time sounding in his words.

"Something tells me your buddies ain't coming to help…"

The three other men crouched along the tree line, listening intently, waiting for their turn to be called into play.

"Come oooon…come oooon," the one with the tattooed face muttered over and over, keeping himself focused so his nerve didn't break.

A sound from one of the others, like a half-stifled cough, reached his ears and made him angry. He whipped his head to face their direction, but he could not see them through the trees.

"My son…he's hurt…"

That was his signal to move, to emerge onto the road and take whoever was there by surprise, but he hesitated.

"Come on! He's right there and there's only one of them!"

Before he could move far enough to stand, a great weight forced itself down on his back and drove all the air out of his lungs.

"If you do not move, I will not have to hurt you," an odd voice whispered in his ear. He couldn't place it. It was nothing like the voice of anyone he had ever known, but still it angered him to be trapped, to be crept up on, and to be told what to do.

His lips peeled back exposing his yellow teeth in a snarl. He moved fast, grasping the hilt of a dagger he intended to shove into the neck of this bastard, but a cold sensation froze his hand.

The cold spread through his back and into his chest, and only when the weight grew heavier, and a crunch sounded from deep inside his body did he realize that he was a dead man.

"Hey, assholes, get out here!"

Weber stood, cleaning the blade he had used to pin the man into the forest floor on the dirty clothes he wore, and announced that he was coming out.

The last man, the youngest of the four, lay in the undergrowth and fought to keep his fear in check. His heart sounded like it was beating a drum, and his breathing was almost uncontrollable.

That wasn't unexpected, given how he'd just witnessed the forest come alive, how he'd seen a giant emerge from the trees like he was invisible to cut the throat of one man and stab another through the back.

He waited until that huge man had stood tall and walked out of the trees, heard the angry shouts of their leader, and fled as silently as he could to warn the rest of them.

Chapter Twenty-One

Onwards, Dear Friends

Anderson

Our collective mood was pretty good as we continued flying north. After the dreadful start a few days ago, for the moment at least, I felt like we'd turned a corner and things seemed to be going our way.

Hendricks must've read my thoughts or something because he brought us down to earth by reminding us that no matter how it seemed now, we still had a long way to go. That minor balloon bursting made me think of Rishi, and it worried me how I'd forgotten about him until reminded. Then I told myself I hadn't forgotten, I'd compartmentalized it. Whatever, Cat would know what to do to unpack it when I got back.

We stopped a total of six more times until even Hendricks had to admit that things had gotten better and were staying that way. At every stop we had over the next few days as we continued over the seemingly endless forest, we were either left alone completely or Annie alerted us to some middle of the night delivery of food, branches, and trinkets.

On day six—I think—the forest started to thin out and the landscape started to look more like the savanna. The drums were still beating, and bundles of foliage were delivered every time we landed. Our supply of suitable gifts was getting severely depleted and we strained our imagination by the time we'd left the forest region.

We barely even set a guard when we landed, and Hendricks and Amir set up their hammocks to get some proper sleep while we leisurely fed the fuel generators.

"Three heat signatures approaching from the east," Annie announced, although without any hint of alarm in her voice.

"Amazon," Marco declared, looking in the right direction and seeing the bundles of leafy branches being carried into the clearing.

"Ha! Literally!" I said, finding the joke funnier than it was but I chalked that up to a lack of solid sleep.

We didn't see any more movement that night, and I didn't know if it was my imagination or if I'd gotten used to it, but the drums seemed that much quieter than before.

Not long after we had left the last of the forests and entered the savanna area proper, we needed to look for the next refueling area. Due to the time of day, it would have to be an overnight stop as the light would soon be fading. From the images received from the drone we'd sent ahead we knew the area still contained stands of trees. Turned out it was a lot easier to find trees in a flat landscape than it was finding a little flat landscape among trees. Go figure.

The first stop was at a small cluster of trees centered around a dip in the land, probably indicating a water source not far beneath the surface.

Following our now well-practiced routine, the first thing we noticed when we landed was the lack of drumbeats. Having become so accustomed to them over the last few days the absence of them was…disconcerting.

From the air, I was expecting my view to be grassland interspersed with the occasional tree, stretching as far as I could see in all directions. During the flight over the seemingly endless forest, I'd longed to reach the savanna region if only for a change in scenery.

I thought I'd feel safer, less enclosed, with the ability to see for a long way in every direction, but that turned out not to be the case. The grasses ranged from waist height to above head height making it impossible to see more than a few feet in each direction, which was worse than the forest, and for some dumb reason I couldn't get that scene from one of the *Jurassic Park* movies out of my head.

We were in a small area of grass that had been flattened by the downwash of the helicopter when it landed, but were surrounded on all sides by a wall of grass.

Don't go into the long graaaass, my stupid brain yelled at me.

"I can't see a damn thing," I complained.

Hendricks walked up behind me, then walked around the small perimeter obviously deep in thought. He bent down and studied the grass that the downwash had flattened for a while before standing back up.

"Get the drone up asap please, David. At least that'll give us some idea of what's out there…"

I turned and got the drone case out of the helicopter.

"Weatherby?" Hendricks then called over the radio to the helicopter that was still hovering above us. "We need to flatten the grass around us so we can get a field of fire cleared. Fly a few low circuits around us to see if that's a quick fix please."

"On it," came the reply.

By the time I had the drone ready, Amir was on his second circuit around us. The plan was working and most of the grass he had flown over was pushed flat. As soon as Annie had flown the drone on a circuit around the area, we breathed a sigh of relief when she reported that she could detect nothing untoward within the range of the cameras and sensors on the drone.

"It's working," Hendricks confirmed to Amir. "Widen the circle until I tell you to land. Good job."

Five minutes of precision flying later, Hendricks told Amir to land. As he, Ozzie, and Marco joined us, the pilot admired his handywork.

"Well, if that's how much fun gardening is, I'd have tried it years ago! And to think, I paid people to cut my lawns before."

I raised my eyebrows at him behind his back, like that guy had ever cut grass. Hell, I bet he didn't even know the name of the person who employed the people who organized for the grass to be cut at any of the ten thousand buildings his company owned.

"Okay, everyone," Hendricks said, changing the subject with a small shake of his head at Amir's comments. He waved us in to gather around him.

"Annie, can the drone see far enough to give you a heads-up of anything sneaking up on us?"

"Affirmative, Mister Hendricks. I believe with the new terrain we are in I can give you far greater warning than before."

"Thank you, Annie. Can you please watch over us while I brief everyone?"

She bleeped a tone in reply and Hendricks continued.

"Okay, people. New environment, new tactics. First of all, due to the lack of the percussion section, I believe we're now out of the territorial range of our new friends. Which is a shame, but there you go. Secondly, we don't know what's out here, but as Annie has informed us, she can now see further."

I shifted uneasily at the thought that we'd survived the apes and now we'd leveled up or something. I just hoped we hadn't stumbled into a boss level. Hendricks had more to say so I shook it off and paid attention.

"I don't need to remind you all of the continual need for vigilance—"

"You just did," Nathalie interrupted, smirking at the intentional annoyed expression he sent her way.

"Also, we don't have much in the way of barricade building stuff around here, so our only protection is a clear field of fire, and advance observations."

He smiled and sighed before he continued.

"So, let's get a camp set up. Weatherby, Anderson, while we're doing that can you see how good this grass is for fuel production?"

"Grass?" I asked, looking around us and looking confused. "What grass?"

My joke was obviously so bad that only Hendricks acknowledged it, and that was because I knew the guy was too polite not to.

Over the previous few days, we'd elected not to bother building a barricade around our nightly camps as it was clear the locals had no hostile intentions toward us, but we had to acknowledge we weren't in friendly territory now. We had no reason to think there was anything out here to get us, but if experience taught us anything since we woke up it was that there was probably something out there to get us.

The tall trees that grew where we'd landed by were too large to fell and move, and the small number of immature branches that grew around their base wouldn't make much of a barricade, plus, we might need those to turn into fuel if the grass turned out to be unsuitable. It was an oversight in planning the mission, but as Hendricks liked to say, no plan survived something or other about contact with the enemy.

With the drone hovering above us like a protective eye in the sky we got on with our tasks. Hendricks went off to do his daily radio update with base, something I'd noticed over the past few days he was doing more and more out of earshot of us. Maybe it was my imagination, but I'd noticed. I wanted to ask him about it, to ask if everything back home was okay after he'd let slip the whole renegade comment, but I never seemed to get the chance to talk to him alone.

Weatherby reported that even though the grass didn't produce as much fuel as the heavier foliage, the hoppers could deal with it a lot quicker and so the quantity we had available made up for the quality of it. Fuel could be produced at an acceptable rate which was good news, and I was grateful that this was a lot lighter to haul around than the stuff in the forest.

I was almost running on autopilot when I bent to pick up an armful of head-high grass and it moved.

"Shitballs!" I yelped, letting myself down big time in the manly stakes.

I staggered backward, tripping over the cut stalks as I fought to get my rifle from my back and point it in the right direction.

I heard others shouting, heard transmissions over the channel in my ear, but none of it reached my brain because all I could imagine was a damn velociraptor jumping out at me.

Before I could aim the rifle, a beady eye fixed me, and I froze.

The thing was like a rabbit, only it looked more like a mouse. It had massive, round ears and buck teeth, and the overly long back legs looked too skinny for it to move. It thumped one of those skinny feet into the dirt to make a sound like a machine gun, and the grass rippled before a bunch more of the goofy little bastards poked their heads into the clearing we'd made.

"Stay down!" a British accented voice barked from behind me. I stayed the hell down, because I could guess what was coming next.

Far from the eruption of automatic gunfire mowing the grass ahead of me, I heard the disciplined reports of single shots in a flurry before the animals disappeared from view.

An hour later, when my dignity had returned along with a healthy heart rate, I accepted a chunk of roasted meat on a stick from Jones.

He'd expertly skinned and roasted the mouse-rabbits over a small fire of dry sticks, but only after Annie had used the biofuel generators to test the flesh for toxins.

Turned out that the dark meat of mouse-rabbits—and I definitely needed to come up with a better name for them—tasted goddam divine.

As soon as the dawn gave us enough light the following day, we were on our way again. Apart from a few animals we observed as we flew over them, we encountered no sign of any settlements or habitation, which I took as good news.

The animals we saw herding on the plains seemed to belong to either the antelope or deer family. We were unsure which, but noticed they were different to anything any of us recognized. Another new species we could add to the whole 'no animal can survive the end of the world' list, and of course, Jonesy wanted to shoot one and eat it.

As we flew, I had Annie show me on my tablet our location superimposed over the world map from the database. The readout was super low-res and glitchy, but I got enough of what I wanted to see. It showed we were flying over what was once the Middle East and that meant we were over halfway to our destination, which was good news. As far as the surveillance we had showed us, the terrain, until we reached another temperate forest region that grew in the area around Echo site, was very similar to what we were travelling over now.

If we encountered no more problems, then we were probably only five days away from Echo site.

The new routine of using the helicopters to flatten a clearing for us to land in developed over the next few refueling stops, but we still opted to stop near the trees because that meant water and it meant animals. Once a suitable spot was chosen, Hendricks would fly a pattern around the area flattening the landing zone. Then, while we landed and got the drone in the air to provide top cover, Amir would widen the area until the all clear was given and then he'd swoop in and land.

The next few days passed in the endless routine of fly, land, refuel, fly, land, refuel, sleep, and eat.

No dangers were encountered, and it was hard not to let the current ease of the journey uplift our mood. I spoiled that mood as we sat around a fire eating mouse-rabbit—mabbit?—and asked Annie a question.

"This is a herbivore, right? I mean...eyes on the side of the head, no canine teeth, pretty twitchy things makes them prey animals, doesn't it?"

"That assumption is most likely correct, David."

"So, stands to reason, that there's something out here other than us that eats them?"

As far as conversation pieces went, my observations went down about as well as a bad fart in a crowded elevator.

The stands of trees started to thicken over the course of the next day, and the flat grasslands gave way to the thick, dark vegetation of the northern forest area as we'd decided to call it, after one of the long group discussions that served to keep us sane as we flew over the monotonous terrain.

At the first refueling stop in a suitable clearing we had spotted, Hendricks ordered us to make a barricade as a precaution against whatever the new environment might hold for us. Even though there were no drums, the environment was close enough to where we'd encountered the apes originally to not assume there were similar animals up here.

"We just don't know what's out there," Hendricks explained unnecessarily as we reached for our machetes and began hacking at branches, dragging them into place to build the familiar fort we'd constructed many times before.

Our eyes and ears, backed up by the drone that flew in wider circles around our position, didn't detect anything untoward, other than the usual forest noises made by the myriad small animals and birds that called the place home.

I quickly grew familiar with those sounds; with the screeching and whistling running on loop, so the call of a particular bird or the honk of a small animal didn't make us reach for our weapons as they had in our first few training missions.

Another thing I'd noticed that was different was me was my fitness levels had increased; I could swing my machete with more power and for longer than I would ever have thought possible. I had...what was the word? Guns. I had guns. Like, visible muscles in my arms and shoulders, and I kinda liked it!

When I stripped to change clothes or to have a rudimentary wash with a cloth and water, I couldn't help but admire my growing muscles and general hardness of my body where it had previously been pale and a little on the squishy side. I just hoped I'd get back to show off my new physique to Cat.

The foliage was premium grade now we were back in the forest, and I found myself missing the open grasslands. Now I had the familiar feeling of claustrophobia replacing my panic at being unable to see over the grass, and I guessed I couldn't win.

With the tanks filled with premium in record time, we were on our way again.

Chapter Twenty-Two

So Close...

The next day we stopped for our second refueling halt at about midday. We knew that this would be our last stop of the day because, according to our coordinates, we were less than an hour's flying time from our destination.

Less than fifty miles.

It hadn't felt like we'd been on the move for weeks, but the stubble on my face had become an actual beard, even if it was a little patchy in places, and Rishi's death felt like a lifetime ago.

Hendricks suggested it would be best to arrive at Echo site as early in the morning as we could, so we could take advantage of as much daylight as possible to first observe and then investigate whatever we'd find there. I couldn't fault the logic in that, and it wasn't as if rushing to get there before nightfall made my life any easier.

Once the rough barricade was built and Annie was flying the drone as our first line of defense and observation, the pace relaxed. Because the greenery was so...green, the usual frenetic process of manufacturing fuel as fast as possible had calmed down. It still had to be done, but we knew that we had the rest of the afternoon and all of the night to get everything we needed completed. Also, we knew that today could be our last day of relative leisure for the foreseeable future, because once we'd done everything we needed to at Echo site, all of us would want to return home as quickly as possible.

The return journey, though, didn't hold the trepidation for me that the outward one had initially, as we knew what to expect and could only foresee a long but otherwise hopefully uneventful trip home.

Discussions had even begun to think what gifts we would leave if, as we expected, the same happened and we had offerings of cut foliage and other stuff left for us. It had already been discussed and agreed that we would refuel at the landing zones we had established on the way out, because why not? We knew where they were because Annie had marked their exact locations, and we reckoned on getting a friendly welcome there.

One spot would be avoided, and that went without saying, because none of us wanted to revisit the place where we'd been attacked.

When the tanks were brimming and we reckoned we had the time to spare, we set to filling our few spare fuel containers.

With our bellies full of a roasted mouse-aroo and the guard rota allocated, we settled down as the darkness descended and tried to get as much sleep as possible, planning to be gone the second there was enough light to fly.

Hendricks, the flashlight illuminating his bearded face heroically, gave us his final briefing as we waited for the pre-dawn light to brighten the eastern sky.

"Okay chaps and chapess. We've gone through this before, but repetition never hurt anyone. Plan is to locate a suitable LZ within a mile of the site. Annie's detailed a few options from the drone footage, but worst-case scenario we'll have to lower someone to clear some trees."

Ozzie, recognizing when one of the few jobs he was better qualified for came up, raised a hand to acknowledge his involuntary volunteering.

Hendricks continued. "Jonesy and Marco will take the lead. Weatherby, Anderson, Ozzie center. Nat and I tail end Charlies. Annie will provide us overhead coverage with the drone as usual, so we'll be able to get a move on as hopefully she will spot anything before it becomes a problem for us."

"How come he doesn't get called by his last name?" I asked, thinking I'd gauged the mood right with a nod at Ozzie.

"Because your nickname's shit, mate," the Australian answered matter-of-factly.

"Nickname? I don't have a nickname?"

"Exactly," Ozzie said, seeing Hendricks' raised eyebrows asking permission to carry on, accepting the blame for the interruption that was my fault.

"Anyway. Keep in formation and follow the lead. Once we get eyes on the target, Jonesy and I will observe for a while. Annie will do a sweep of the area before we both scout it out on foot. Depending on what we find—hopefully a whole chunk of nothing—I'll either call you in or we'll exfil to your location and make another plan."

He patted the tablet computer he held in his hand.

"We've all studied the site layout from the plans, satellite images, and the footage from the drone sweep but if you want to familiarize yourselves one last time during the flight, I'd recommend that."

I liked it when Hendricks did that. He made a simple order sound like a friendly suggestion that you appreciated the mental nudge for, but somehow left you with the impression that his suggestion was one hundred percent what you had to do without fail.

Nathalie picked up the briefing. "Okay. We know what the ground conditions should be like, so if the area is clear we'll 'ead straight for the main bunker entrance and do what we need to do."

"Any questions?" Hendricks asked, but we'd all been over this so many times that any last-minute question would likely be a dumb one.

When no one answered other than with a firm shake of their heads as we all got our game face on, he finished with a look at the sky which was visibly brightening by the second.

"Let's mount up and get going."

Two minutes later the light level was just high enough to lift off. We knew in the short journey ahead of us it would strengthen enough for us to pick out a suitable landing spot, and I hoped there was one because the alternative meant hovering for a while until someone made one.

We'd only practiced it once, and it was our emergency procedure in case we got ourselves stranded over dense forest with nowhere to land before we ran out of fuel. It basically meant adapting a special forces jungle tactic whereby someone would get lowered through the canopy and they'd blow up a few trees to make a hole big enough for the helicopter to land.

We'd adapted it slightly by using the electric chainsaws—much to Jones' disgust—but the practice still sucked if you weren't a participant. Given how nothing needed programming or hacking, I was the last person to ever be a participant in that task.

Forty-five minutes later a small but open area in the forest below afforded us our first potential landing site.

"Annie, mark it for me. Let's fly on for a few minutes first and if nothing else turns up, that's our boy," Hendricks announced after hovering over it for a few seconds. "Annie, location to Echo site?"

"Current surface distance is approximately one thousand seven hundred and thirty meters from the main bunker, with a twelve percent margin for error given topographical anomalies. Given the density of the foliage, the journey would be difficult on foot."

"Thank you, Annie," he responded curtly. "Keep looking, folks. Every yard we don't have to cut our way through the forest counts."

"Remind me again why we don't just land at the site?" I asked, knowing exactly why we weren't going to just land at the site and misjudging my comedic timing. Hendricks took the question seriously and gave me one of his confusing answers.

"My dear Doctor Anderson, one doesn't simply park outside the address where one plans to execute a warrant."

I took that to mean what I already understood and said nothing, keeping my eyes open for the subtle changes in the forest canopy that indicated a clearing.

"There," I said, rolling my eyes at my own stupidity because our pilot couldn't exactly see what I was looking at. "Um, left...ten o'clock?"

I'd planned to give him degrees from starboard like I was on the bridge of the Enterprise before I remembered I didn't know how to do that, nor did I even understand which was port and which was starboard. Ten o'clock seemed to get the job done though, because the break in the treetops came into sight as Hendricks turned our helicopter to head that way.

It looked ideal, if a little tight for both helicopters, and once Hendricks had confirmed the location with Annie he landed after completing our usual sweep of the area. He ordered Amir, hovering overhead, to land. I set up the drone and quickly established the comms links so Annie could operate at her best capability.

"Thank you, David. I am now connected and ready to operate the drone to full capacity."

I was about to respond but she must have included Hendricks in the last part of our conversation as he replied instead. "Thank you, Annie. Let's go everyone."

He pulled the charging handle on his weapon, peering into the breech to see brass, and waited for us all to file past before taking his place at the rear of our little column. We went with backpacks stuffed with the gear we might need, but the rest would have to stay there until we could bring the helicopters closer when everything checked out.

If everything checked out.

The forest surrounding us was similar to the one at Charlie site and to what we had flown over, but there were subtle differences. Instead of the warm, almost tropical forest this was darker, damper, and the temperature was noticeably lower.

So damn much of the world had been overtaken by dense greenery over the last thousand years. I reckoned any environmentalists left who'd campaigned that man was destroying the planet with industry and pollution; well, I'd imagine they'd be feeling a little smug right now.

It wasn't carbon emissions or rising sea levels or disappearing glaciers that had screwed us. It wasn't our technology advances. It was a chunk of rock hitting our chunk of rock at about a billion miles an hour, and no amount of nuclear power could've broken it up enough to save everyone.

I found myself getting a little philosophical about it all as we patrolled carefully through the trees, hoping that we as a species wouldn't make the same mistakes again.

Probably not, I thought, as I told myself off for daydreaming and got back to my job of following the man in front of me and watching out for any danger in the forest around me.

Maybe not…not for a while at least.

My eyes stayed focused, my ears alert for alien noises, but my mind still wandered. It wandered to a presentation I'd attended at a tech seminar where the guy had eventually been escorted off the stage when his allotted time was up, and he refused to stop talking.

His talk had been called "The Human Infection" or something, and he basically posed the theory that the earth was the organism, and we were just like flu on a large scale. He said that all the infectious diseases that killed us off—Spanish Flu, Black Death, AIDs, the Cocoliztli epidemic, COVID-19 to 26 and a dozen pre-historic outbreaks, polio, H1N1, Ebola, Zika—weren't pandemics, but were the earth's own immune system upping its game.

He was crazy, like clinically, but like a lot of crazy people he said a lot of stuff that just made sense. It's a side effect of being human to think that the world revolves around us, when the truth is that we've just evolved around our world. And it had been doing just fine without us for hundreds of years.

Thirty sweaty, absent-minded, tiring minutes later Jones held up his fist, indicating for us to stop immediately. I crouched, nerves spiking, and pointed my weapon in the opposite direction to Ozzie in front of me. Out of the corner of my eye I watched as Jones crawled up to the crest of the gentle slope we'd been ascending where he lay unmoving for five minutes. Hendricks, after signaling that everyone else was to stay put, made his way stealthily up the slope and lay down beside him.

That's it. It has to be Echo site, I thought excitedly.

We'd made it. A journey of over four thousand miles across unknown and uncharted territory. We'd fought against hostile inhabitants of the forests, until—for reasons beyond our understanding—they started to treat us as gods.

We'd crossed lands where deserts once stood and navigated ourselves to a pinprick on a map. A pinprick we hoped would give us more answers than questions, and ultimately help us to survive going forwards.

Chapter Twenty-Three

Echo

The minutes dragged as the five of us waited for Hendricks and Jones to complete their initial surveillance of Echo site. Eventually, Hendricks crawled back from the crest and crouch-ran back to our position.

"It looks clear," he said in a low voice. "Annie, can you do a sweep please? Then Jonesy and I will do the recce of the buildings and the surrounding area. If it's clear, we'll call you down to our position."

With that he turned, and half crawled back to his overwatch position. Annie launched the drone from where she had landed it to conserve battery life as soon as he'd requested it, and it buzzed over our heads to disappear ahead.

Annie communicating over an open channel to inform us a few minutes later the drone's cameras and sensors had detected nothing untoward, and she recommended the next stage of the mission could commence.

Hendricks agreed with Annie.

"Confirm, go for human reconnaissance phase, I have overwatch," she answered, sounding pleased with herself. Maybe it was only me that picked up on that, though.

I was caught up in the moment for a second when she said that. She was an artificial intelligence program, and she was a more useful member of the team than the person who created her. If I didn't make it back then a few people would be upset for a while, but life would go on. If Annie somehow didn't make it back, everyone would be in big trouble.

The rest of us could do nothing but wait as we listened, concentrating on our earpieces to try and pick up any clues to what was going on. Hendricks and Jones were too professional to make any noise, let alone talk out loud when they were conducting what they called a CTR—close-target recce, which I learned was British for recon—and would have been relying on hand signals to communicate as they approached the buildings to do their thing.

I jumped when eventually Hendricks' cheerful, confident voice sounded in my ear.

"It's all clear. Make your way to us so we can begin. Annie will lead you to our position."

Nathalie stood and spoke. "Okay everyone, let's get going. Remember, now is not a time to relax."

I took those words to heart as we moved, Marco up front and Nat tucked in behind.

I'd studied the photos and footage plenty before and during the journey, so the buildings had a familiar feel to them when they eventually came into view.

The twisted ruins and dilapidated shells of the accommodation. The office blocks used in the construction of the underground bunker. The familiar yet different crater viewed from a new angle.

The buildings had the appearance of a lost city of the jungle, vine-covered and tumbled down, just waiting to be rediscovered by an intrepid explorer.

Annie guided us to Hendricks and Jones who were standing in a large undergrowth-covered, portal-type entrance that was sunk into the side of a hill: the main bunker entrance.

I looked up at the rising hill Echo bunker had been built into, and I couldn't help but feel this had a far more industrial feel to it than Charlie site or our ARC.

I peered into the gloom of the tunnel. It looked to have collapsed in places and the floor was littered with large slabs of decaying concrete and piles of rubble and rocks.

Hendricks looked at Ozzie. "Time for our engineer to shine. Can you survey the tunnel? Give us an idea of its stability or lack thereof? Marco will accompany you to watch your back."

Ozzie, who had preempted this request already, had shrugged out of his backpack and was fitting together the metal poles he had pulled from it.

"What's that?" I asked out of curiosity and a need to fill the silence as we all watched him work.

"It's a lightweight carbon fiber and titanium poly-alloy collapsible pry bar," he stated simply, as if the whole world would instantly know what the thing was.

"Oh, yeah, silly me," I replied, hearing the sarcasm in my voice turned up a little too high because of the stress.

"Bloody computer geeks," the Australian muttered, his tone implying friendly banter. That banter we had between us was primarily about the differences between the rough and dirty world he had mainly lived in, against the sterile sedentary world I had, and which made the better man.

"I'll use it to test the roof and walls and knock off any loose bits that might want to fall on our heads." He stood up and looked down the tunnel, holding the long bar easily in one hand. "It's what we call man's work, computer boy, so stand aside and let the real men through."

I snapped to attention and gave him a one-fingered salute as he passed.

We waited, guns facing out. The only sounds apart from the ones nature made around us were the regular metallic ringing sounds as Ozzie tested the tunnel behind us. Eventually he reappeared.

"It looks good enough," he called to us. "It's a bit rough in places but should hold up for now. I got as far as a big steel door like the one at Charlie site," he said as he blinked in the sunlight and started taking apart his magnetic carbon titanium fiber poly-pry thing.

"Jones, Marco, guard the entrance while we try and gain access. Nat, take point," Hendricks ordered, not wanting to waste any more time as he turned and walked down the tunnel activating his weapon-mounted flashlight as he went. The rest of us trooped after him, one by one our own lights turning on, and I knew he'd given himself the most important job of all: protecting the VIPs.

When we reached the circular door, I knew Ozzie was right because it looked exactly the same as the one at Charlie site.

"Hey, Amir, you get a bulk-buy discount on these things?" I joked.

"No, I had the company contracted to design the US government's nuclear shelters bought out and their chief designer created these for me. Only four existed in the world, so I believe the saying is, my shit's custom."

Okay, he owned me on that one, I'll admit it.

Amir approached the door and held his wristband up. We all waited, hoping the next noise we heard would be the locks disengaging and the door rolling open, but nothing happened. He turned and looked at me with a deflated expression on his face.

"What's up? Your custom shit not working?" I asked, lowering my rifle and pulling out the wire attachments for the tablet hanging around my neck. "Annie, are you picking up anything? Active power supply maybe?"

"Yes, David," she replied immediately. "I am detecting a low-voltage current and a very weak data signal utilizing my original primitive code emanating from inside the facility. I have only just begun to detect it as we approached the door."

"We'll revisit the word 'primitive' another time. Can you do anything to increase the voltage here?" I asked, trying to lever open the access panel so I could attach my wires and do my nerd thing. I was thwarted by a thousand years of grime that acted like Gorilla Glue.

"Hey, real man, give me a hand here?" I said, seeing Ozzie's smile in the flashlight beams.

I ignored his intentionally manly noises as his carbon weave whatever popped the metal panel open after it flexed his tool so much I worried it would snap. There seemed to be some unspoken agreement to drop the comedy as I clipped my wires to the control panel and asked him his professional opinion.

"Ideas on boosting the power supply?" I asked.

"Easy option is to rig up the spare drone battery and give it a little extra juice, but it might not have the guts to get it open."

"Annie, can you interface with this panel?" I asked.

"Not yet. I do not have the data range to do so, as I believe from site schematics that all wireless data receivers are inside the complex, hence beyond my ability at this time. Can I request we set up the comms gear that is in the helicopter so I can access my full capabilities?"

"Negative on that for now," Hendricks answered firmly. "We'll move the helicopters in when we've got inside unless we have no option."

That told me that I had to earn my keep and get creative, but Ozzie was way ahead of me.

"Annie, is the voltage on this door the same as the standby voltage on Charlie site?"

"Affirmative."

"So that means the facility's on standby mode."

"Affirmative."

Where he was going with his train of logic hit me then.

"So we just need to give it the wakeup signal!" I said, thumping the fingertips of my right hand into the tablet's screen after bringing up the terminal application.

"David, wait…"

Annie's interruption stopped me in my digital tracks just as I was about to hit enter on a line of code.

"Annie?"

"The root code for this facility has been radically altered. I do not believe that your command will have the desired effect."

"Annie, what are you saying?" Hendricks asked suspiciously.

"She's saying someone screwed with the system and wired the mains electricity to the front door handle," Ozzie replied for her.

"That is an incorrect metaphor, but I do believe the altered programming is indicative of someone not wanting this facility to be tampered with by any outside influence."

My hand, still hovering over the tablet, slowly retreated like it had made its own mind up about messing with it.

"Hey, err, Hendricks? I…I can't de-bug the system from a tablet…"

"What do you need?"

"What do I need?"

I need ten of me working multiple screens around the clock for about eight months to check every single line of code against the master system which I don't even have a record of. One wrong move and the place could be wired to detonate the damn power core!

"That's impossible," Hendricks argued. "Aren't there… *fail-safes* or something?"

"Yeah, but I don't know about any nuclear power sources left on standby mode for hundreds of years, do you? I need a little time," I said. "And I need Annie with a full uplink to do the leg-work for me."

"Marco, Weatherby, head back to the LZ. Marco, stay there, Weatherby fly one back, then Nat escort him back here and all three of you get back here. Jones, stay on watch out there. Annie, are you able to keep the drone up?"

"Affirmative."

"Good, do it. You two good in here if I go out and take up the watch with Jonesy?" he asked, speaking softly to just me and Ozzie. I looked around at the empty tunnel and told him we were good.

I carefully scrolled through the available code on the tablet before Annie warned me to stop.

"I am unable to cross reference the facility's programming against my record of the original code. Please wait for me to reconnect to the uplink before attempting anything."

"I'm not attempting anything, Annie, just taking a look."

It sounded sullen even to me, but I stopped messing and waited for the distant buzz of drone rotors to whip a light breeze down the tunnel at us.

Another few minutes passed as Hendricks set up the commlink, then my tablet came alive and started to work by itself, and a lot faster than I could make it go.

"I am connected with the system, but do not worry—I am presenting as a routine maintenance checklist that the system is designed to complete periodically."

"What are you seeing?" I asked, trying to keep up with the code exploding over my screen but it was harder than trying to read the subtitles on an Eminem music video.

"The override for the door has been altered to initiate a subcommand," she said, just as the lines of code stopped scrolling and the cursor sat there, blinking at me like it was calling me a bitch and asking what I was gonna do about it.

"Eades, you sneaky son of a bitch," I breathed, seeing the extent of the code he'd changed.

"I concur with that assessment," Annie said. "It appears that Mister Eades did not want anyone gaining access to this facility."

"Update?" Hendricks asked from way outside.

"Eades rigged the system wakeup to kill the power to the door if someone outside tried to remote access it," I said.

"I have also located coding that blocked all communication from the ARC via satellite," Annie said.

"Blocked it? Why would he block it?" Hendricks asked.

"To be more precise, there is additional coding that prevents any data signal from outside the facility to make any override changes, such as an instruction to open the door."

"So he blocked you in space from down here?" Ozzie asked. "The hell was this crazy bastard smoking down here?"

"I believe I have located fourteen additional sub-routines for simple commands. I am isolating them now."

"Can you undo them, Annie? Safely, I mean."

"Yes. The basic code changes are simple to locate as they are not very well hidden. It appears that Mister Eades, or whoever changed the programming, lacked your finesse for such things."

I took that compliment happily enough, but I was more concerned about why Eades wanted to shut everyone else out of his controls.

Hendricks came jogging back down the tunnel with the spare drone battery under one arm. He handed it wordlessly to Ozzie who began unscrewing a panel in the wall to snake wires out and connect them to the door supply.

"Okay, we good to go?"

"Hold! Don't open that door yet!" Hendricks sounded adamant on that front, so I took my finger away from the tablet for the second time.

"Wait for the second helicopter and the full team to be ready first. I already don't like this."

The second helicopter took less than ten minutes to arrive, and this time only Annie in the form of the drone remained outside to keep watch.

Hendricks, his calm British demeanor at odds with the grim expression on his face, stacked up on the door with the other three trained warriors acting like the rest of his caterpillar. He gave me a terse nod and I activated the door, expecting it to roll back and for them to burst inside with their guns up.

Instead, with what sounded like only one tired motor, the door gave off a metallic judder and began to roll open so slowly it was almost amusing.

It was like some dumb action-comedy movie where the fight stops to let some old lady cross the street with her stroller on the way to buy cat food or something, and the stress of everything made me bark out a laugh that only succeeded in making Ozzie jump.

"Hey! Ya bloody bastard," he complained, swiping at me with his left hand.

A huff of stale air wafted out of the tiny gap and made me wrinkle my nose.

"The door requires additional power," Annie said. "The motors are straining and are in danger of failing."

"Hold on," I said. "I think I can reroute—"

"Gah! Bloody nerd!" Ozzie barked, standing up and rolling his shoulders. He spat on his hands and rubbed the palms together which looked more like a psychological thing than any kind of way to increase friction, then shoved his favorite new tool into the widening gap and hauled, bending the bar as his body weight was transferred through it. He grunted, hauling on the bar, to be rewarded with an increase in the pitch of the whining motor. The door moved faster, and he staggered, trying not to fall over as it moved freely to eventually roll into its recess, revealing the room beyond.

Hendricks said nothing, just led the armed caterpillar into the room to split off in different directions as if controlled by a single consciousness, the light from their weapons illuminating the area.

We knew from the plans that the antechamber and control room was similar to the one at Charlie site, but similarities between the two felt very different when we got inside.

They swept through, checking every crevice of the antechamber and calling "clear" before opening the doors to the control room. The exterior rooms were like massive garages or small aircraft hangars, but going deeper the rooms grew smaller.

"Control room clear," Hendricks announced, giving me the signal to move in and do my thing.

Hendricks was looking and tapping his finger on a flickering display of the bunker's schematics.

"Accommodation and storage areas don't concern me too much...Mister Weatherby? You're certain that this site contains no secret VIP bunker like Charlie site?"

"Certain. Nothing was off the books here."

"Yeah, that you knew about," Ozzie muttered, getting ignored by everyone who heard him clearly.

I went straight to the main control panel and busied myself connecting my tablet to it.

"Annie? Are you with me?"

"I am connected, David."

"What about...Echo Annie?"

"The command AI system for this facility has been deactivated."

I sat, sweeping about an inch of dust off the work surface and closing my eyes to blow the crap off the keyboard. Luckily it was one of those sealed, rubbery bastards that made programming slow but at least it kept dust and ramen out from the keys. I flexed my neck and fingers ready to go to work.

"I suggest we reformat and re-initialize the communication array from the original coding."

"Good idea," Amir added, sitting down at another terminal and tapping keys to wake it up.

"Is it formatted as a backup?" I asked, waiting for a full three seconds—about a day in Annie speed—before she came back to say it was.

"Okaaaay...downloading the communications drive now."

"Downloading it?" Amir asked. "I thought you were wiping it and starting again?"

I was too busy tapping away to come back with a retort to the obvious red flag he was waving, but luckily I had an Australian with a carbon fiber thing he was itching to use.

"Why you so keen to wipe the comms logs, mate?"

"Wipe them? I'm not..."

"Thank you, Ozzie…How long?" Hendricks asked with annoyance, turning his attention to me.

"Can't say. The download should be fast enough, but it'll take some time to reformat that part and upload the original code."

"And you'll have Annie's full assistance when it's ready? She won't be limited?"

"I will have full functionality outside of all corrupted systems when the link is established," Annie said, but Hendricks was peering closely at the display again.

"The power system isn't performing as I'd expect. Could it be indicative of reactor damage?"

The question was intended for Ozzie, but I looked around at the mention of reactor damage. "Maybe, maybe not…could be losing power at a dozen places."

"Annie, are any of the corrupted systems going to prevent us inspecting the reactor?" Hendricks asked.

"Negative. I am reactivating the air recirculation systems to full capacity in the areas you require. The facility is not generating sufficient power to reactivate everything at once."

"Okay. Nat, Marco, go with Ozzie and let me know ASAFP if we need to be a few hundred miles away."

They left, and with Jones back outside guarding the tunnel and the helicopters it felt a little frosty with just the three of us there.

"Amir," Hendricks said calmly. It was so calm it was almost a threat. It took me a second to figure out I'd only heard him speak without transmitting, and I wondered how he'd communicated to Annie that he wanted her to mute our mics.

Amir turned in the dusty chair and fixed him with a look of bland innocence.

"I distinctly recall the last time we did this you intentionally withheld information from me. That…misunderstanding cost lives. I'll ask you now: is there anything you know about this facility, about Eades or any other person here, that you haven't told me?"

"No."

He answered a little fast for my liking. If he was giving the question its full consideration then he'd at least have paused before answering.

"Okay, so why in the hell would Eades run a bunch of hidden malware commands hidden among the operating code for the site?" I asked. I was more annoyed at myself for not seeing the obvious booby trap, but I had an avenue to vent that annoyance.

"I have no idea. I'd suggest we ask the man himself, but I don't think that's possible."

"Communications drive downloaded. Commencing reformatting and reinstallation of original code," Annie announced, breaking the tension between the three of us. Amir relaxed, rubbing his face like he was exhausted, and seemed more human than ever.

"I have no idea, but if he is the one behind this then I might have some information that is circumstantially circumspect," he said.

He looked at me, but I just blinked.

"What?" I asked.

"Annie?" Amir said, looking up out of old habit now that we were back under a roof. The up-tone was his only answer.

"Please contact Ms. Cole and ask her to locate and forward the psychiatric evaluation for Mister Eades conducted at the Texas—"

"I have located the document, Mister Hendricks. It is on your personal device now."

Hendricks sat in the corner reading, making the occasional noise that told me nothing. I waited for the comms drive to come fully online under Annie's control, checking the other corrupted systems to kill time.

Now that I knew what I was looking for I could see the amendments easily enough. To put it in terms that normal people can understand, it was like reading a book where somebody stuck their own words into the text on a sticker. At face value it looked right, but when you checked it a little closer you could see where it'd been changed.

My biggest worry wasn't the sheer volume of changes, it was the risk of not finding one that was better hidden than the rest.

"Annie, can you check all of these code variations and see what they're designed to do?"

"Yes. The first one we encountered was—"

"I don't mean tell me now, I mean write it all down and check it later. It's more important to get the facility up and running than it is to pick it all apart. I want to do the same with each drive and system in turn when we're done with the comms drive."

"I will record the changes and prepare a prioritized list for reformatting site systems."

I didn't know if I'd pissed her off or if she was just busy, but she didn't let me know when the drive was good to go, because I just got a system admin box appear on my terminal informing me.

I ran the new code, waiting as the array did its thing and gave Annie the burst she needed to be at full power. Just when it looked like things were starting to work out, it all fell down.

"Err, Hendricks, this is Marco…"

"Go ahead."

"Listen, we have…we have bad news and really bad news," the American said. In the background I could hear Ozzie grunting and cursing up a swarm with a lot of C-bombs being dropped on inanimate objects.

"Send," Hendricks said flatly.

"Bad news is the reactor wasn't damaged before, it was just leaking power into the containment unit."

"And the really bad news?"

"Really bad news is that it wasn't damaged before, but by us activating the facility it…well, it kinda is now. The additional power drain must've screwed it."

"Hendricks! I am detecting a critical power core failure," Annie said, like she'd fallen asleep and woken up a second too late to break the news.

"So I'm hearing," Hendricks grumbled, closing his eyes like he couldn't believe his life could get any more difficult.

"I anticipate a loss of containment in under twenty-four hours if mechanical repairs are not made to the cooling system."

"Do you know what repairs are needed? Are the requisite parts available at this site?" Hendricks asked.

"The answer to both is yes. I will be able to direct one of the team to the correct storage area to locate the parts and tools before assisting Ozzie in making the repairs."

"Well lucky fuck'n me!" Ozzie grunted.

"Do what you can," Hendricks said softly.

"Mister Hendricks, I have Mister Weber on comms stating that he has important information to share with you," Annie interrupted.

I saw the look on his face and heard the urgency in her voice. He walked away, telling her to put the comms through to him.

~

Dieter Weber tapped his heels together in his customary fashion. He wasn't sure if he was meant to show military respect to the young man leading Three Hills, but he showed the respect anyway because it was genuine. He had fought alongside Harrison and Tori and knew both to be, as his American friends would say, *ze real deal*.

Dexter had carried their prisoner the last mile of their journey after his third, futile attempt to escape them. The short, squat man had declared his patience had run out before encircling the prisoner's neck in one huge arm and seemed to give him a long hug until his arms stopped flailing and he went to sleep.

He watched him now, more to prevent the locals from carving pieces off the man.

"Tell us what happened," Tori said.

Weber glanced at the older man he did not know by name until he was reassured that he could speak freely.

"This is Clarke, he is the leader of The Springs and here at our invitation. He wants the same thing we do."

Weber offered the man a brisk, stiff bow of his head and explained. "We have been sent here to assist you, but on our way, we have found three men who would be trying to rob us."

Tori and Harrison exchanged a glance, frowning, as they both deciphered his unique grammar.

"You said three, but only one prisoner?" Clarke asked innocently.

Weber gave a small shrug before answering. "The others are still where we found them."

"You left them out there?!" Clarke gasped.

"Ja, it was not possible to be bringing them with us..."

"So they can just attack someone else?"

Tori held up a hand to calm the older man, having read between the lines of Weber's literal report. "They won't be attacking anyone, I don't think. Isn't that right, Weber?"

Weber laughed disconcertingly. "Ja, unless they are rising from the dead?"

The sentiment rose eyebrows in the room and Weber's laughter coughed its way into awkward silence.

"And the prisoner?" Harrison asked, wanting to get the conversation back on track. He alone sat in the room, and he wore a ponderous, troubled expression.

"He is...asleep. He is not harmed."

"And where is he from?"

Weber frowned, unsure of the meaning of the question.

"Which town is he from?" Clarke asked gently.

"Oh, I believe he is from The Springs. He has…" he gestured at his face, searching for the right word. "Tattooings? All over his face."

"I know this man," Clarke said once he had approached and studied him closer, his face a mask of anger. "His name is Brian. He is a warrior, but not one many people liked. He claimed the successes of better warriors as his own."

Tori rolled her shoulders back as if preparing for action. She bent to Harrison and made an impassioned plea. "Let me find out what he knows! He won't hold out, I—"

She stopped talking as the young man held up a hand to silence her. His eyes never left Weber's, and Tori knew that he was scheming. That his calculating mind was looking to earn favor with other, powerful people.

"Do you have ways of making people…talk?"

Weber almost burst out laughing again, but he knew that the stereotype would take more explaining than he had the patience for.

"Ja, I am trained in interrogation."

Tori shifted again but Harrison raised the hand a second time without looking at her.

"Would you…interrogate him on behalf of both Three Hills and the Springs?" he asked formally, glancing at Clarke for a nod of acceptance. It was a clever political move, Weber realized, because neither faction could be accused of forcing a confession from a man where their own agendas would be served. It was a political move of impartiality, and it made accepting the truth easier for everyone.

"Rise and shine, motherfucker!" Dexter said cheerily, sending a stinging slap across the face of the bound man. He startled awake, looking left and right desperately, groggily, before writhing to try and free himself from the ropes binding his arms and upper body to his chest.

"Let me go! I'll kill you!"

"Relaaaax!" Dexter said calmly, patting his cheek again with a meaty palm. "And besides, you had your chance to do that, so now you're gonna talk to us."

Weber stepped forwards, looming over the bound captive from behind and above like some demonic golem. His features, so quickly softened with a smile or his quick laugh, were set in granite to lend him a terrifying appearance.

Brian looked up, swallowed, and lowered his head in silence.

"Tell me, do you know what waterboarding is?" Dexter asked. His tone was light and friendly, as if he was asking about a bird or a piece of culture. The tone was soft, but the implied danger was evident.

The tattooed face shook slowly, cautious of the trap.

"Never mind. I'll explain it to you. What we'll do, is we'll tip your chair back and my big-ass buddy here'll hold a piece of cloth tight over your face. Then I'll take a bucket of water and I'll pour it, nice and slow, in your mouth. It won't actually drown you, but what'll happen is your brain will tell your body that you're drowning, and that'll make all kinds of stuff happen."

He walked slowly to the side of the room and hefted a wooden bucket, carrying it over to set it down and slosh water onto the dirt floor.

"So, you'll think you're drowning, like I said, and you'll try to break free at first, try to hold your breath, but that won't work. In the end you'll choke on the water, and your body'll send all sorts'a good stuff into your blood to help you. The adrenaline'll make your heart beat out your chest, give you the extra power to get away, but all it'll do is make you breathe faster, and that'll make my job easier. Best advice I can give is to stay calm, got it?"

Without another word, and at the prearranged signal, Weber tipped the chair back to drop him on the deck and throw a filthy sack over his face. He stood a massive boot on either side of it to pin him down, and Dexter tipped the first splash of water onto his chest.

Before a drop even touched the sacking, the muffled shriek of submission rang out.

"I'll tell you anything!"

Dexter looked up at Weber, disgust and disappointment clear on his face, and he set the bucket back down.

Brian was tipped back up, his breathing ragged and terrified, and the chair dripped fluid that had not come from the bucket.

"It's not me...okay? It's...the new guy..."

"Good start. Who's the new guy?"

"He found...us a few...weeks ago...he—"

Dexter slapped Brian again, shocking him into silence.

"I ask a question," he said, gesturing to his left. "And you answer it," he finished, moving his hands to his right.

"He...he said—"

Dexter stood, stepping back to avoid the flailing feet as Weber tipped the chair a second time and dropped the cloth over his face.

"No! Noooo!"

The water began to pour, but the spluttering screams formed into words.

"Jacob! He's called Jacob!"

Chapter Twenty-Four

The Truth is Out There

"Wait, you said twenty-four hours?" I asked, not liking what I was hearing.

"I have revised that initial estimate based on further information," Annie answered.

"And what is that estimate?" Hendricks barked.

"Given the physical examination by Ozzie, I can now say that without intervention, the power source will lose containment in approximately eleven hours and fifty minutes, with a margin for error of—"

"Let's not worry about margin for error this time, shall we?" Hendricks said tiredly.

"How?" I asked, dumbfounded. "Is it our fault? Did we do this?"

"Technically yes. By activating the startup sequence, we have inadvertently accelerated the containment drain. The likely result of a loss of containment is an explosion with a yield of—"

"Annie, we won't be anywhere near the place when that happens, believe me," Hendricks cut in.

She didn't need to explain what the destruction of a nuclear reactor would mean to anyone standing within the blast radius or fallout zone, and it still annoyed me that she couldn't read a room sometimes.

Hendricks paced, clearly pissed about the private call from Weber he hadn't told anyone else about, and he transmitted that mood over the channel.

"Ozzie, Hendricks. What's the estimate for repairs?"

Ozzie's voice came back, grunting as he talked and worked. "Assuming all the parts are good, and assuming I don't have to manufacture anything and nothing bloody breaks, eight hours."

"That doesn't leave us much wiggle room," Hendricks answered, as if a mild complaint could make the job miraculously go faster.

It wasn't like him to act that way, so I knew there was more than just the one catastrophic event happening.

"What about if we just download what we need and get the hell out of here?" I asked, earning his full attention. "Think about it, if we can't stop this place from going Chernobyl on us, what's the harm?"

"Other than a devastated area uninhabitable for hundreds of years?" Hendricks snapped back.

I didn't get why he was so pissed about it. It wasn't like we needed the area or would be at risk from the fallout.

He eyeballed me for a few seconds past comfortable, then snapped down the comms at Ozzie to "Shift his arse."

The way I saw it, we were only here for information. Annie was on fire, now that she had the linked processing power of all three sites running to her via the orbiting ARC.

I was reduced to an overqualified spectator as she located and identified files for me to inspect, all the while fixing the system with the original code. She found all the communications between Kendall and Eades—Charlie and Echo site's version of me—and they made for interesting reading, but they didn't tell us how to control The Swarm. She downloaded everything for later analysis, but kept a running commentary as she worked.

"I can find no reference to The Swarm in any of the files. I am confused, David, because everything he did would have been recorded and stored."

I sat back and thought for a while. "You know what, Annie, I always thought Eades was a sneaky little bastard, no matter how nice he was to everyone. If he was working on stuff like that, and he knew the system, he'd know to encrypt it. Annie, scan every line of code inputted by Eades again, but this time search for something anomalous, something that just doesn't fit or make sense."

"Scanning now."

A few moments later, which showed how fast she could work now she was Super Annie, she came back with something.

"I believe I have found it. Hidden in a letter he emailed to his mother. I checked his personnel files and both his parents died before he entered Mister Weatherby's employment, which is why I highlighted it. There are references to the pets he was keeping at the site along with a picture of a puppy. Within the picture is hidden a code which opens the files we are looking for."

"Great, Annie, download everything for later," I replied with a smile of satisfaction knowing we'd outsmarted a man who'd been dead for hundreds of years, but his creation still had the power to destroy us or, maybe, save us.

"I think it more prudent to give you a synopsis now," she replied. "I have studied the files in detail. For safety I have already transferred the relevant files to the main hub so if anything happens to us the knowledge will not be lost."

With that rather morbid statement Hendricks filled in the silence it caused.

"Tell me now, please."

"Very well. Please be patient and leave any questions you may have until I have finished…What Mister Eades created can only be described as remarkable. When he went into cryo he also, in the separate laboratory he had built offsite, preserved biological samples he had been working on in cryostasis. These pods, however, were most likely irradiated when the fragments of the asteroid impacted near the site, and some were damaged. The ones that escaped the damaged pods survived a nuclear winter in excess of a century, apparently by feeding off the power supply that was still functioning in the laboratory."

"Power supply?" Jones' voice muttered. Annie ignored his interruption.

"In their isolation, the effects of the radiation altered and mutated the development of the genetic modifications he had been experimenting with. Eades himself, when he emerged from cryo, could not fully explain it. It appears that when he went to his laboratory and saw what was in there, he abandoned all other works and isolated himself away in his laboratory to continue the experiment. There are video logs of his updates, and I believe they document his descent into ill health."

"Give us the highlights, Annie," Hendricks said.

"The Swarm had been in what he described as hibernation, surviving by feeding off the power supply and evolving. The main change was in their physical appearance, as his test subjects had multiplied in size dramatically. He continued to alter their genetic programming and improved on what the radiation had started. Now the subjects were much larger the electronic organic elements were easier to design and integrate into the living tissue."

I couldn't believe what I was hearing. It was like the guy had totally lost it and had never seen literally any sci-fi movie ever.

Messing with genetics? Integrating robotics with living tissue? What the hell, Eades, you insane son of a bitch!

"He overcame the reproductive issue by manipulating the parthenogenetic tendencies of the bullet ant's genetic code that made up a significant portion of the mutated hybrid, into the dominant reproductive process. To put it in simple terms, he enabled reproduction without any external fertilization, and they could be programmed to do so on receipt of the correct transmission."

"Remote controlled asexual reproduction of a killer cyborg beetle-ant. Got it," I said sourly.

"The one limitation he could not overcome was the effect direct sunlight had on The Swarm. The electromagnetic radiation absorbed from daylight overloaded their internal organic electronic elements, rendering them inoperable and killing them."

"Wait, back up," I said, not caring that she didn't want to be interrupted. Some things you can't just wave your hand at and gloss over by saying quantum or whatever. "Sunlight kills them? What are they, vampires?"

"It is more likely an evolutionary side effect that they developed during the time when the atmosphere was heavily clouded with reduced ultraviolet rays able to penetrate the dust cloud in the atmosphere," Annie answered, shutting me down and continuing her story.

"It appears that Mister Eades overcame this problem by programming The Swarm to only leave their hive when the moon was full, so the solar-generated power required to keep their organic electronics working, using their carapace as an effective solar charger, would generate enough power from the earthlight shining to function."

Annie hesitated. "Are you still following this explanation? Do you want me to pause briefly so you can absorb the information?"

"No, carry on, Annie," Hendricks growled.

"His work continued over the years. Life at Echo site also continued, and he worked tirelessly with his creation to the detriment of his health and interpersonal relationships. It ended with him being effectively ignored by the rest of the community, as he rarely emerged from his laboratory. He appeared content maintaining the computer systems when necessary and enhancing his creation. The video logs show no evidence that he felt threatened by anyone, so he did not feel the need to utilize the potential weaponizable capability he had created. That was until Mister Kendall contacted him and explained the tyrannical dictatorship that the original Mister Tanaka had created."

I groaned internally at the memory of that asshole, but I kept it to myself.

"It was then he hatched his plan to help. The tiger beetle and bullet ant, which are the two species he used to create the hybrid creatures, both have the capability to fly. This trait he had suppressed as he did not want his creations escaping. He created a new genetic strand which had their flying capabilities enhanced instead of suppressed, and once they were ready, he programmed them to fly to a location he and Mister Kendall agreed upon."

"So Kendall was the one who set those things loose?"

"Please, allow me to continue," Annie said. "Mister Kendall, who at the time had not fallen under suspicion by Tanaka, had free reign to enter Charlie site and perform maintenance on the computer facility. He used this freedom to establish a power source at a site many miles away from any community. And yes, I do have the coordinates now and so we know where their nest is."

"Wait, they have a nest? Near our home?" I almost yelled. I looked at Amir for some backup, for someone else to take this shit as seriously as I was, but he just looked shocked.

No, scratch that, he didn't just look shocked, he looked betrayed and shocked.

"The video logs end soon after that event. There is not much data to explain why, apart from the final entry where he states he is sending out his creations to try and eliminate their attackers."

"When was that, Annie?" Hendricks asked.

"The time stamp on the file does coincide with the appearance of the new craters at the site which I had previously incorrectly hypothesized were caused by the asteroid strike; however, I now believe were caused by low-yield nuclear detonations."

"So…what you're telling us…" I began hesitantly, once my racing mind was back in a semblance of order. "Is that we know how he created them, and we know where their nest is near us…But do you know how to control them?"

She sounded a little smug when she replied.

"Yes, I do. While I was just informing you of the facts I had discovered, I found and decrypted the command-and-control program he coded to give The Swarm its instructions. The work is not overly complicated, but now that we have the knowledge, I will be able to recreate it with ease."

"So, the signal they emit, you can control it?"

"I believe I can, yes."

Okay, I couldn't be sure, but I had a sudden worry of the Skynet variety. If Annie decided we weren't doing the right thing, it was only her self-programed morals keeping her from letting the damn bugs loose on us.

"Annie," Hendricks said in a tone of disbelief. "Download everything. I want a physical copy with us and send encrypted backups to yourself at the other sites just in case Ozzie can't work any magic on the reactor."

~

Ozzie was working his magic. He was doing the best that he could, as fast as he could, and it was totally, utterly pointless.

Marco had brought him the right materials in the form of the spare parts Annie had directed him to, deep in the bowels of the facility on shelves oddly devoid of dust.

The lack of dust was what Ozzie called a head-scratcher, but Annie had told him that the facilities had a complex air circulation and filtration system that effectively made parts of the bunker a vacuum.

"S'pose that'd keep the critters under control too, eh?"

"Correct. It is highly unlikely that even highly resilient arthropods such as cockroaches could survive in such an environment. In fact, it is…"

Ozzie turned a smart wrench, tightening a fixing on a coolant pipe he'd replaced, but when Annie didn't complete her sentence, he stopped and frowned. "Annie?"

A single, flat tone sounded in his earpiece. It was short and sharp, and his mind translated it as, "Wait!"

He waited, not moving, barely breathing, as if to do so would break some spell and bring all the superstitious bad luck in the world down on him.

"Containment failure imminent," Annie said.

She did not sound alarmed, or panicked, but more that she was sad and resigned to the failure which came across as a personal one.

"Yeah, I know, that's why we're fixin' the bloody pipework—"

"Negative. There are now three other containment leaks detected."

"Where?" Ozzie was tense, fired up, and determined to fix every last leak even if he had to stick his fingers in holes.

"One in this sector and two in the crawl spaces one level up."

"Shit!"

The curse tore from him like a ripping hiss. If the leaks were simple valve replacements like the one he had literally just fixed he had a hope, but the crawl spaces were too difficult to reach and even harder to work in.

"How? Why're the bloody seals popping?" he asked, half wailing the question as if knowing the answer made any difference.

"I do not know. I hypothesize that the sealant rubber has degraded over time."

Ozzie said nothing. There was no point in a smart comment about the facility's complex air circulation system keeping parts of the place in vacuum, because the rubber had degraded and the containment would fail. When it failed, it would go into meltdown. When it went into meltdown, it would look like Hiroshima underground.

"Hendricks?" he called into the channel, dragging out the last syllable of the name as he gathered his tools. He started up a loping jog towards the long tunnel leading back to the outside world when the response hit his earpiece.

"What's going on?"

"What's goin' on is this place is gonna do an impression of a mushroom a lot sooner than we thought. It's time to go home, mate."

"Wait! What about the safe shutdown?" Weatherby asked. The tone of his voice made it clear he was trying to protect his expensive toys like a vestigial habit he couldn't break.

"You volunteering, mate? Coz I tell you one thing for free, I'm not."

"There are hazardous material suits by the reactor—"

"Yeah…" Ozzie's boots rang a steady, metallic rhythm on the floor as he ran. "Thousand-year-old hazmat suits, and you'd trust the decon process?"

"Annie?" Hendricks asked.

"I have to concur with Ozzie. I cannot assure the suits will offer sufficient protection, nor can I confirm that the decontamination process would adequately protect the wearer."

Hendricks took that as a firm no. He barked orders over the channel, rallying their team back to the helicopters for a rapid exit, just as Jones broadcast the words nobody wanted to hear.

Chapter Twenty-Five

Unexpected Guests

"I'm getting movement out here! Stand to, Stand to!"

"What are you seeing?" Hendricks commanded.

"Uncertain, but we both had the feeling something or someone was watching us and now we can pick up movement in the forest surrounding us," Marco answered.

"Apes?" Hendricks asked, a hint of hope in his words.

"Can't say, boss," Jones reported.

"Annie? Drone?"

"Already up," she replied. "I have not entered the trees, but overhead surveillance shows multiple heat sources approaching from the northeast. They will be in visual range in roughly two minutes if they keep up their current pace. From their size, shape, and movement I am confident that they are human."

"Human?"

"Affirmative."

"Jones, Marco. Did you copy?" Hendricks asked. They did copy, and Annie's next report made my blood run cold.

"Thermal imaging shows them carrying weapons."

"Confirm?" Hendricks snapped.

"Kalashnikov pattern, eighty-two percent certainty," Annie answered, clipping her tone and speaking with fast accuracy to match Hendricks' style.

"Everyone outside, front and center. Weatherby, get your bird in the air and be ready to have Annie take over autogun control."

I ran outside, choosing a rubble pile of cracked concrete covered in vines as my spot, and asked for a direction. Annie told me, which was good because I was aiming way off, and I fought to control my breathing.

"Annie. How many do you estimate?" Hendricks asked. The channel was open so we could all hear.

"Between thirty-eight and forty-one. Some shapes are larger than others and I only have one camera angle to track them as they cross paths."

"Time until visual?"

"Ninety seconds," Annie said, giving by far the most human response to an estimated time I'd ever heard. Just thinking about her lack of detail and the total absence of a margin for error estimate killed a third of that time.

Ninety seconds became two minutes. Two became two and a half, became three, and still nothing emerged from the trees.

"Annie?" Hendricks asked quietly. It must've showed how long I'd spent with him that I could tell from his voice his cheek was pressed into the stock of his rifle.

"Still no visual. I am detecting thirty-nine heat signatures in the tree line."

"No flanking moves?" Marco asked.

"Negative."

"I'm going to call out to them," Hendricks said, standing from cover and lowering his rifle. He ignored the hissed warnings from some of the others and walked toward the trees until he stood very much alone in the open. Gathering himself he let his gun drop slightly as he cupped his hand to his mouth.

"Hello out there. We know you're watching us. We mean you no harm and will be leaving very soon, but you need to leave too! This place is not safe!"

Nothing.

He tried again.

"Hello. My name is Hendricks...we need to warn you that this place is dangerous!"

"Pochemu ty zdes!"

The shouted response was distant and echoing, and I blinked at the response.

"Annie...Was that Russian?"

"Affirmative. Do you want me to translate?"

"You ever heard me talk Russian?" My stress levels made me snap, but for a super-intelligent...thing, she'd just asked a dumb question.

"He asked why we are here."

Hendricks again raised his hand to his mouth and shouted out, "Druz'ya, Druz'ya."

"Mister Hendricks is announcing that we are friends."

"Or he just ordered a coffee," Ozzie joked. It wasn't the time for jokes, but that literally never stopped an Australian from making one.

A long torrent of words came from the forest.

"Um...Annie?" was all Hendricks said.

"He would like to know how we can be friends when you are pointing guns at him and trespassing on his lands."

Hendricks walked ten paces backward. He unclipped his rifle and rested it on the ground, stepping forward again. I knew he could draw the pistol off his thigh and shoot fast, but I also knew the magazine didn't hold thirty-nine rounds.

With a low murmur of, "Wish me luck" he stepped forward a few more paces and just stood there with his arms held out wide.

He stood for either ten seconds or five minutes, I couldn't be sure, before a figure emerged from the cover of the trees. He was heavily bearded, wearing rough spun, homemade clothes, the only 'old world' item he carried was an old-looking, but clean rifle.

There was no mistaking the silhouette of that weapon, but Jones still felt the need to explain that it was indeed an AK47 he was carrying.

With his weapon pointed straight at Hendricks' chest he slowly walked forwards, his face showing both anger and fear.

Hendricks stood stock still, his arms spread wide with a smile on his face trying to look as friendly and unthreatening as possible as the man approached.

When he was ten yards away Hendricks raised his arms more, offering complete submission to the man's hard gaze, and repeated his claim of friendship.

"Druz'ya, druz'ya. Friend, friend."

The man stopped and stared at him for a long time. His eyes also flicked to the rest of us he could see crouching around the entrance to Echo site, and to the one remaining helicopter in the clearing. He took in their modern clothing and clean, untarnished weapons. He looked up at where Amir's helicopter hovered quietly in the air with the nose pointed right at the trees.

He spoke, rattling loudly and gesturing with his right fist. I didn't know if he was angry or if it was just part of being Russian, but the guy looked like he was giving a rousing speech to troops about to go to war.

Before my imagination ran too wild, Annie muttered the translation in my ear.

"You do not look like our enemies. Where are you from? Why are you here? We have raided many of your places and have never taken things such as the items you wear and possess…have you come from the east in your flying machines?"

I didn't hear Hendricks' response, but I could tell from the way his shoulders moved that he was answering the guy.

The man lowered his weapon a few inches, frowning his heavy brow. He looked pained, and spoke again. The force and tempo of his words were far softer this time.

"He is asking if we are truly from before…"

The man dropped the Kalashnikov on the sling and mimed an asteroid coming down with a fist pummeled into his free hand. The two hands came up, fingers splaying outward, like he was miming an explosion.

Hendricks, once he had comprehended and translated the words he had said, smiled, nodded his head, and said that we truly were from before.

The man, who by now had stopped waving his arms around recreating explosions, smiled as Hendricks responded and confirmed they were who he thought they were. He stepped forwards and grabbed the surprised Hendricks' hand and began pumping it up and down vigorously. As he did he turned and called in the direction of the ones who were waiting back in the forest in a rapid burst of speech.

"Annie?" Hendricks asked in the quiet voice of a ventriloquist. I imagined his teeth clenched together in a smile.

"I think it is okay," Annie said. "I could not pick up all of his words as they do not match the database, but I believe he is asking if we are here to help them kill the Chinese."

"The Chinese?" Hendricks whispered back sharply. "Kill them? What does he mean?"

"I am in the dark as much as you are, but we may find out soon as all the others in the forest are now approaching our location," Annie replied.

"We're going to get more company...First impressions count, people. Nobody shoot while I'm out here," Hendricks said in his ventriloquist's voice again.

"Fingers off triggers, please," Annie said, picking the absolute worst time to rip off a Hendricks line.

The handshake soon developed into a bear hug as the guy grabbed Hendricks and picked him up, covering his cheeks in kisses as he spun him around. Unable to escape the embrace, Hendricks smiled and went along with it, trying his best not to get crushed.

He only stopped when all his comrades started to approach. Still with his arm around Hendricks, he shouted with joy and started talking loudly to his audience. Annie translated automatically for us.

"The people from the legends are here...look at their clothes...look at their weapons, with them on our side...we will be able to stop the enemy raiding our lands…and killing our people. Let us welcome them to our land," Annie said, quickly adding, "I am condensing the translation as he is using many hyperboles which bear no relevance to what we are capable of. I think we need to try and set the record straight as soon as possible to avoid more confusion."

"I agree, Annie," Hendricks said, and then called through the open channel to the whole team. "Can everyone join me please. It's time we proved we're not the messiah…Keep your weapons slung and a big smile on your face, everyone. This is going to be an exercise in bush diplomacy and gentle letting down, I believe."

"Hendricks, want me to land?" Amir asked eagerly, earning the same smiling, ventriloquist response.

"You stay where you bloody well are! They don't know you're our top cover!"

Hendricks released himself from the grip the man still held him by and stepped forwards, raising his arms in the air in the universal "please be quiet" gesture. It was ignored, so his bearded bull of a counterpart balled them out and slashed his own hand through the air in the universal "shut the fuck up" gesture.

"Can you translate for me please, Annie?" Hendricks said, unplugging the radio earpiece so the speaker would work.

There was a ripple through the crowd as the rest of us approached. As ordered, no weapons were in hands, and everyone was grinning as if our lives depended on it.

Scratch that. I was pretty sure our lives *did* depend on it.

As soon as Hendricks, with his arms held aloft again, had quietened them down once more, he began talking.

"Hello friends," Hendricks said, pausing as he waited for Annie's voice to broadcast from the radio in translation."

The slight consternation of a Russian voice booming from the little device was soon overcome as they listened to what Hendricks was telling them.

"It is good to meet you all…to know that others survived what happened…many hundreds of years ago. I am eager to hear your history…but we are not here to help you fight anyone."

He paused, waiting for them to digest the information. A lot of them shifted uneasily when they found out we weren't their reinforcements.

"We have come only to access information…from this site…to help us control a deadly swarm of mutated insects…that we are in danger from."

More mutters. More uneasy shifting at the mention of The Swarm.

"We have traveled thousands of miles to get here. We have slept for many years…in the sky…waiting to come back."

He raised his arm to point upwards, but the head guy started talking again, acting like he couldn't believe what he was hearing.

"He is saying that such a journey is not possible…that the mountains cannot be crossed…that the forests are dangerous places…"

Hendricks placed his hand on his heart in the sincerest gesture he could make. "It is true."

"And you chose this place…you chose our home…"

"Shit, Annie, where's their town or base or whatever? They said this is their territory?" Ozzie asked, his voice desperate.

The realization hit me at the same time, and my mouth dropped from false smile to "oh shit."

"Annie, find out how far away it is right now," ordered Hendricks rapidly as the same thought dawned on him too.

A rapid exchange of Russian between Hendricks' radio and the top guy followed as Annie questioned him herself. He looked confused and a little put out by the demand for information about their home.

"They operate a series of linked homesteads and settlements in what appears to be a feudal system. Their nearest settlement is…Hendricks, I cannot be certain of the distance from his description. Permission to direct Mister Weatherby to conduct reconnaissance?"

"Do it."

The hovering helicopter shot upwards and flew north.

"Annie, how far north of here did we send the drone?"

"Only four miles. I realize now that this was an oversight."

"By all of us," Nathalie answered, clearly upset at herself as she was part of the mission planning group.

"Annie, what's the blast radius if this place—when this place—goes up?" I asked.

"There are many variables. The models I have predicted are all in agreement at a blast radius of one-point-one miles."

"That's okay, right? They're more than four miles away?" I asked.

"Got it!" Amir reported. "A little under eleven miles away."

"Annie, prevailing wind?" Nathalie asked.

"All models show radioactive fallout spreading in all directions between thirteen and twenty-six miles."

"Ah, fuck it," Ozzie growled. He turned and ran for the entrance, and I followed him before I knew what I was doing.

Chapter Twenty-Six

You Have Been, and Always Will Be, My Friend

Ozzie ran hard, and I struggled to catch up to him. I didn't call out for him to slow down, to wait for me, because me going with him wasn't part of his plan.

I could hear him talking, raising his voice to shout over the sound he made running, but I couldn't decipher the few words I made out. My guess was that he was talking to Annie, so I tried the same thing and just got a down-tone response.

Not now, that's what my brain said she was telling me.

Ozzie hit the stairs and pounded down. I could count the levels he was descending by the sounds; the rattle of bootsteps, a moment of silence, the heavy clang of him landing after jumping half the flight.

I kept up as best I could, and if I'd stopped to ask myself why I'd run after him I wouldn't have been able to put it into words. It was a feeling. An instinct. Some sixth sense that the guy was about to do something dumb or heroic.

Or both.

I caught up to him as he was waiting for a revolving door to grind its way around, and before I could get to him, he slipped inside, and I had to pull back or lose my hand.

"Dammit, Ozzie, what the hell are you doing?"

"What I have to, mate," he yelled, his voice barely reaching me through the glass that looked about eight inches thick. I tried to make the door revolve but it wouldn't move, and I saw him looking up at the ceiling and moving his lips.

Gone was the joker, the guy always looking to wind the others up, and I saw a resignation on his features that frightened the ever-living shit outta me.

"Annie, connect me to him," I said, standing back so I could see him through the glass. He was stripping off his gear and fighting his way into a yellow hazmat suit.

"He has requested that nobody—"

"Annie, I don't care what he requested. Connect me!"

He stopped, looking at the radio on his gear first then up at me through the glass.

"Ozzie…I…" It dawned on me that I didn't know what to say. I'd overheard enough of the earlier conversation to know that the only chance of stopping Echo site going boom was likely a suicide mission, and I was looking at the only volunteer.

"You don't have to do this," I tried.

He smirked at me, that annoying, cocky half grin that usually preceded some joke at my expense.

"I know, couldn't have you wankers takin' all the glory though, eh?"

The comedy was bravado, but it was a bravado that made what he was about to do easier for both of us. He carried on trying to fit the bulky suit to him, but I could see his hands were already shaking.

"The decontamination procedure, tell me what I have to do," I tried, looking around for another suit to put on and resting my eyes on his rifle and the carbon fiber tool he was so damn proud of.

Son of a bitch even left the good gear behind so it didn't get contaminated.

"Nah mate, forget about it, alright? Just get goin'."

"Ozzie, no—"

"Mate, how many people'll die when this place goes up? Not just in the blast but long term? I'll tell ya: maybe fifty thousand, and that's not countin' the four generations of mutated babies. Trust me, mate, you're not getting me to change my mind here."

"Ozzie—"

"Annie, tell this bloody Yank to get gone and mind his business?"

Before Annie said anything I cut over the channel that I was pretty sure was just the three of us because everyone else was oddly silent if it wasn't.

"Bullshit. There has to be something I can do!"

"There is, mate," Ozzie said as he stood by another thick door marked with the radioactive logo. "You can help me make this story sound so fuck'n cool that your grandkids'll talk about it."

He stuffed the helmet over his head and pressed the seal down before wrenching open the next airlock door and disappearing from sight.

Out of respect for his wishes, Annie cut all communication to and from him while he was inside the reactor chamber. She recorded it so it could be played back, after any appropriate editing, but she let him work without interruption, talking him through the procedure for the manual shutdown sequence. He cried at first, sad for himself and all the things he'd never see or do again, but those tears of self-pity did not last long.

At thirty seconds of exposure, even through the flimsy protection of the defunct suit, he started to suffer a headache that seemed to originate in his sinuses. He blinked, shaking his head to try and clear the pain, and forced himself to continue.

At sixty seconds he was fighting the uncomfortable, fizzy sensation of sudden nausea, forcing him to swallow repeatedly so he didn't fill the inside of the flexible helmet with his last meal of rabbit-mouse.

At ninety seconds, when three of the four overrides had been forced into position, his hearing and vision threatened to white out like lightning was flashing inside his head. He gasped, steadied himself on the reactor, then recoiled at the intense heat of the metal casing.

He sweated profusely, and he didn't know if that was a side effect of radiation poisoning or from the effort, but he forced himself onto the last one and turned it stiffly, sending the core into shutdown.

There was no winding down noise, no rapidly decreasing hum or whine, just the click of the last override sitting neatly and the satisfaction that he had just saved more lives than he thought possible.

No act of bravery he'd ever heard of had saved so many people in one event. Sure, saving a family from the holocaust created hundreds of lives, but saving fifty thousand people at the cost of his own life?

That was the stuff of legends, and as he always told people, he was a fuck'n legend.

"Annie...link me up to the two poms," he gasped as he staggered and bounced his way out of the chamber like a drunk.

He said his farewells, refusing to accept thanks or sympathy, just laying a heavy burden on each of them. He left the computer geek to last, planning on one last prank at his expense, if only as payback for scoring the hot nurse back home.

He crawled toward the thick glass where Anderson sat crying on the other side. He leaned up against the glass with his back to him and made him swear the same promise he had the others.

~

I frowned, my tears stopping as my brain saw through the whole dying a horrible death from radiation poisoning prank.

"You hear what I said, nerd? You...earn this..."

"Dude, did you just quote *Saving Private Ryan* at me?"

"Earn...this..."

"You're totally quoting *Saving Private Ryan*! You jackass, I thought you were really dying!"

"David, I estimate that Ozzie will go into cardiac arrest in less than a minute," Annie said quietly.

"Wait, what?"

"I estimate that Ozzie will go into cardiac—"

"I heard you, I…you're really dying? And you're still playing tricks on people?!"

A weird raspy sound came back to me, and I turned my head to see he was grinning widely and huffing a weak laugh. His eyes were red from all the burst blood vessels, and he looked, well he looked goddam terrifying.

"That's…not even the best…part…"

"What is?"

"I need you…to do…one last thing…for me…"

I had no idea why I did it. Grant a dying man his last wish? Whatever, it felt pretty twisted to do it, then to watch it back on my tablet with him on the other side of the glass.

Annie recorded it, and I gotta say she did a good job with the lighting and sound, too.

"One more—" Ozzie broke off to cough up blood and wipe it over his chin with a lazy fist, "one more time…mate…"

I held up the tablet up again, watching myself press a hand to the glass as Ozzie staggered to collapse in front of me. I sank down with him, listening to him gasp out the words before his head fell.

I laughed in anticipation of what came next, watching as I threw my head back and roared the name at the top of my voice.

"Khaaaaaaaaaan!"

I laughed harder, breaking into my own coughing fit, and when I turned to see if he wanted to watch it again, I saw those blood red eyes had lost their shine. Whatever made Ozzie himself was gone. What made him him was what he'd just made me do, and I both loved and hated him for it.

I stood, tears flowing down my cheeks without shame, and lifted both of our rifles before returning to the stairs and making my slow way back up.

Epilogue

"My names is Eadesavich. What is your names?"

The bunch of people from the trees had sent word back for their chief guy to come up to Echo site. Everyone was surprised when he started talking a kind of English.

"Eadesavich is a not a traditional Russian name that I have any record of being used before. It may be possible its origination comes from Eades, the site's programmer," Annie said helpfully.

We all knew who Eades was, but it was nice to know Annie thought we were dumb.

Hendricks held out his hand. "Hendricks. Pleased to meet you. Annie, can you ask him what he's doing here?"

The two of them conversed in Russian for a while before Annie reported back.

"He says that he will build a statue to Ozzie here, forever standing sentry over this place."

That irony was a painful one, because Ozzie would be doing exactly that, preserved in the sealed chamber for eternity now that no power supply was capable of opening that door, even if the safety protocols could be overridden.

I had no stomach for diplomacy. I sat in the helicopter and pretended to be asleep so nobody tried to talk to me.

I was done crying. I'd gone back to letting out inappropriate laughter every time I remembered what he made me do, and I guessed that was the genius of his plan all along. It would be hard for anyone to forget him now, statue or no statue, because he was right all along. He truly was a fucking legend.

Hendricks made a show of presenting Ozzie's rifle to their head guy. We handed over a good amount of ammunition for it too, because we had the limited means to make more along with a stockpile that would—hopefully—last us decades.

The gifts were treated with the respect they were due, but the ceremony was dragging on to cover the fact that Annie was working with Jonesy and Nat to transform our spare parts for the drone and comms array into a solar-powered comms relay so they could talk to us.

When that was running and tested, Hendricks gave us a loud whistle and spun his trigger finger in the air.

"Helicopters fully refueled and ready to go? Good. We're going home."

~

Many miles away, a bored young soldier sat staring at a screen in a forward observation outpost set up just within their border. The main function of the base was to patrol that border and send occasional sorties across it to control the few scattered tribes of rebels. Rebels who occasionally made a nuisance of themselves when raiding for supplies. Not enough to illicit a stronger response, but enough to deem the remote outpost an important first line of defense for their territory.

His superiors never told him what it did or what it was for, just to report anything immediately that showed on the screen. Not in his living memory or by conversations with others who had served at this remote outpost of the Chinese Nation far longer than he, had anything ever been seen. Neither, according to legends told, had anything ever been seen on the screen in hundreds of years.

The blip, when it appeared, immediately hit his subconscious brain, numbed after many thousands of hours staring at the screen. His eyes and brain saw it, but he did nothing to respond at first. He blinked as he knew something had happened and it took him a few seconds to realize that a faint and intermittent blip was blinking at the far edge of the screen.

Trying to remember what to do next, he eventually hit the record button, picked up the ancient telephone receiver and reported the incident up the chain of command.

Now fully awake and in a near state of panic, his complete attention rested on the screen. The image blinked faintly once more and then disappeared.

He didn't know what it meant, but as his captain crashed into the room after being woken by his call, he knew it was important.

At another desk in another monitoring station further away from their border with the rest of the known world, alarms began ringing as unknown burst of signals over many bands and medium were being received. After the initial panic and excitement that something had actually happened, their training and professionalism turned back on, and they began tracing and analyzing what they had detected.

~

The reports from the distant outposts on their westerly border had begun a frenzy of activity in all levels of the military who had ruled China with total authority since they had emerged from their vast underground shelter after the dust clouds had settled and the climate had returned to some semblance of normality.

Instead of developing cryogenic technology, they had chosen to send carefully selected young subjects to live and survive in a vast series of excavated subterranean caverns. Using advanced hydroponics and immense underground farms where, under artificial light, they could grow and nurture all the food they would ever need.

Entire manufacturing plants for everything from military equipment to technology were relocated underground, along with the primary production facilities to manufacture the steel and other materials they would need. The huge site had been carefully selected and they could directly mine the ore, coal, and other minerals from seams within the caverns.

Everything was carefully controlled by the existing leaders who, as time passed, handed over the reins of power to their own siblings, who then handed it onto theirs.

The 'peasants' as they were called by the leaders, even though everyone chosen to enter had been very carefully selected for their high mental and physical capabilities, were set to work to provide for their leaders. Highly indoctrinated, some would call it brainwashed, they dumbly and meekly fulfilled their masters' orders until they were deemed too old to be of any use and were summarily executed. Breeding between these people was carefully controlled. The population needed to be maintained so it would not become a drain on their resources.

Eventually when the world above their subterranean city was deemed safe enough, they emerged into the new world. Initially, they concentrated on rebuilding the grand residences their leaders thought they deserved. The land was so vast and empty it took centuries for the population to spread to cover even a small fraction of their original country. The military, though, still harbored the memories of their old empire and they wanted to keep their land for themselves and not allow any foreign invaders to lay claim to any of their old territory. As soon as they emerged into the daylight, they sent out expeditions to create outposts to watch over their borders.

The outpost that was nearest to Echo site was developed to be their largest, after they detected a signal coming from what their data showed was a suspected cryogenic storage site. They learned that it had been created by the billionaire Amir Weatherby in his attempt to survive the asteroid strike. They also knew of his other projects both in Africa and space.

Not wanting what was a potential technologically equal enemy close to their borders, the Chinese did not even consider diplomacy and chose the military option without any qualms. Their attacking force was overrun and virtually wiped out by a swarm of huge and aggressive insect-like animals, which they assumed correctly could only have been created and controlled by whatever strange science their enemies had been working on. They then upped the ante and immediately ordered a strike of low yield nuclear armed cruise missiles which destroyed the site and its insect protectors.

The few survivors of the strike, they knew, were still in the area and over the past few hundred years had proved little more than an annoyance with their petty raids for a few miserable supplies. These bases at the extremities of their territories and the stories behind them of keeping the filthy foreigner away from their blessed land were constantly used by the military to justify why large amounts of their resources were still directed to the military when very little had happened for a lot longer than living memory.

Now the frenetic activity was tinged with more than a shred of jubilation that at last they had something to direct their anger and full resources at.

Direction finding pinpointed that both the radio signals and radar detection came from the site they had dropped nuclear weapons on. The track that the signal had departed on when they extrapolated the line, led back to the approximate location of the other site in Africa they had records of.

The coincidences were too much to deny. And within hours of the signals being detected they were planning to go to war.

About the Authors

Devon C Ford is from the UK and lives in the Midlands. His career in public services started in his teens and has provided a wealth of experiences, both good and some very bad, which form the basis of the books ideas that cause regular insomnia.

Facebook: @decvoncfordofficial
Twitter: @DevonFordAuthor
Website: www.devoncford.com

Chris Harris was born in south Birmingham and proudly declares himself to be a true Brummie, born and bred.

He has a wife, three children and one grandchild, all of whom are very important to him and keep him very busy. His many interests include tennis, skiing, racquet ball, darts, and shooting. He's also been an avid reader throughout his life.

Facebook: @chrisharrisauthor
Website: www.chrisharrisauthor.co.uk